Michael Strogoff or, The Courier of the Czar

Modern English Translation Book II - Illustrated

Juan José Piedra

QuantumDigitalPublishing.io

Copyright, Michael Strogoff - Book I & II

Contact us: Reviews@AuthorJuanJose.io

Book Design, Cover & Chapter Illustration Art and NFTs by:
Juan Jose Piedra

Michael Strogoff Printable Art &

NFT Collections: QuantumDrive.io/MichaelStrogoff
Author WebSite: AuthorJuanJose.io

Author X.com: AuthorJuanJose

Manuscript Editor: Dr. Jessie Keener - https://drjessie.life/

Book I - Old English - Author Jules Verne - First edition
March 2025

ISBN 978-1-967405-00-8 (eBook) – ISBN
978-1-967405-01-5 (Paperback) – ISBN
978-1-967405-02-2 (Hardcover)

Book II - Old English - Author Jules Verne - First edition March 2025

ISBN 978-1-967405-03-9 (eBook) – ISBN 978-1-967405-04-6 (Paperback) – ISBN 978-1-967405-05-3 (Hardcover)

Book I - Modern English - Author Juan José Piedra - First edition April 2025

ISBN 978-1-967405-06-0 (eBook) – ISBN 978-1-967405-07-7 (Paperback) – ISBN 978-1-967405-08-4 (Hardcover)

Book II - Modern English - Author Juan José Piedra - First edition April 2025

ISBN 978-1-967405-09-1 (eBook) – ISBN 978-1-967405-10-7 (Paperback) – ISBN 978-1-967405-11-4 (Hardcover)

Box Set - Book I & II - Modern English - Author Juan José Piedra - First edition August 2025

ISBN 978-1-967405-22-0 (eBook) – ISBN 978-1-967405-23-7 (Paperback) – ISBN 978-1-967405-24-4 (Hardcover)

Contents

About The Author

Juan José Piedra

John Joseph Stone, Juan José Piedra

John Joseph Stone, writing under the pen name **Juan José Piedra**, is a **Science Fiction, Steampunk Science Fiction, and Historical Fiction** author and artist whose work seamlessly blends rich storytelling with visually captivating artwork.

His notable works include **illustrating the cover and chapter art** for *Michael Strogoff, or the Courier of the Czar* by **Jules Verne**. With **17 chapters in the first book and 15 in the second**, John's illustrations bring the adventurous world of 19th-century Russia to life. Additionally, he has created **full-color, high-resolution printable images**, available as **NFTs and free downloadable artwork**, along with meticulously designed **Asiatic Russian maps and illustrated scenes** from the novel.

Currently, **Juan José** is developing an **eight-part Steampunk Science Fiction novella series**, chronicling the **evolution of steampunk technology;** from the age of **steam, coal, and wood to high-tech advancements and space travel**. This ambitious project aims to **span the entire fictional history of steampunk innovation**, offering readers a deep, immersive journey through time and technology.

Inspiration & Background

John Joseph's writing is fueled by **extraordinary real-world experiences**. Having spent **over 40 years in the Secret Space Program** while serving in the **USMC Special Section Division**, he brings to life ideas and themes that stretch the boundaries of what most would believe possible; making science fiction the perfect medium to share his vision.

His experiences go beyond classified operations; John has **traveled and lived all over the world**, immersing himself in diverse cultures and perspectives. These global experiences have **broadened his understanding of life and humanity**, giving him a unique lens through which he crafts his stories; offering readers more than just fiction, but reflections on **our world, its possibilities, and its hidden truths**.

Attention to Detail & Creative Vision

A meticulous creator, John Joseph is deeply committed to **historical and technical accuracy** in his works, ensuring that every **story, illustration, and world-building element** is both immersive and authentic. His dedication to precision, combined with an artistic vision, results in stories that are **both intellectually rich and visually stunning**.

Personal Life & Creative Passions

John Joseph is **happily married** and currently resides in **Mérida, Mexico**, where he finds peace in cultivating a lush garden of **Taro, Avocado, and native Mexican trees**. His love for **creating visually compelling imagery** extends beyond writing; he designs **art pieces that inspire, tell stories, and stand as works of art in their own right**.

Connect & Explore More

X: https://x.com/AuthorJuanJose
Books: QuantumDigitalPublishing.io
NFTs, Illustrations and Printable Art: QuantumDrive.io
Contact: authorjuanjose@proton.me

Forward - Michael Strogoff

How Are These Books Unique?

1. Clear & Comfortable Reading: Designed for an enjoyable reading experience, this edition is formatted in 12pt EB Garamond font for excellent readability.

2. Expanded Glossary for Old English Editions: A comprehensive glossary is included at the back of the book to help readers easily understand historical terms and phrases.

3. Beautifully Illustrated: Both volumes feature high-resolution 300dpi illustrations, ensuring stunning print quality. Book I includes 17 chapter illustrations, while Book II has 15, totaling 32 unique images. Plus, enjoy a FREE downloadable version, perfect for printing or setting as wallpaper!

4. Modern English Edition – Coming Soon! We're currently working on a modernized version that updates the language to a smooth, reader-friendly 20th-century style, making this classic adventure even more accessible.

5. Exclusive NFT Collection – Coming Soon! We've also created a series of exclusive NFTs for Michael Strogoff, offering a unique way to collect and engage with this timeless story. Stay tuned!

Jules Verne's Michael Strogoff, or The Courier of the Czar is a thrilling adventure novel set against the vast and treacherous landscapes of

19th-century Russia. The story follows Michael Strogoff, a loyal courier entrusted by Czar Alexander II with a perilous mission: to deliver an urgent message to the governor of Irkutsk and warn him of an impending Tartar rebellion. With telegraph lines cut and enemy spies lurking at every turn, Michael must travel over 5,000 miles from Moscow to Siberia, crossing forests, rivers, and the formidable Ural Mountains while evading capture by treacherous forces. His duty demands unwavering courage and resilience, as failure could mean the fall of Irkutsk and disaster for the Russian Empire.

In Book 1, Jules Verne's Michael Strogoff, or The Courier of the Czar follows the fearless courier of Alexander II on a perilous mission across the vast, treacherous Russian Empire. Tasked with delivering a crucial message to the governor of Irkutsk, Strogoff braves Tatar invasions, the Siberian wilderness, and relentless foes while maintaining his disguise. Along the way, he encounters journalists, spies, and the cunning Ivan Ogareff, a traitor bent on bringing the empire to its knees. His journey is a test of endurance, loyalty, and sheer willpower.

In Book 2, the saga deepens as Strogoff faces greater trials after being captured and subjected to a brutal mock execution, leaving him presumed blinded. Against all odds, he pushes forward, relying on his instincts and unwavering patriotism to reach Irkutsk before Ogareff can unleash his treachery. As the Tatars tighten their grip, Strogoff's final confrontation with his nemesis becomes a defining moment for Russia's survival. Verne masterfully blends historical drama, adventure, and espionage in a gripping tale of duty and heroism at the heart of the empire.

Prologue - Michael Strogoff I & II

Michael Strogoff I & II

From the frozen wastes of Siberia to the fortified cities along the Irtysh, whispers of rebellion rode upon the air, carried by merchants, Cossacks, and exiled men who knew too well the signs of coming strife. Across the vast and treacherous expanse of Asiatic Russia, where the Czar's grip stretched thin over steppe and mountain, the great empire trembled beneath the weight of an unseen enemy.

To the west, Saint Petersburg schemed in its gilded halls, while in Moscow, generals pored over maps marked with the ever-shifting borders of loyalty and betrayal. To the east, beyond the great rivers and dense forests, lay the frontier, a world where the authority of the Russian crown was measured not in decrees but in the speed of a courier's horse.

It was upon the Postmaster Roads that the empire lived and breathed. These arteries of communication, stretching thousands of versts through perilous terrain, were the veins of the Czar's will, binding the farthest reaches of his dominion. Across these routes, the couriers rode, men of iron endurance, bound by duty, carrying dispatches that could mean the difference between war and peace, between loyalty and rebellion.

And now, as the Tartar hordes gathered under the banners of an unseen leader, the fate of the empire depended more than ever on those men who rode alone into the storm.

In the city of Omsk, where the Siberian winds carried the scent of damp earth and the whisper of fate, one such man prepared for the road ahead. Michael Strogoff, a courier of the Tsar, stood at the threshold of history, unaware that he would soon become its author.

For the empire could not afford failure. The enemy moved in silence, striking in the darkness where no warning could be given. The couriers of Russia were all that stood between order and chaos, and of all those who rode, none would bear a burden greater than the one that now approached.

The dispatch was coming. The message that would change everything.

And when it did, Michael Strogoff would ride.

ASIAT

SSIA
Juan Jose Piedra
© 01/01/2025
QuantumDigitalPublishing.io
Michael Strogoff
or, The Courier of the Czar
Book I

Chapter One

A TARTAR CAMP

At a day's journey from Kolyvan, several miles past Diachinks town, a vast plain extends, dotted with towering trees, pines and cedars stretching toward the horizon. During warmer months, Siberian shepherds graze their abundant flocks in this section of the land, their bells echoing across the grasslands as sheep and goats feast on the rich vegetation. However, at this time, the approaching danger had driven away every nomadic resident. Yet the plain was far from empty. It was bustling with an ominous activity.

Fearsome Emir Feofar-Khan, at the heart of his Tartar army, commanded a landscape dotted with white tents like sprouting mushrooms, his pavilion a pinnacle of power. The next day, August 7th, saw the arrival of captives from Kolyvan, where Russian forces had failed to halt the invaders' advance despite their valiant resistance. The Russian army had suffered devastating losses, of the two thousand troops who had faced the enemy's twin columns extending from Tomsk and Omsk. Only a few hundred survived, their defeat marking another victory in the Tartars' relentless march westward.

The situation looked grim. Imperial control seemed to have crumbled beyond the Ural frontiers, though this setback would prove temporary, as Russian forces would prevail against the barbaric invaders. For now, though, the invasion had penetrated deep into Siberia's heart, spreading through rebellious territories both east and west like wildfire through dry grass. Irkutsk, Asiatic Russia's capital, stood vulnerable to its insufficient garrison, its walls a thin line of defense against the surging tide of invaders. Without timely reinforcements from the Amoor and Takutsk provinces, their troops still days or weeks away on forced marches through treacherous terrain, the city would fall to the Tartars, leaving the Grand Duke, the Emperor's own brother, at the mercy of Ivan Ogareff's vengeance.

Had Michael Strogoff succumbed to his hardships, worn down by the endless classes of hostile territory? Had the mounting calamities since the Ichim incident, each more devastating than the last, broken his iron spirit? Was he ready to admit defeat, to surrender to the overwhelming odds that seemed to multiply with each passing day, believing his mission was impossible and his orders futile in the face of such widespread devastation?

But Michael belonged to that rare breed who persists until their last breath, who finds strength in adversity and courage in despair. He yet drew air; the imperial message remained secure in his possession; none had penetrated his disguise. He found himself among countless prisoners being herded like beasts by the Tartars, stumbling through dust and mud beneath the merciless sun. Each step toward Tomsk brought him closer to Irkutsk. He maintained his position ahead of Ivan Ogareff, a minor victory that sustained his resolve.

"I must make it!" he vowed, his jaw clenching with determination.

After what happened at Kolyvan, his thoughts focused on a single goal: freedom! How could he slip away from the Emir's guards? Every moment brought fresh scrutiny from the watchful Tartar soldiers, their curved sabers glinting in the harsh light as they prowled the edges of the prisoner column.

The sight of Feofar's encampment was breathtaking, a sprawling city of tents that stretched across the plain like a sea of silk and canvas, banners snapping in the wind.

Countless tents made of hide, felt, and silk sparkled under the sunlight like gems scattered across the steppe. Tall plumes adorned their pointed peaks, fluttering among flags, banners, and streamers of every imaginable hue, from deep crimson to brilliant azure. The most lavish tents belonged to the Seides and Khodjas, the khanat's most distinguished figures, their dwellings adorned with intricate patterns and precious ornaments that spoke of wealth and power. A distinctive pavilion, decorated with a horse's tail emerging from an array of woven red and white poles, marked the exalted status of these Tartar leaders, its shadow stretching long across the trampled grass. Beyond stretched thousands of Turcoman tents, known as "Karaoy," which were transported on camelback, their dark shapes dotting the landscape like islands in a vast sea.

The massive encampment housed 150,000 troops, split between cavalry and infantry, all united under the Alamanes banner that rippled in the wind. The Tadjiks stood out among these forces as the quintessential representatives of Turkestan, distinguished by their classical features, fair complexion, tall stature, and dark hair and eyes that seemed to hold the mysteries of the ancient silk road. Making up the largest portion of the Tartar military, they came in equal numbers from the khanats of Khokhand and Koundouge as from Bokhara, their diverse origins clear in the subtle variations of their dress and weaponry. The air hummed with the sounds of their different dialects mixing, creating a constant murmur that drifted across the camp like music.

Interspersed among the Tadjiks were warriors from various neighboring peoples. The short-statured, red-bearded Usbecks, similar to those who had chased Michael, stood alongside flat-faced Kirghiz warriors who resembled Kalmucks. These Kirghiz bore an array of weapons: Asian-made lances, bows and arrows, sabers, matchlock guns, and the deadly "tschakane", a short-handled ax known for inflicting fatal wounds. Their skill with these diverse weapons matched their fierce battle reputation; each warrior carried three or four different weapons.

The Mongol soldiers presented a distinctive appearance with their medium build, black hair braided into back-hanging pigtails, circular faces, dark complexions, and sparse beards. Blue nankeen, trimmed with black plush leather, composed their clothes. Their attire also included sword-belts with silver buckles, braided coats, and fur-edged silk caps adorned with three trailing ribbons. The ribbons, dancing in the wind like serpents, served as markers of rank and experience, their colors and patterns telling stories of battles fought and victories won. Supple leather and metal studs reinforced their boots, suiting them for riding and fighting on foot, a testament to their versatility as warriors.

The army's diversity extended to dark-skinned Afghans with their weathered faces and battle-hardened expressions, Arabs displaying the classic features of ancient Semitic peoples - aquiline noses and deep-set eyes, and Turcomans with their distinctive pupilless-appearing eyes that seemed to reflect the vast steppes of their homeland. All these varied peoples served together under the Emir's banner, a flag that symbolized destruction and pillage across the lands it conquered.

Within the ranks of these independent warriors were several slave soldiers of Persian origin, led by their own countrymen as officers. Feofar-Khan's military forces highly regarded these Persian units for their disciplined approach to warfare and the mastery of both bow and blade. Their reputation for unwavering loyalty, even in captivity, had earned their positions of trust.

The army's composition was further diversified by Jewish servants, distinguished by their cord-bound garments and small dark cloth caps worn in place of the turban (which their faith prohibited). They moved through the camp, maintaining supplies and tending to essential logistics. Hundreds of "kalenders", religious beggars dressed in tattered clothing and leopard also supplemented the ranks of skins, their wild appearance masking their fervent dedication to both faith and combat. These wandering warriors carried curved daggers beneath their ragged garments and were known for their fearless charges into battle. This diverse assembly of peoples and tribes, each bringing their own fighting traditions and survival skills, formed the Tartar army.

The scene was a masterpiece of visual splendor that would challenge even the most talented painter to capture its full magnificence, a tableau that seemed to blend earthly wealth with divine authority.

Feofar's grand pavilion dominated the encampment. Luxurious silk, cascading in elegant folds and secured with ropes and gold tassels, adorned the tent; the tassels' metallic sheen caught the sunlight like frozen streams. Tall, graceful plumes crowned its peak, swaying like elegant fans in the breeze, their shadows dancing across the dyed fabric below. The majestic shelter stood in a spacious clearing, embraced by towering birch and pine trees whose ancient trunks seemed to stand guard over this temporary palace. A gleaming lacquered table, embellished with precious gems of sapphire and ruby that sparkled like morning dew, sat before the tent, supporting the holy Koran. Master artisans designed its sacred pages from delicate gold leaf, executing each letter and flourish with exquisite precision. The Tartar standard flew overhead, displaying the Emir's coat of arms in its quartered design, the fabric snapping in the mountain air as if proclaiming its master's authority to the heavens themselves.

The ornate tents of Bokhara's highest officials formed a precise semicircle around the mountain clearing, each dwelling marked by distinctive pennants that fluttered in the crisp air. Among these distinguished residents was the master of stables, who held the unique privilege of accompanying the Emir on horseback right into the palace courtyard, a right guarded and passed down through generations. Nearby dwelt the grand falconer, keeper of the royal hunting birds, and the "housch-begui," keeper of the royal seal whose touch could transform a mere document into imperial law. The artillery commander, known as "toptschi-baschi," also maintained his quarters there, his tent marked by crossed bronze cannons above the entrance. The council head, the “khodja,” enjoyed special honors, like receiving the prince's kiss and appearing with an untied girdle, signifying great trust and intimacy. Verses from the Koran distinguished the religious authority rested with the "scheikh-oul-islam," leader of the Ulemas, embroidered in gold thread along its edges. The "cazi-askev" handled military disputes when the Emir was away, wielding power over life and death in matters of martial discipline. Completing this circle of power was the chief astrologer, whose primary duty involved consulting the stars whenever the Khan contemplated moving, his tent adorned with celestial symbols and charts mapping the heavens' secrets.

The Emir remained secluded in his tent when the prisoners arrived at the camp, choosing not to appear behind its embroidered curtains. This was likely a blessing, as even the slightest gesture or command from him could have sparked a massacre among his zealous followers. By maintaining his distance, he embodied the mysterious power of Eastern monarchs, whose very invisibility inspired both awe and terror among their subjects, a tradition dating back to the great Khans of antiquity.

The captives faced a grim fate. Guards would herd them like cattle into a crude enclosure ringed by sharpened stakes, where they would endure harsh treatment, meager rations of moldy bread and brackish water, and the full force of the elements while awaiting Feofar's judgment. The Tartar soldiers took particular pleasure in tormenting these captured enemies, prodding them with spear butts and showering them with jeers in their guttural dialect.

Michael Strogoff proved to be the most compliant and composed among them. He submitted to being guided, knowing they were taking him to his intended destination under safer conditions than if he had traveled alone from Kolyvan to Tomsk. His calm demeanor and apparent acceptance of his fate drew suspicious glances from the guards, who were accustomed to more resistance from their captives. Attempting an escape before reaching Tomsk would have risked encountering the Tartar scouts patrolling the steppe, their mounted units sweeping across the grasslands like hungry wolves searching for prey. The easternmost boundary of Tartar control lay at the eighty-fifth meridian, which intersected Tomsk, creating an invisible line between captivity and freedom that consumed Strogoff's thoughts. Once beyond this meridian, Michael believed he would be clear of enemy territory and could journey through Genisci to reach Krasnoiarsk before Feofar-Khan's forces could spread into the province.

Michael silently repeated, "Once at Tomsk" to himself, trying to suppress his mounting impatience, his fingers tapping against his leg as he walked. "Just a few minutes more and I'll be past the outposts. Twelve hours gained on Feofar and Ogareff would give me enough of a head start to Irkutsk." The thought of outpacing his enemies gave him a grim satisfaction, though he kept his face neutral as the guards prodded the group forward.

What troubled Michael most deeply was the thought of Ivan Ogareff being present in the Tartar encampment. Beyond the risk of being identified, he sensed this traitor was the one person he had to outrun. He realized that once Ogareff's forces merged with Feofar's, it would create a complete invasion force that would sweep toward Eastern Siberia's capital as one overwhelming unit. These thoughts consumed him, and he listened for any trumpet signals that might herald the Emir's lieutenant's arrival, his shoulders stiffening at every distant sound carried on the wind.

Thoughts of his loved ones weighed heavily on his mind - his mother imprisoned in Omsk, and Nadia, now held captive aboard the Irtych boats just like Marfa Strogoff. He felt powerless to help either of them. The possibility that he might never see them again made his heart sink with despair. His jaw clenched as he imagined their faces, wondering if they still held hope, if they were being treated, if they had enough food and water. The burden of their fates pressed down on him like a physical weight, making each step forward feel like an act of will against his desire to turn back and attempt their rescue, however foolish and impossible such an action might be.

Within the same Tartar encampment where Michael Strogoff was being held, his former traveling companions, Harry Blount and Alcide Jolivet, were also being held captive. Though aware that the telegraph office had captured them all and that guarded walls now confined them together, Michael kept his distance. Their opinion of him since the Ichim incident meant little to him now. He preferred solitude, wanting the freedom to act if needed, and thus maintained his isolation from his onetime acquaintances. He sometimes glimpsed them across the compound, huddled together in earnest discussion, no doubt planning their next newspaper dispatches should they ever regain their freedom. The two journalists seemed to have formed an unlikely alliance in their captivity, their previous professional rivalry set aside in the face of their shared predicament. Michael found a bitter irony in how circumstances had pushed the competitive reporters together while driving him further into self-imposed seclusion.

During the journey from Kolyvan to the camp, Harry Blount depended on Jolivet's unwavering support. After being wounded and falling at Jolivet's side, Blount kept pace with the other prisoners only by leaning on his companion's arm for several hours. Though he attempted to declare his status as a British subject, the barbaric captors showed no concern, responding only with threatening jabs from their weapons. Left with no choice, the Daily Telegraph's correspondent had to endure the same harsh treatment as everyone else, though he resolved to lodge a formal protest and demand recompense later. The journey proved especially difficult because of his painful wound, and without Jolivet's constant aid, Blount would not have survived the march to reach the camp. Each stumbling step sent waves of agony through his injured leg, and the freezing wind cut through his inadequate clothing like knives. Jolivet, despite his own exhaustion, maintained a steady stream of quiet encouragement in his peculiar mix of French and English, helping to keep Blount's mind focused on placing one foot in front of the other rather than dwelling on the growing infection he could feel taking hold in his wound.

The correspondent Jolivet, ever practical in his outlook, had done everything possible to boost his companion's physical and mental condition. Once they were inside the enclosure, his immediate priority was to check Blount's injury. He helped remove Blount's coat and discovered that the bullet had grazed the shoulder, though the surrounding skin was an angry red from exposure and strain.

"Nothing serious," he assured him, prodding the area with experienced fingers. "Just a surface wound. You'll be fine after I dress it a few times. The inflammation will subside."

"But who will dress it?" Blount inquired, his British reserve clear, even through his obvious discomfort.

"I'll take care of that myself," Jolivet responded, already rolling up his sleeves.

"Oh? You have medical training?" Blount's skepticism was obvious in his voice.

"Every Frenchman knows a bit about medicine," Jolivet replied with confidence, a familiar twinkle returning to his eye. "We learn it somewhere between wine-tasting and philosophy."

Alcide ripped his handkerchief in two, fashioning one piece into lint and the other into bandages with practiced movements. After drawing water from a well in the center of the enclosure, its rusty chain creaking in protest, he cleaned the wound and applied the damp cloth to Harry Blount's shoulder, his touch gentle but assured.

"Water is my treatment of choice," he explained, dabbing at the wound's edges. "It's the most effective pain reliever we know for wounds, and it's now the most widely used. Can you believe it took doctors six thousand years to figure this out? Yes, a full six thousand years, give or take! Such a simple solution, right under our noses the whole time."

"Much appreciated, Monsieur Jolivet," Harry said as he reclined on the cushion of dried foliage that his companion had prepared for him beneath a birch's cooling shadow. His face had already showed signs of relief from the treatment.

"Oh, think nothing of it! You'd do the same for me," Jolivet replied, adjusting the makeshift bandage with practiced care.

"I wouldn't be so certain," Blount replied with frank honesty, though a hint of amusement played at the corners of his mouth.

"Don't be absurd, you fool! Every Englishman has a generous heart," Jolivet declared, patting his handiwork with satisfaction. "It's written into your constitution."

"Perhaps, but what about the French?" Blount countered, his eyes twinkling despite his apparent discomfort.

"Ah, the French, they're savages, if that's what you want to call them! But their saving grace is their Frenchness itself. Now, let's drop this topic, or better yet, let's have complete silence. You must rest," Jolivet insisted, his tone growing more stern with each word.

Despite needing rest for his wound, Harry Blount, the Daily Telegraph correspondent, couldn't keep quiet. The journalist in him was far too restless to succumb to silence.

"M. Jolivet," he inquired, shifting against the tree trunk, "what do you think? Have our recent dispatches made it past the Russian lines?"

"I don't see why not," Alcide replied, busying himself with organizing his travel pack. "I'm certain my dear cousin is already well-informed about everything that happened at Kolyvan."

For the first time addressing his companion, Blount asked, his professional curiosity getting the better of him, "How many copies of her dispatches does your cousin distribute?"

Alcide chuckled, a knowing gleam in his eye. "My cousin is quite the private person," he said, adjusting his cravat with deliberate care. "She doesn't appreciate being discussed and would be upset to think she's keeping you from the rest you need."

"I have no interest in sleeping," the Englishman retorted with concealed impatience. "What's your cousin's take on the situation in Russia?"

"The situation may look dire for now. But damn! The Russian government has such might - they can't be worried about some barbarian invasion," he said, waving his hand as if brushing away an annoying insect. "We will crush these Tartars like all the others before them."

"Even the mightiest empires have fallen because of overconfidence," Blount countered, betraying a hint of the typical English skepticism toward Russia's ambitions in Central Asia. His fingers drummed against his knee as he spoke.

"Please, let's avoid politics," Jolivet interjected, adjusting his position with a slight wince. "Doctor's orders. It's terrible for shoulder wounds - almost as bad as making you fall asleep. And I've had quite enough of both for one day."

"Then let's discuss what our next move should be," replied Blount, leaning forward with renewed intensity. "I don't plan on being these Tartars's prisoner any longer than necessary, Mr. Jolivet."

"Good heavens, neither would I!" Jolivet exclaimed, his voice dropping to a whisper despite their relative privacy. "The accommodations are up to standard."

"Should we make a run for it when we get the chance?" Blount's eyes darted toward the tent entrance as he spoke.

"Yes, if we can't find another way to get free." Jolivet rubbed his wrists where the ropes had chafed them earlier.

"Have you thought of something else?" Blount asked, eyeing his companion with a mixture of skepticism and hope.

"Of course. We're not combatants; we're neutral parties, and we can demand our release. Any civilized army would recognize that fact."

"From that savage Feofar-Khan?" Blount scoffed, shaking his head at the notion.

"No, he wouldn't grasp the concept," Jolivet replied, drumming his fingers on his knee. "But from his second-in-command, Ivan Ogareff."

"That man's a scoundrel." Blount spat the words with obvious distaste.

"True enough, but he's a Russian scoundrel. He understands you can't ignore human rights, and keeping us serves no purpose for him. Still, I'm not keen on asking that man for any favors." Jolivet grimaced at the thought.

"Where is that man? I haven't spotted him anywhere in the camp," Blount pointed out, peering through the tent flap again.

"Don't worry, he'll show up. It's inevitable. He needs to meet with the Emir. With Siberia split in half now, Feofar's forces are just waiting for his arrival before they march on Irkutsk." Jolivet's voice took on a grim tone as he considered the implications of such a military advance.

"And once we're free, what's our next move?" Blount asked, touching the makeshift bandage on his arm.

"We'll keep up our mission, trailing the Tartars until we can make our way to the Russian forces. We can't back down now, we're just getting started. You've already earned your battle scars for the Daily Telegraph, while I have faced no hardship yet for my publication. Though I must say, this entire ordeal has given me enough material for a dozen articles." He paused, studying his companion's face. "Ah, look at that," Alcide Jolivet said, "he's drifted off. Nothing that a few hours of rest and some cold compresses won't fix. These Englishmen are built like tanks. Perhaps getting knocked around by those guards was a blessing in disguise, forcing him to get some sleep."

During Harry Blount's rest period, Alcide maintained a vigilant watch nearby, his notebook at the ready, filling it with detailed observations. His pencil moved swiftly across the pages, capturing not only the events but also the charged atmosphere of uncertainty that hung over the camp. He intended to share these notes with his colleague, ensuring Daily Telegraph readers would receive comprehensive coverage that reflected both their perspectives. Recent events had forged an unexpected alliance between the two men, dissolving their previous professional rivalry into something resembling genuine friendship and mutual respect. Ironically, what Michael Strogoff feared most had become the journalists' greatest hope, Ivan Ogareff's arrival would provide them with the story they sought, a tale of intrigue and conflict that would captivate their readers back home. This put their interests in direct opposition to Strogoff's objectives, creating an unspoken tension that none of them acknowledged. Recognizing this conflict, and mindful of several other concerns about maintaining his cover and protecting his mission, Strogoff kept his distance from his former traveling companions, taking care to remain out of their sight whenever they crossed paths in the crowded encampment.

The situation remained unchanged for four days. The captives received no word about the Tartar camp dismantling. Under constant surveillance, they faced an impenetrable ring of guards, both on foot and on horseback, monitoring them around the clock. Their meager rations arrived twice daily, charred goat intestines or portions of "kroute," a tart cheese crafted from sheep's milk. This cheese, when mixed with mare's milk, creates the Kirghiz specialty known as "koumyss," a staple that even their captors seemed to relish.

Violent storms, lashing rain, and howling winds tore through the camp like angry spirits, turning the weather brutal. The prisoners, lacking any protection save what threadbare garments they still possessed, endured these harsh elements without relief, huddling together in desperate attempts to preserve warmth. The toll was especially heavy on the injured women and children, with several succumbing to their conditions despite the valiant efforts of their fellow captives to share what little they had. Their captors added to their degradation by forcing them to dig graves for their dead, refusing even this basic duty and watching with cruel indifference as grieving families struggled with frozen ground and inadequate tools to bury their loved ones.

During this difficult time, Alcide Jolivet and Michael Strogoff labored in their assigned sections of the compound. Being strong and in good health, they endured the harsh conditions better than most others and could withstand the challenges they faced. Their guidance and support proved invaluable to their fellow prisoners, who were suffering and losing hope. Through quiet words of encouragement and minor acts of help, they helped maintain what little dignity remained among the captives, sharing their meager rations with the weakest and organizing small work groups to improve their desperate situation.

Could these circumstances continue? Would Feofar-Khan, content with his initial victory, delay his advance on Irkutsk? These concerns seemed likely to materialize. However, events unfolded differently. On August 12th, the situation Jolivet and Blount expected, yet Michael dreaded, transpired. As dawn broke, an unusual stirring among their captors created a palpable tension that spread through the compound like an icy wind, leaving the prisoners to wonder what fresh torment awaited them.

Across the desolate plains echoed the cacophony of trumpets, drums, and cannons. A massive dust cloud billowed across the Kolyvan road as Ivan Ogareff led his army of thousands into the encampment of the Tartars, their horses' hooves pounding the earth like rolling thunder. The air grew thick with the metallic scent of weaponry and the acrid smoke of gunpowder as column after column of mounted warriors emerged from the haze, their standards snapping in the wind and their armor glinting in the morning light.

Chapter Two

CORRESPONDENTS IN TROUBLE

The vast army of the Emir advanced under Ivan Ogareff's command. His forces, comprising both mounted soldiers and foot soldiers, had taken part in the capture of Omsk. Ogareff had failed to seize the elevated citadel where the governor and his troops had taken shelter, he chose not to linger. The fortified position had proven too strong for a direct assault, and a prolonged siege would have delayed his broader objectives. Determined to press forward with the campaign to conquer Eastern Siberia, he stationed a defensive force in Omsk, gathered additional troops from those who had taken Kolyvan, and merged his strengthened forces with Feofar's army. The combined might of their forces stretched across the horizon like a dark tide.

The troops under Ivan Ogareff's command stopped at the camp perimeter, their weapons gleaming in the fading light. Their leader did not instruct them to set up camp, as he intended to push straight through to Tomsk with minimal delay. The soldiers remained mounted or stood at attention, awaiting orders to continue their march. This strategic town would serve as a crucial base for their upcoming military operations, its position and resources, making it an ideal staging ground for further conquest.

Along with his military force, Ogareff was transporting a group of Russian and Siberian captives taken during the battles at Omsk and Kolyvan. Harsh conditions confronted these prisoners; instead of placing them in the full main enclosure, guards forced them to remain unprotected on the outskirts, without adequate food or protection from the elements. The relentless march wounded many, and their injuries went poorly treated, while others showed signs of exhaustion. Their fate remained uncertain, would Feofar-Khan have them imprisoned once they reached Tomsk, or would he order their execution, as Tartar leaders did when prisoners became burdensome? Only the unpredictable Emir knew what he had planned for these unfortunate souls.

Trailing behind the army that had marched from Omsk and Kolyvan was the usual collection of vagrants, bandits, traveling merchants, and nomadic peoples, the typical hangers-on that follow military forces on campaign. These opportunists set up their own makeshift camps each night, trading goods and information, offering services to soldiers, and scavenging what they could from the army's wake. Some were spies, others survivors trying to profit from the chaos of war, but all contributed to the swelling mass of humanity that stretched for miles behind the dominant force.

These followers stripped the land bare wherever they went, leaving almost nothing in their wake - not a stalk of wheat in the fields, not a head of livestock in the pastures. The army had no choice but to keep advancing, if only to find enough food to sustain the soldiers, pushing ever forward like a swarm of locusts across the steppes. The army plundered the entire territory between Ichim and the Obi, exhausting all resources down to the last root vegetable and dried grass blade. In the Tartars' path lay only barren wasteland, a desolate stretch of earth that would take years to recover its former fertility.

Moving from the western regions, a notable Tsigane band stood out among the arriving gypsies, the same group that had journeyed with Michael Strogoff to Perm, their colorful wagons and fierce horses drawing wary glances from other travelers. Among them was Sangarre, the ruthless spy who served Ivan Ogareff with unwavering loyalty, her dark eyes missing nothing as she surveyed the countryside. While Ogareff made his way to Ichim, Sangarre led her band through the province's southern territory to reach Omsk, gathering intelligence and marking the movements of Russian forces along their circuitous route.

Sangarre proved invaluable to Ogareff's operations. Her gypsy group could slip unnoticed into any location, acting as his eyes and ears throughout the occupied territories. Through this network, Ogareff maintained a constant awareness of developments deep within the conquered provinces. He rewarded this surveillance, knowing well the strategic advantage it provided him.

The Russian officer had once rescued Sangarre when she found herself entangled in a grave situation. The debt of gratitude remained forever etched in her mind, leading her to pledge unwavering loyalty to him. Her dedication went beyond mere obligation, she had developed an almost fanatical devotion to Ogareff's cause, directing her fellow Tsigane with ruthless efficiency. They moved like shadows through villages and military outposts, their aimless wandering concealing a orchestrated web of espionage. Local authorities, who might have otherwise questioned their presence, often dismissed them as simple nomads, never suspecting the crucial intelligence flowing through their network.

Ivan Ogareff, upon choosing the path of betrayal, recognized how he could use this woman's dedication. Sangarre would carry out any command he issued without question, executing his will with a single-minded focus that bordered on obsession. Beyond mere gratitude, an unexplainable force drove her to become subservient to the traitor, having been bound to him since he first arrived in Siberian exile, where their paths had crossed amid the harsh winter winds.

A loyal associate, Sangarre, who lived as a nomad without ties to any nation or family, had offered her services to the invaders that Ogareff had unleashed upon Siberia. She moved through the land like a phantom, her dark eyes missing nothing, her network of informants growing with each passing day. She possessed remarkable cunning and fierce determination, showing neither mercy nor forgiveness to those who stood in her way. Her ruthlessness made her a formidable ally in Ogareff's campaign, and her reputation alone often extracted information from those who might otherwise resist.

After arriving in Omsk with her fellow travelers, Sangarre had remained at Ogareff's side, her dark presence like a shadow that never wavered. She knew about Michael and Marfa Strogoff's meeting and shared Ogareff's concerns about a courier traveling for the Czar, her instincts telling her there was more to this situation than met the eye. With Marfa Strogoff in her custody, Sangarre could employ cruel methods to extract information from the prisoner, methods she had perfected through years of practicing her dark craft. However, Ogareff had not yet decided it was time to force the old Siberian woman to speak, preferring to let fear and isolation do their work first. So Sangarre waited, keeping Marfa under constant surveillance, studying her every movement and word, trying to catch any mention of the word "son," her keen ears attuned to even the slightest whisper or mumbled prayer. Despite her vigilance, Marfa's silence remained unbroken, a testament to the old woman's iron will.

When the trumpets first sounded, their brass notes echoing across the encampment, a group of high-ranking officers, accompanied by an impressive contingent of Usbeck cavalry in their distinctive armor and flowing robes, advanced to the camp's entrance to welcome Ivan Ogareff. Upon meeting him, they showed him profound respect, bowing and speaking in reverent tones, and requested his presence at Feofar-Khan's quarters, where matters of great importance awaited discussion.

Maintaining his characteristic composure, Ogareff responded to their courtesies with cold detachment, his face a mask of calculated indifference. His attire was plain, yet exuded an air of rebellious pride. He continued to wear his Russian military uniform, its brass buttons gleaming in the harsh light.

Just as he prepared to enter the camp, Sangarre emerged from among the officers like a shadow taking form, stopping in front of him. Her presence caused several nearby horses to stamp. "Nothing?" Ogareff inquired, his voice barely above a whisper.

"Not a thing," she replied with apparent frustration.

"We must wait."

"Will we soon make the elderly woman reveal what she knows?" Sangarre's fingers twisted at her sleeve as she spoke.

"Indeed, we will, Sangarre," Ogareff answered with quiet certainty.

"Tell me when she'll talk."

"Once we arrive at Tomsk."

"And that journey ends..." she pressed, leaning closer.

"Three days from now," he cut her off.

A mysterious light flashed in Sangarre's dark eyes before she walked away, her silhouette melting into the shadows between the tents. Ogareff dug his spurs into his mount's sides with unnecessary force, causing the horse to snort in protest, and, trailed by his contingent of Tartar officers who maintained a respectful distance, made his way toward the Emir's pavilion, where the silk banners snapped in the rising wind.

The high-ranking Tartar leader Feofar-Khan sat awaiting his lieutenant in his opulent tent, surrounded by braziers that filled the air with sweet-scented smoke. His council gathered around him: the keeper of the royal seal, his face lined with age and wisdom; the stern-faced khodja in his dark robes; and several senior military officers with their curved sabers at their sides. Ivan Ogareff arrived on horseback, dismounted with practiced ease, and stepped inside, the tent flap rustling behind him.

At forty years old, Feofar-Khan cut an imposing figure, tall and pale-skinned, with fierce features, malevolent eyes that seemed to pierce through men's souls, and a thick black beard that cascaded down his chest like silk. His battle attire was a dazzling display of wealth and power: a coat of mail inlaid with gold and silver that caught the lamplight, a jewel-encrusted cross-belt and scabbard that spoke of plundered riches, boots fitted with golden spurs that clinked as he moved, and a helmet crowned with sparkling diamond plumes that trembled with his slightest motion. Yet despite all this finery, his appearance struck one as more peculiar than majestic for a Tartar ruler, a self-indulgent Sardanapalus who held absolute power over his subjects' lives and fortunes, and wielded that power with capricious cruelty.

As Ivan Ogareff entered, the high-ranking officials remained in their positions atop cushions adorned with golden thread and intricate Eastern motifs. However, Feofar stood up from an ornate divan at the rear of the tent, where a luxurious Bokharian carpet with a thick velvet pile covered the ground, its deep crimson and azure patterns telling ancient stories of conquest and glory.

The Emir moved toward Ogareff with calculated grace and given upon him a significant kiss, one whose importance was unmistakable to all who witnessed it. This gesture elevated Ogareff to the head of the council, placing him in authority even above the learned scholar, whose weathered face betrayed a flicker of displeasure at this unexpected honor.

Feofar then broke the silence, his voice carrying the weight of absolute authority through the perfumed air. "There's no need for me to interrogate you," he declared, settling back onto his divan with fluid ease. "Speak freely, Ivan. Everyone here is most eager to hear what you have to say." His jeweled fingers traced idle patterns on the arm of his seat as he waited, the assembled dignitaries leaning forward almost imperceptibly in anticipation.

"My lord," said Ogareff, conveying his message with the ornate flourishes typical of Eastern speech, "I bring vital information." He continued in the Tartar tongue, his voice dropping to a conspiratorial timbre that made the assembled dignitaries lean closer still. "My lord, now is the time for action, not idle talk. You've witnessed my achievements leading your forces. We've secured both the Ichim and Irtych frontiers, and your Turcoman cavalry now water their steeds in what are now Tartar-controlled rivers. The Kirghiz tribes have rallied to Feofar-Khan's banner, swelling our ranks with their fierce warriors. Your armies can now advance either eastward toward the rising sun, or westward toward its setting."

"And should I follow the sun's path?" inquired the Emir, his expression remaining inscrutable beneath his jeweled turban, fingers still tracing those meaningless patterns.

"To follow the sun's path," Ogareff replied, drawing himself up with contained excitement, "means to strike at Europe itself, to conquer the Siberian territories of Tobolsk all the way to the Ural Mountains. The very heartland of Russian power lies vulnerable before us."

"What if I venture forth to confront this celestial messenger?"

The Tartars target Central Asia's most prosperous regions, including Irkutsk, for inclusion in their rule.

"What of the forces under the Sultan of St. Petersburg?" asked Feofar-Khan, using this peculiar title to refer to the Russian Emperor. His fingers drummed against the ornate arm of his chair, a steady rhythm that matched the tension in the air.

"They pose no threat," Ivan Ogareff assured him, his scarred face twisting into a confident smile. "Our attack came without warning; Irkutsk and Tobolsk will fall to your control before Russian reinforcements can arrive. The Czar's military crushed at Kolyvan, and they shall meet the same fate wherever they dare face your forces. Their scattered remnants flee before our advance like leaves before a storm."

"What direction should we take to serve the Tartar mission?" inquired the Emir after a thoughtful pause, his calculating gaze fixed on the detailed maps spread before him like a tapestry of conquest.

"We must advance eastward, toward the rising sun," Ivan Ogareff replied with conviction, tracing his finger along the map's eastern territories. "Let our Turcoman steeds graze upon the eastern steppes until their hooves shake the very foundations of Russian power. We shall capture Irkutsk, the eastern provinces' crown jewel, and with it claim a hostage more valuable than any territory, the Grand Duke himself, the Czar's own brother, who cowers behind its walls."

This was Ivan Ogareff's scheme, crafted through years of festering resentment. His passionate words revealed his true nature, he seemed cut from the same cloth as Stephan Razine, the infamous pirate who had terrorized Southern Russia during the 1700s, with similar dreams of chaos and revenge. Ogareff's deepest desire was to capture and eliminate the Grand Duke, thus satisfying his burning hatred that consumed him like a fever. Seizing Irkutsk would deliver all of Eastern Siberia into Tartar hands, from the Ural Mountains to the Pacific shores.

“Do it as you say, Ivan,” Feofar declared, drumming his jeweled fingers against the wooden table.

"What are your commands, Takhsir?" Ogareff asked, his head bowed in deference.

"We shall move our headquarters to Tomsk today," the Emir pronounced, rolling up the maps with deliberate precision.

Ogareff bowed, his scarred face concealing a triumphant smirk, and departed with the administrative officer to carry out the Emir's instructions, their boots echoing against the wooden floor as they left.

Just as he prepared to mount his horse to return to the outposts, chaos erupted from the prisoners' section of the camp. Several shouts pierced the air, followed by the crack of two or three gunshots, the sounds echoing off the wooden barracks. Perhaps some captives had attempted to escape or start an uprising, something that would require immediate and harsh response to maintain iron discipline among the ranks.

Ivan Ogareff and the administrative officer strode toward the commotion, their faces dark with contained fury. Within moments, two men burst through the gathering crowd, their clothes torn and muddy, having overpowered the guards who tried to restrain them with rifle butts and bare hands. All the other surrounding Tartar soldiers raised their weapons, ready to fire.

Lacking further information, and adhering to standard procedure, the administrative officer ordered the prisoners' deaths; however, Ogareff's intervention prevented the execution. Because these prisoners' manner and dress, different from the local captives, revealed their foreign nature to the Russian, who ordered them brought for questioning, his cold eyes studying their features.

Harry Blount and Alcide Jolivet stood before Ivan Ogareff. Earlier, they had insisted on seeing him upon his arrival at the camp, but the soldiers had denied their request with rough shoves and harsh words. What followed was chaos. A scuffle broke out when Blount attempted to push past a guard, the journalists attempted to flee through the gathering crowd, and shots rang out, the bullets whistling past their ears and kicking up dirt at their feet. Their lives would have ended there in the dusty camp thoroughfare had the Emir's lieutenant not stepped in, raising his hand to halt the execution.

The lieutenant studied these unfamiliar prisoners with scrutiny, noting their European dress and bearing. Though they had witnessed the violent encounter at the Ichim post-house where Ogareff had struck Michael Strogoff, the cruel traveler had paid no mind to anyone else present in that common room too focused on his own dark purposes to notice the watching journalists huddled in the shadows of the crowded space.

The two men, Blount and Jolivet, identified him, prompting Jolivet to whisper with contained revulsion, "Well, well! So the Colonel Ogareff we see here is none other than that brute from Ichim!" He then leaned closer to his companion, his breath hot against Blount's ear as he murmured, "Please handle this conversation, Blount. I'd be grateful. Something about seeing this Russian colonel in a Tartar camp turns my stomach. Though I owe him my life, I don't trust myself to look him in the eye without revealing my disgust. The very sight of him makes my blood run cold."

With these words, Alcide Jolivet composed his features into a mask of supreme, disdainful indifference, drawing himself up with the practiced hauteur of a Parisian gentleman who has encountered something unpleasant.

Ivan Ogareff may have noticed the prisoner's contemptuous demeanor, but he gave no sign, his face remaining as impassive as carved stone. "Your names, gentlemen?" he inquired in Russian, his voice cool and measured, lacking its characteristic harshness, though an undercurrent of menace lingered beneath the polite words.

"We're reporters from British and French newspapers," Blount stated, his clipped English accent lending authority to the simple declaration.

"I assume you have documentation to verify your credentials?" Ogareff's eyes narrowed as he studied their faces, searching for any sign of deception.

"These letters from the British and French chancelleries confirm our authorization in Russia," Blount declared, withdrawing the preserved documents from his leather satchel.

Ivan Ogareff examined the papers Blount presented, turning them over in his gloved hands and scrutinizing the official seals. "You're requesting permission to cover our military campaign in Siberia?" he asked, his tone neutral.

"All we want is freedom of movement," the British journalist replied curtly, his stance rigid and professional despite the tension in the air.

"Consider it granted, gentlemen," Ogareff responded, handing the papers back with practiced precision. "I look forward to reading your coverage in the Daily Telegraph." A ghost of a smile played at the corners of his mouth.

"The cost is sixpence per issue, delivery included," Blount stated with remarkable composure, as if discussing subscription rates in a London drawing room. He then rejoined his associate, who seemed to endorse his handling of the situation, a slight nod passing between them.

Showing no sign of annoyance at the journalist's impertinence, Ivan Ogareff mounted his steed with fluid grace and, taking his position at the front of his military escort, vanished into a swirling cloud of dust kicked up by dozens of hooves.

"Tell me, Jolivet, what's your impression of Colonel Ivan Ogareff? Who commands the Tartar forces?" Blount inquired once the soldiers were well out of earshot, brushing dust from his sleeve.

"My dear friend," Alcide responded with a sardonic grin, adjusting his cravat with theatrical flair, "I must say the administrator displayed quite an elegant form when he signaled for our execution. Such impeccable posture, is truly the mark of a gentleman."

Ogareff's motives aside, the two correspondents now found themselves unrestrained, able to move throughout the war zone. Rather than part ways, they stayed together, their previous antagonism having transformed into genuine camaraderie. Their shared experiences had forged a bond between them, erasing their former competitive spirit. Harry Blount remained grateful for his companion's help, though the latter never mentioned it. This newfound friendship enhanced their reporting capabilities, benefiting their readership from both the Daily Telegraph and Le Constitutionnel.

"Now that we're free," Blount inquired, adjusting his wire-rimmed spectacles with a thoughtful expression, "what's our next move?"

"You might as well take advantage of it," Alcide responded, pulling out his leather-bound notebook and studying the scrawled maps within. "We should head to Tomsk and observe the situation there firsthand."

"Until we can reconnect with a Russian regiment, I assume? Hopefully that won't be long," his companion replied, squinting at the distant horizon where dust clouds still marked Ogareff's departure.

"Exactly, my dear Blount. We mustn't become too comfortable among the Tartars. The civilized army has the advantage here. These Central Asian invaders have nothing to gain and everything to lose, while the Russians will push them back. It's a matter of time," Alcide declared with the confident air of a seasoned war correspondent who had witnessed countless similar conflicts.

While Ivan Ogareff's arrival had granted freedom to Jolivet and Blount, it posed a serious threat to Michael Strogoff. If chance brought the Czar's courier face-to-face with Ogareff, he would surely recognize Michael as the traveler he had treated so harshly at the Ichim post-house. Though Michael had restrained himself from responding to that insult, unlike how he might have reacted in different circumstances, any recognition would draw unwanted attention to him and complicate executing his mission. The memory of that confrontation still burned in his mind, making him all too aware of how precarious his position had become.

The situation had its drawbacks. Yet his presence brought one welcome development, the command to break camp and move headquarters to Tomsk. This aligned with Michael's deepest wishes. As mentioned before, he aimed to reach Tomsk by blending in with the other captives, reducing his chances of being spotted by the many scouts patrolling the town's outskirts. However, with Ivan Ogareff's unexpected appearance, he questioned whether his original strategy remained viable or if he should attempt an escape during the transfer instead. The chaos of moving an entire camp might provide opportunities, but it would also mean increased vigilance from the guards. Every option carried its own risks, and Michael knew one wrong choice could doom not only himself but his vital mission to warn Irkutsk.

The plan to continue on would have held firm in Michael's mind if not for the news that Feofar-Khan and Ogareff were already moving toward the town, accompanied by thousands of mounted warriors. "Perhaps it's best to bide my time," he reasoned. "Unless fortune presents an extraordinary chance to break free. The dangers are considerable on this side of Tomsk, but once I push beyond it, I'll have cleared the easternmost Tartar positions within hours. Just three more days of endurance, Lord willing!" His muscles tensed at the thought, but he forced himself to maintain an appearance of defeated resignation.

Watched by a large contingent of Tartar guards, the prisoners faced a grueling three-day trek across the steppe. The journey stretched one hundred and fifty kilometers from their camp to their destination, a manageable distance for the Emir's well-provisioned troops but a brutal ordeal for the captives, weakened by hunger and hardship. The bodies of those who couldn't survive the journey would soon mark the path they would take. Already, the elderly and infirm among them cast desperate glances at the horizon, knowing their chances of reaching Tomsk were slim.

The sun blazed overhead at two o'clock on August 12th, without a cloud in sight, when the toptschi-baschi commanded the group to begin their journey. The harsh rays beat down on the assembled crowd, and the dry grass crackled beneath their feet as they shuffled into formation.

Having gained horses, Alcide and Blount had already departed for Tomsk, where fate would bring together the key figures in this tale, their hoofbeats fading into the distance as dust clouds marked their progress across the barren landscape.

Among the captives in Ivan Ogareff's Tartar camp was an elderly woman who remained silent, keeping to herself and avoiding the other prisoners. She never uttered a sound, resembling a living monument to sorrow, her weathered face bearing the deep lines of untold hardships. This woman received close supervision, with the gipsy spy Tsigane Sangarre watching her, her dark eyes never straying far from her charge, though the old woman seemed oblivious to this surveillance. Despite her advanced years, she was forced to march alongside the other prisoners on foot, receiving no mercy or special consideration for her age, her steps growing more labored with each passing hour.

In their midst stood a young woman, placed there by fate's merciful hand to provide solace and aid. Among the other captives, this beautiful yet quiet girl had appointed herself as guardian to the elderly prisoner, moving with grace despite the harsh conditions. Though they exchanged no words, the young woman stayed beside the old woman, offering her support on difficult terrain and sharing her meager water ration whenever needed. Yet as time passed, the girl's straightforward gaze, modest demeanor, and the unspoken bond that forms between fellow sufferers melted Marfa Strogoff's reserve, creating a silent alliance against their shared misfortune.

Nadia, for this was indeed her name, returned to the mother the same care she had once received from the son. Her natural compassion guided her actions twofold. By dedicating herself to the older woman's care, Nadia's youth and beauty found shelter beneath the protective mantle of the elderly prisoner's age, shielding her from unwanted attention in these dangerous times.

The silent pair, a grandmother and granddaughter, commanded a certain respect from the crowd of suffering, embittered people around them. Even the most hardened among their fellow captives would step aside to let them pass, perhaps reminded of their own mothers or daughters left behind.

Tartar scouts captured Nadia along the Irtych and transported her to Omsk with other unfortunate travelers. There she remained a prisoner, sharing the same fate as all others taken by Ivan Ogareff, including Marfa Strogoff. The girl's quiet strength never wavered, even as the harsh conditions of their captivity tested the limits of human endurance.

Only Nadia's remarkable strength of spirit kept her from collapsing under these twin blows. The halting of her journey and Michael's death had left her oscillating between despair and agitation. She faced the anguish of being separated, perhaps, from her father, just when her determined efforts had brought her so close to him. Adding to her sorrow was the loss of her brave companion, whom Providence seemed to have sent to guide her. She couldn't banish from her thoughts the image of Michael Strogoff being struck by a lance before her eyes and vanishing into the Irtych's waters, his body swept away by the merciless current while she stood helpless on the shore.

Was it possible for such a noble person to meet such an end? Why would God not intervene if this virtuous soul, driven by an honorable mission, was destined for such a tragic fate? Her sorrow soon gave way to fury, burning hot in her chest. She recalled the humiliating incident at the Ichim relay station, where her companion had shown remarkable restraint in the face of cruel provocations. The memory made her blood surge with indignation, and her hands clenched at her sides as she relived those moments of helpless anger.

"Who shall seek justice for one who can no longer seek it himself?" she wondered, her whispered words carrying the weight of both a prayer and a promise. The question echoed in her mind, unanswered but persistent, as she gazed through the bars of her prison toward the distant horizon.

Deep within, she declared, "Let it be me!" The words burst forth with fierce determination, though she spoke them only to herself. Had Michael shared his secret with her before his passing, despite her being a young woman, she might have been able to complete the unfinished mission of her brother, whom the Lord had claimed . The weight of this lost opportunity pressed heavily upon her conscience.

Nadia, lost in her own reflections, noticed the hardships of her imprisonment, the cold stone walls, the meager rations, the endless hours of silence. A twist of fate placed her alongside Marfa Strogoff, and she remained unaware of the woman's true identity. How could she know that this elderly fellow prisoner was the mother of the man she knew only as

Nicholas Korpanoff? The weathered lines on Marfa's face held no clue to their connection. Marfa couldn't understand that this young woman beside her was her son's connection, and owed him an unrepayable debt of gratitude. They sat together in their shared confinement, each harboring secrets that might have changed everything had they only known.

What caught Nadia's attention about Marfa Strogoff was how they both endured their misfortunes with similar resilience. The elderly woman's steadfast demeanor in the face of daily trials and her indifference to physical discomfort could only stem from an emotional anguish that matched Nadia's own. This understanding was correct. An unspoken connection formed between them, as Nadia recognized in Marfa the same deep suffering that lay beneath the surface. The young girl's proud spirit admired this dignified way of handling hardship. Rather than offering help, Nadia provided it, leaving Marfa neither the burden of accepting nor declining help. Whenever the path grew challenging, Nadia was there for support. During food distribution, while the older woman would remain still, Nadia would share her meager rations with her, often placing the better portions near Marfa's hands when the guards weren't looking. This arrangement helped them endure the grueling journey across the harsh terrain, where each step seemed to drain more of their strength. With Nadia's support, Marfa could keep pace with the prisoner-guarding soldiers without suffering the fate of many other unfortunate captives who were bound to saddle-bows and pulled along this trail of misery, their feet bloody and raw from being dragged across the unforgiving ground.

The aged Marfa Strogoff could only exclaim, "May the Lord bless you, dear child, for your kindness to me in my twilight years!" These heartfelt words marked their sole exchange for some time, hanging in the air like a fragile thread connecting their shared misfortune.

Though the days stretched before them like centuries, both women remained quiet about their circumstances, finding solace in their silent companionship amid the harsh realities of their journey. Marfa, exercising careful discretion, shared minimal details about herself, avoiding any mention of her son or their fateful encounter, her weathered face masking the pain of secrets held close.

Nadia, too, kept to herself, though her composure gave way under the weight of her burdens. One day, as they huddled together during a brief rest, her emotions spilled forth as she recounted everything, from leaving Wladimir to witnessing Nicholas Korpanoff's last moments, her voice trembling with the raw memory of those events.

The elderly Siberian woman listened with strong attention as her young friend spoke, her lined face betraying a flash of recognition that she concealed. "Nicholas Korpanoff, you say?" she inquired, her voice carrying an unusual urgency. "Please, tell me more about him. In all my years, I've known only one person who might act in such a way. Are you certain that was his name? Think, my dear." Her gnarled fingers gripped her worn shawl as she waited for the answer.

"He was honest with me about everything else," Nadia responded, her fingers tracing patterns on the rough wooden table between them. "Why would he lie about his name? Everything about him spoke of honor and truth."

Driven by a strange inner feeling that seemed to quicken her aged heart, Marfa Strogoff pressed on with her questions, leaning forward in her chair.

"You mentioned his bravery, child. Did you witness this courage yourself?" she asked, her eyes searching Nadia's face.

"Brave doesn't describe him," Nadia declared with conviction, her cheeks flushing with remembered admiration. "He faced dangers that would have broken lesser men."

Marfa whispered to herself, her voice stirring the air, "That's exactly how my son would have behaved."

"Did you not mention," she continued, her voice growing stronger, "that he remained undaunted and unshaken by any challenge? That his gentle strength made him like both a brother and sister to you, watching over you with a mother's care?"

"Yes, that's true," Nadia confirmed, clasping her hands together. "He was everything to me, brother, sister, and mother, all in one! Through the darkest nights and coldest days, he never wavered."

"And he protected you fiercely, like a lion?" Marfa's voice quavered with suppressed emotion.

"Indeed, he did!" Nadia exclaimed, rising from her seat in enthusiasm. "Like a lion, an authentic hero! Nothing could stop him when danger threatened."

'My son, my son!' thought the elderly Siberian woman, her heart pounding beneath her worn dress. But aloud she said, maintaining her composure with visible effort, "Yet you mentioned he endured a terrible insult at the post-house in Ichim?"

"He endured it," Nadia replied, lowering her eyes, her fingers twisting the fabric of her dress.

"Endured it!" Marfa whispered with a shudder, her weathered hands trembling in her lap.

"Mother, please," Nadia pleaded, leaning forward with earnest intensity, "don't judge him! He carried a secret, a secret that only God can jüdge right now! There was purpose in everything he did."

Marfa lifted her head, her eyes searching Nadia's face as if trying to peer into her very soul, studying every minute expression that crossed the young woman's features. I'm curious. Did his public embarrassment cause you to despise Nicholas Korpanoff?

"No," Nadia answered, her voice filled with conviction despite its gentleness. "I was in awe of him, even though I couldn't comprehend his actions. Never had I felt he deserved more respect than at that moment. His dignity seemed to grow even as others tried to diminish it."

The old woman fell quiet, considering this for a moment, her fingers tracing the worn wooden arm of her chair.

"Was he a tall man?" she asked, breathing as she waited for the answer.

"Yes, very tall," Nadia confirmed, straightening her posture as if the mere memory made her stand prouder.

"And his looks?" the old woman pressed, her voice gentle, almost caressing the words. "Tell me, my dear girl."

A blush crept across Nadia's cheeks, coloring them like rose petals at dawn. "He was... very handsome. Noble in bearing, with eyes that could pierce your very soul."

"My son!" the old woman cried out, throwing her arms around Nadia with surprising strength. "It was my son, I tell you! My Michael!"

"Your son?" Nadia gasped in astonishment, her hands trembling as they clutched the fabric of her dress. "Your son?"

"Let me understand this, my dear," Marfa said, her weathered fingers reaching out to grasp Nadia's hands. "This man who traveled with you, who protected you, he had a mother. Did he ever mention her?"

"His mother?" Nadia's eyes softened with remembrance, a gentle smile playing at her lips. "He spoke of her, just as I spoke of my father. He loved her. Sometimes, on frosty nights by the fire, he would tell me stories of her strength and kindness."

Marfa's voice trembled with emotion, her grip tightening. "Nadia, you're describing my son. Everything you say matches what I know in my heart."

She leaned forward, her eyes bright with desperate hope. "Surely he was traveling to Omsk to see this mother he cherished so much?"

"No," Nadia replied, the weight of truth heavy in her voice, "he wasn't."

"What?" Marfa exclaimed, her voice rising as she pulled back, color draining from her face. "How dare you say he wasn't!"

"Let me explain: Despite what I've said, I realize that Nicholas Korpanoff had compelling reasons, unknown to me, for traveling through the region in complete secrecy. His very survival depended on it, and more importantly, his honor and duty were at stake. There were things far greater than personal desires driving his journey."

"Yes, duty, an overwhelming sense of duty," the elderly Siberian woman responded, her weathered hands clasping together. "The kind that forces someone to give up everything, including perhaps a last embrace with their mother. Nadia, there's so much you don't know, so much I didn't understand until now. You've helped me make sense of it all, like pieces of a puzzle falling into place. But while you've illuminated the shadows in my heart, I cannot do the same for yours. If my son chose not to share his secret with you, I must honor that silence. Please forgive me, Nadia; I can never repay your kindness in bringing me this understanding."

"Mother, I'm not asking you to tell me anything," Nadia replied, reaching out to touch the older woman's arm with gentle reassurance.

Understanding dawned on the elderly Siberian woman, everything made sense now, including her son's behavior toward her at the Omsk inn, his distant manner and careful words. Without question, the young girl's traveling companion had been Michael Strogoff himself, concealing his identity as the Czar's courier because of his secret mission through enemy territory. The pieces fit together with painful clarity, explaining both his presence in Siberia and his necessary deception.

"My courageous son," Marfa thought to herself, her weathered hands clasping in her lap. "I shall guard your secret. No amount of torture could make me reveal you were the one I encountered in Omsk. Not even to ease this child's pain."

With just a few words, Marfa could have repaid Nadia's kindness and devotion. She could have disclosed that her companion Nicholas Korpanoff, or rather Michael Strogoff, hadn't died in the Irtych River after all, since she had met and spoken with him several days after that incident. The truth burned in her throat like a coal, demanding release.

But she held her tongue, keeping silent, knowing the gravity of her son's mission and the lives that might depend on her discretion. Instead, she said, her voice gaining strength with each word, "Keep hope alive, my child. Misfortune won't defeat you. You'll be with your father. I feel it in my heart. And perhaps the one who called you sister still lives. God wouldn't let such a brave companion perish. Hold on to hope, dear child! Look at me, I wear this mourning dress, but not yet for my son." Her eyes gleamed with the conviction of one who knew more than she could say.

Chapter Three

BLOW FOR BLOW

The current circumstances had brought Marfa Strogoff and Nadia together. The old Siberian woman now comprehended their connection, and while Nadia remained unaware that the companion she mourned was still alive, she had at least discovered her link to the woman she now called mother. Nadia felt blessed to serve as a surrogate child to this woman who believed she had lost her son, finding solace in their shared grief and mutual support during these dark times.

Yet both women remained oblivious to one crucial fact: Michael, who had been taken prisoner in Kolyvan, was traveling in the same group of captives, heading toward Tomsk alongside them, separated by mere yards yet distant in the chaos of their forced march.

The captives delivered by Ivan Ogareff joined those already imprisoned in the Emir's Tartar encampment. These victims, a mix of Russian and Siberian military personnel and ordinary citizens, formed a massive column stretching several miles long, their footsteps raising clouds of dust in the summer heat. The most potentially threatening prisoners were bound in chains and shackles, the iron clanking with each weary step. The group included both women and children, many youngsters strapped to saddles, their faces streaked with tears and dirt, while the women were forced to march on foot or driven forward like livestock, their expressions haunted by exhaustion and despair. Mounted guards maintained strict order in the column, brandishing whips and rifle butts at any sign of rebellion or weakness, and none dared fall behind, save for those who collapsed, never to stand again, their bodies left as grim markers along the harsh Siberian road.

Because of these circumstances, Michael Strogoff found himself positioned among the front lines of those departing the Tartar encampment, with the Kolyvan captives. This placement made it impossible for him to interact with the prisoners who had arrived at the camp from Omsk after him. As a result, he remained unaware that his mother and Nadia were part of the convoy, while they too did not know he was marching ahead of them. The trek from the camp to Tomsk proved devastating, with many perishing under the brutal treatment of soldiers who drove them forward with whips and spears, showing particular cruelty to those who stumbled or pleaded for water. The soldiers forced the captives across the steppe on a path made even more suffocating by the dust kicked up from the Emir's advance guard, the chalky clouds stinging their eyes and coating their parched throats. Their commanders ordered them to maintain a swift pace, allowing very few breaks, only when the mounted officers needed to water their horses or adjust their equipment. Though covered as quickly as possible, the hundred-mile journey beneath the scorching sun felt endless to the suffering prisoners, each step bringing fresh agony to their blistered feet and exhausted bodies, while the horizon seemed to stretch before them, offering no hint of respite or salvation.

The region stretches eastward from the Obi River to where the Sayanok Mountains jut out their rocky spur, a harsh expanse of desolate terrain that seems to mock any attempt at human passage. This barren landscape offers little vegetation, with only occasional withered shrubs dotting the endless plain, their branches twisted and bleached by relentless winds and merciless sun. The soil supports no farming, lacking the essential water that the exhausted prisoners craved during their grueling march, their tongues swollen and lips cracked from dehydration. To find any flowing water, they would have needed to travel fifty miles east, right to the mountain foothills, a detour that seemed an impossible dream to the suffering column.

In those mountains runs the Tom, a modest tributary that flows past Tomsk before joining one of the major northern rivers, its waters cutting through ancient valleys carved by centuries of persistent flow. That route would have provided plentiful water, more hospitable terrain, and milder temperatures, sheltered from the worst of the steppe's punishing heat by towering rock faces and scattered pine forests. However, the convoy commanders had strict instructions to take the most direct path to Tomsk, their orders brooking no argument or deviation. The Emir feared Russian forces from the northern provinces might outflank and isolate his position if he deviated from the shortest route, a strategic concern that outweighed any humanitarian considerations for his captives' welfare.

There was no point in describing the torment of those wretched captives. Countless prisoners died on the open plains, leaving their remains to scatter across the steppe until the cold season brought the wolves to devour the remaining bones. The guards seemed indifferent to the mounting death toll, viewing their charges as little more than cargo to be delivered.

Just as Nadia aided the elderly Siberian, Michael did what he could to support his weaker fellow prisoners, despite his own circumstances. He moved among them, offering words of hope to some and physical help to others, continuing until a guard's spear forced him back to his designated position in the line. His quiet defiance earned him both admiring glances from the other prisoners and suspicious stares from the guards.

What kept him from attempting to flee?

He had waited until he could traverse the steppe. His plan to reach Tomsk "courtesy of the Emir" remained unchanged, and his reasoning was sound. Watching the many patrols that swept across the plain sometimes to the south, sometimes to the north, he knew he wouldn't make it even two kilometers before being caught. Tartar cavalry seemed to materialize everywhere, like insects emerging from the soil after a storm. Attempting to escape under such circumstances would have been impossible. The guards maintained constant vigilance, knowing their lives would be forfeit for even the smallest lapse in attention. They watched their prisoners with the desperate intensity of men who knew their own survival depended on preventing any escape.

As night fell on August 15th, the convoy arrived at Zabediero, a small village thirty miles from Tomsk. The settlement's few wooden buildings cast long shadows in the fading light, their windows dark and unwelcoming.

Armed guards prevented the prisoners from dashing toward the Tom River, keeping them in formation until proper arrangements were made. Even though the river's fierce current could have aided an escape attempt by the more daring captives, the authorities had implemented rigorous security measures. They had commandeered boats from Zabediero and positioned them across the river, creating an impassable barrier. Vigilant sentries who paced along their assigned routes, their rifles gleaming in the twilight surrounded the camp it, on the village outskirts,.

Michael Strogoff assessed the situation, considering his own escape. After examining their predicament, he concluded breaking free was impossible under such tight security. Unwilling to risk capture in a futile attempt, he bode his time. Despite: Guards, with torches placed at regular intervals, eliminated shadows that might have offered concealment, providing no comfort in the growing darkness. The sound of the rushing river, its waters unreachable, mocked the held prisoners.

Along: The army ordered its prisoners to make camp along the Tom River for the night. Planning: The Emir planned a grand military celebration to mark the Tartar headquarters' establishment in Tomsk, delaying his troops' entrance into the important city. While Feofar-Khan had taken control of the fortress, most his forces remained camped outside its walls, awaiting their ceremonial entry, their campfires dotting the landscape like fallen stars.

Ivan Ogareff, having arrived at Tomsk with the Emir the previous evening, departed for the Zabediero camp where he would spend the night in prepared quarters. The next day, he would lead the Tartar army's rear-guard, a position that allowed him to maintain his watchful eye over both the prisoners and his own troops. At dawn, the cavalry and infantry would march to Tomsk, where the Emir planned to welcome them with the lavish ceremony typical of Asian rulers, complete with flowing banners and the thunderous beating of war drums.

Once the camp was established, guards let the exhausted prisoners, who had endured three days of travel and suffered from severe thirst, drink and rest. Many collapsed on the spot, their legs too weak to carry them further. The sun had already dipped below the horizon when Nadia, supporting Marfa Strogoff, reached the Tom's riverbank. They had struggled to make their way through the crowds gathered at the water's edge, but at last quenched their thirst, the cool water bringing momentary relief to their parched throats.

The elderly woman leaned down toward the pristine stream while Nadia dipped her hand in the water and brought it to Marfa's parched lips. After helping the older woman, Nadia quenched her own thirst, cupping the water in both hands. The cool waters restored their vigor, washing away some of the day's exhaustion from their bodies. Without warning, Nadia jerked upright, letting out an involuntary gasp that drew curious glances from nearby prisoners.

There stood Michael Strogoff, mere paces away. The setting sun's dying light illuminated his figure, casting long shadows across his weather-worn features and travel-stained clothing.

Michael flinched at Nadia's outcry, his shoulders tensing. Though startled, he maintained enough self-control to remain silent, knowing any word might betray him. Yet when his gaze fell upon Nadia, he recognized his mother beside her, and his hands trembled ever.

Realizing he couldn't maintain his composure much longer during this unexpected encounter, he shielded his eyes with his hands and strode away, pushing through the crowd of prisoners still gathered at the riverbank.

Nadia moved to pursue him, her feet already carrying her forward, but the elderly Siberian woman caught her arm and whispered in her ear, "Remain here, my child! There are too many eyes watching."

"It's him!" Nadia exclaimed, her voice thick with emotion, her hands clasped against her chest. "He's alive, mother! It's him! I can believe my eyes!"

"That's my son," Marfa replied with practiced calm, though her heart raced beneath her composed exterior, "that's Michael Strogoff, and notice how I remain still, not taking a single step toward him! Follow my lead, my daughter. Our actions now could mean life or death."

Michael felt his heart surge with the most powerful emotion he had ever experienced, threatening to overwhelm his maintained facade. Before him stood his mother and Nadia, looking worn but unbroken by their ordeal!

Divine providence had brought together these two prisoners, forever linked in his heart, in their shared misfortune. Each step of their separate journeys had led to this moment. He wondered if Nadia knew his true identity, studying her face from afar for any sign. Yes, he had seen Marfa's restraining gesture when she held Nadia back from rushing to him. Marfa had understood everything, and was protecting his secret with the fierce devotion only a mother could muster.

Throughout that long, sleepless night, the urge to reunite with his mother tempted Michael. The urge to embrace her weathered form and clasp his young friend's hand was almost overwhelming, gnawing at his resolve with each passing hour. Yet he understood that even the smallest misstep could prove catastrophic to them all. He had made a solemn vow not to see his mother, and he would honor it despite the agony it caused. Once they reached Tomsk, since escape was impossible that night, he would have to depart without embracing the two people who meant everything to him, leaving them vulnerable to countless dangers that haunted his thoughts.

Michael wished to believe that this unexpected encounter at the Zabediero camp would bring no harm to either himself or his mother. However, he remained unaware that Sangarre the gypsy, Ogareff's spy, had witnessed a portion of their brief interaction, her keen eyes missing little despite the gathering gloom.

The mysterious Tsigane stood a short distance away on the riverbank, her eyes fixed on the elderly Siberian woman as they had been so many times before, studying every minute change in Marfa's bearing and expression. Michael had vanished before she could spot him, but she hadn't missed how the mother had held Nadia back, nor the telling expression in Marfa's eyes, that flash of recognition and desperate restraint that spoke volumes to one trained in reading such subtle signs.

Now she was certain, Marfa Strogoff's son, who carried messages for the Czar himself, was here among the captives in Zabediero, trapped with Ivan Ogareff's other prisoners. Though Sangarre couldn't identify him by sight in the sea of faces before her, she knew without question he was present, like a wolf knowing its prey was near even if hidden. She did not locate him just then, the darkness and the vast crowd of people made such a search futile, but her patience was as endless as the Siberian steppes themselves.

Spying on Nadia and Marfa Strogoff would prove futile. The two women were on their guard, their faces betraying nothing, making it impossible to gather any information that might incriminate the Czar's courier. The Tsigane, the gypsy spy, decided her best course was to inform Ivan Ogareff without delay. Slipping away like a shadow through the gathering dusk, she left the camp and arrived at Zabediero within fifteen minutes, where armed guards escorted her to the lieutenant's quarters. Ogareff, who had been pacing, granted her an immediate audience.

"What news do you bring, Sangarre?" he inquired, his eyes glinting with anticipation.

"Marfa Strogoff's son is here in the camp," she stated with quiet confidence.

"As our prisoner?"

"Yes, as a prisoner," she confirmed, her voice carrying a note of triumph.

"Ah!" Ogareff exclaimed, his thin lips curling into a cruel smile, "Now I shall know..."

"You'll learn nothing, Ivan," the Tsigane cut in, her dark eyes flashing, "for you wouldn't recognize him if you saw him."

"But you know him; you've seen him, Sangarre?" Ogareff demanded, leaning forward.

"I haven't seen him myself, but his mother's unconscious reaction revealed everything. The signs were unmistakable."

"Could you be wrong?"

"I'm certain of it," she replied with unwavering conviction.

"The capture of this messenger is of utmost importance to me," Ivan Ogareff declared, his fingers drumming against the wooden table between them. "If his letter from Moscow reaches the Grand Duke in Irkutsk, the Grand Duke will be warned, and my chance to strike will be gone forever."

The intensity in Ogareff's voice was unmistakable. His agitation revealed just how desperately he wanted to get this letter, and beads of sweat had formed on his upper lip as he spoke. Each word carried the weight of his mounting frustration and anticipation. Sangarre remained composed despite Ogareff's insistent questioning, her stillness a stark contrast to his nervous energy. "I'm certain, Ivan," she replied, her unwavering gaze meeting his.

"But there are thousands of prisoners here, Sangarre, and you've admitted you don't recognize Michael Strogoff," he pressed, rising halfway from his chair as if the very thought of searching through countless faces was too much to bear.

"No," the Tsigane replied with fierce delight, her dark eyes glittering with malicious satisfaction, "I have not met him myself. But his mother will know him. Ivan, we must compel his mother to reveal the truth. She cannot hide her reaction when she sees him."

"Tomorrow she will tell us everything!" Ogareff declared, slamming his fist on the wooden table. He then held out his hand to the Tsigane, who kissed it, a customary gesture of respect among Northern peoples, carrying no connotation of servility. The candlelight cast long shadows across his face as a cruel smile played at the corners of his mouth.

Later, Sangarre made her way back to the camp, her silent footsteps ghosting across the frozen ground as she located Nadia and Marfa Strogoff, and kept watch over them through the night. Despite their exhaustion, neither the elderly woman nor the young girl could find sleep, tossing on their thin blankets. Worry consumed their minds, each passing hour bringing fresh waves of anxiety. They knew Michael was alive but captured, imprisoned somewhere among the masses of other unfortunates. The burning questions remained: Had Ogareff recognized him? If not, how long until he did? Nadia could think only of the joy that he whom she had believed dead still lived, her heart racing whenever she recalled his face. Marfa, however, looked beyond the present moment with mounting dread, her weathered hands clasped in her lap. She was terrified by Ogareff's cold-blooded nature and worried about her son's vulnerability.

Under the cover of darkness, Sangarre had approached the two women and spent several hours listening to them, her form indistinguishable from the shadows that cloaked the camp. She detected no sound, not even a whisper between the prisoners. Out of caution, neither Nadia nor Marfa Strogoff uttered a single word to each other, communicating only through subtle glances and the occasional brush of hands. The following morning, August 16th, around ten o'clock, trumpet blasts echoed across the camp, their harsh notes shattering the morning stillness. The Tartar troops took up their positions, moving with practiced efficiency into neat rows.

Accompanied by many Tartar officers, their uniforms gleaming in the morning sun, Ivan Ogareff entered. His expression was darker than ever, and his furrowed forehead suggested a simmering anger ready to explode at any moment, like storm clouds threatening to unleash their fury.

From within a cluster of captives, Michael Strogoff observed the man's arrival, his muscles tensing. He sensed impending danger, knowing that Ivan Ogareff had discovered Marfa was Michael Strogoff's mother. The weight of this knowledge pressed down on him like a physical burden.

Ivan Ogareff dismounted from his horse with fluid grace that belied his murderous intent, as his soldiers formed a wide circle around him, their weapons at the ready. Sangarre approached with cat-like stealth and reported, her voice barely above a whisper, "There is nothing to tell."

Without responding, Ogareff signaled to one of his officers, his cold eyes never leaving the crowd. With whips and spears, the soldiers drove the prisoners into position around the camp. A sharp crack of leather against flesh accompanied cries of pain and protest. Facing: With armed guards forming an impenetrable wall behind them, their bayonets glinting in the harsh light, the captives had no chance of fleeing.

A tense quiet fell over the scene, broken only by the occasional shuffle of feet and muffled sob. At Ogareff's gesture, Sangarre moved toward the crowd with predatory purpose, making her way to where Marfa stood among the prisoners, her dark eyes scanning faces as she went.

The elderly woman from Siberia noticed her approach and understood what was about to unfold, her weathered face betraying no fear. A look of disdain crossed her features, hardening the lines around her mouth. She then bent close to Nadia and whispered, her breath warm against the girl's ear, "Pretend you don't recognize me anymore, child. No matter what happens, no matter how difficult this becomes, stay silent - don't react at all. This is about him, not about me."

Just then, Sangarre studied her, eyes narrowed with calculating intensity, before placing her hand on the old woman's shoulder like a spider settling on its prey.

"What is it you want?" Marfa demanded, her voice carrying across the tense silence.

"Come with me!" Sangarre ordered with cruel satisfaction, then forced the elderly Siberian forward with rough hands, leading her to where Ivan Ogareff stood in the center of the open space. Michael lowered his gaze to hide the fury that blazed in his eyes, his fingers curling into tight fists at his sides.

Marfa positioned herself in front of Ivan Ogareff, straightened her posture with quiet dignity, folded her arms across her chest, and stood waiting. Her weathered face remained impassive, a mask of stone.

"Are you Marfa Strogoff?" Ogareff demanded, his voice sharp as steel, cutting through the air between them.

"Yes," the elderly Siberian woman answered with unwavering composure, meeting his gaze.

"Do you stand by your words from three days ago during your interrogation at Omsk?" His eyes glittered with dangerous intent.

"No!" The word rang out clear and firm.

"Then you deny knowing that your son, Michael Strogoff, the Czar's courier, passed through Omsk?" Ogareff leaned forward, studying her face for any sign of deception.

"I know nothing of it." Her voice remained steady, betraying nothing.

"And that man you claimed to recognize as your son - you now say he wasn't your flesh and blood?" His tone dripped with concealed mockery.

"He was not my son." Each word fell like ice from her lips.

"You haven't glimpsed him among the captives since then?" Ogareff pressed, circling her like a predator.

"No." The single syllable carried the weight of finality.

"If someone pointed him out, would you know him?"

"No."

Her resolute response rippled through the assembled crowd, drawing murmurs of disbelief. Several prisoners shifted, their chains rattling in the tense silence that followed.

Ogareff's face darkened with rage, his hand jerking upward in a menacing gesture. His fingers curled into a tight fist as veins bulged at his temples, betraying the fury that threatened to overwhelm his calculated demeanor.

"Hear me well," he snarled at Marfa, leaning so close she could feel his hot breath on her face. "Your son is here, and you will identify him to me this instant."

"No."

"Every single prisoner from Omsk and Kolyvan will march before your eyes," he growled, pacing before her with measured steps. His boots crunched against the gravel, punctuating each word. "For each man who passes without you revealing Michael Strogoff, you'll feel the bite of the knout across your back." He snapped his fingers, and a guard stepped forward, uncoiling the dreaded leather whip with deliberate slowness. The metal tips caught the sunlight, glinting with malevolent promise.

Ivan Ogareff saw that, whatever might be his threats, whatever might be the tortures to which he submitted her, the indomitable Siberian would not speak. To discover the courier of the Czar, he counted, then, not on her, but on Michael himself. He did not believe it possible that, when mother and son were in each other's presence, some involuntary movement would not betray him. To seize the imperial letter, he would have ordered all prisoners searched, had he so desired. It was thus not only the letter which the traitor must have, but the bearer himself. His calculating mind had already planned the perfect trap, one that would exploit the most basic of human weaknesses: the bond between mother and child.

Nadia listened and understood Michael Strogoff's true identity and his motivation for traveling incognito through Siberia's occupied territories. Her heart raced as the pieces fell into place, his careful demeanor, his unwavering determination, and his mysterious mission made perfect sense.

She prayed that Michael's iron will would prove stronger than Ogareff's cruel machinations.

Following Ivan Ogareff's command, the prisoners walked single file past Marfa, who stood motionless as marble, her face betraying no emotion whatsoever. Years of hardship had taught her well how to mask her feelings, even in this moment of ultimate test.

Her son came near the end of the line. As he approached his mother, Nadia closed her eyes, unable to bear the sight of what might transpire between them. While Michael maintained an calm demeanor, his fingernails dug into his palms that they drew blood, the physical pain a welcome distraction from the emotional torment that threatened to overwhelm him.

Mother and son, his keen eyes searching their faces for any hint of recognition, any telltale flicker that would confirm his suspicions baffled Ivan Ogareff.

Sangarre, close to him, said one word, her dark eyes glittering with malice: "The knout!"

"Yes," cried Ogareff, who could no longer restrain himself, his frustration boiling over into rage; "the knout for this wretched old woman, the knout to the death!"

A guard approached Marfa with a threatening weapon, the leather strips of the knout trailing behind him as he walked. She knew the punishment that awaited her would be severe, but remained resolute, understanding the gravity of her choice. The weight of the Czar's mission, carried by her son, far outweighed her own safety. She would not speak, no matter the cost, even if every lash stripped away not just flesh but life itself.

Two soldiers forced Marfa to her knees, hustling her shoulders down against the hard ground. Though fear coursed through her veins, she held firm to her convictions, her weathered face a mask of determination, knowing she was making the ultimate sacrifice for what she believed in. She remained dignified, back straight and head held high, even as they prepared to carry out their grim task.

The Tartar soldier straightened his posture, muscles tensing as he gripped the knout, awaiting orders. "Begin!" commanded Ogareff, his voice thick with malicious satisfaction. The whip cut through the air with a menacing hiss, leather strips whistling as they descended.

But before it could strike, a mighty hand seized the Tartar's arm mid-swing, arresting the brutal momentum. Michael had lunged forward from the crowd, unable to bear witness to such cruelty against his own mother. Though he had endured Ogareff's lash at the Ichim relay without retaliation, maintaining his disguise through that torment, seeing his mother about to suffer the same fate broke his maintained restraint. Ivan Ogareff had achieved his aim, drawing out his quarry.

"Michael Strogoff!" he exclaimed, eyes gleaming with vindictive pleasure. Stepping closer, he sneered, savoring the moment, "So, the man from Ichim?"

"The same!" Michael declared, his voice resonating with fury. In one fluid motion, he grabbed the knout from the startled soldier and delivered a fierce slash across Ogareff's face, the leather strips leaving angry red welts. "That's for your blow!" he proclaimed, satisfaction clear in his tone.

"Justice served!" shouted an anonymous voice from within the crowd, echoing the feeling many onlookers.

A score of soldiers descended upon Michael like wolves upon prey, weapons drawn and faces twisted with rage, and death seemed mere moments away as they closed in from all sides.

But Ogareff, who on being struck had uttered a cry of rage and pain, stopped them with an upraised hand. “I reserve this man for the Emir’s judgment,” he said, dabbing at the bleeding welt across his face. "Search him! Every pocket, every seam!"

In Michael’s breast pocket, the soldiers discovered a letter bearing the imperial arms.

Alcide Jolivet himself spoke the words, “Well repaid!” "Par-dieu!" said he to Blount, wiping sweat from his brow as they watched from the crowd's edge. "They are rough, these people. Acknowledge that we owe our traveling companion a good turn. Korpanoff or Strogoff is worthy of it. Oh, that was fine retaliation for the minor affair at Ichim."

"Yes, retaliation," replied Blount, adjusting his spectacles with a grimace; "but Strogoff is a dead man. I suspect that, for his own interest at all events, it would have been better had he not possessed quite so lively a recollection of the event."

"Would you have his mother die from the whip?" Alcide demanded, his face flushing with emotion.

"How does his outburst help either his mother or sister?" Blount countered, his British pragmatism clear in every word.

"All I know is I'd have done the same in his shoes," Alcide responded, his hands clenching into fists at his sides. “Observe that gash on the Colonel!”

"This would make quite the story for our papers," Blount remarked, dabbing at his own minor wounds with a handkerchief, "if only Ivan Ogareff would share what's written in that letter."

After stopping the blood flowing from his face with a strip of linen, Ivan Ogareff broke the seal with trembling fingers. He studied the letter, reading it multiple times as if trying to extract every detail from its contents, his eyes narrowing with each pass over the critical message.

He then ordered Michael to be bound with thick hemp ropes and taken to Tomsk with the other captives under heavy guard. Taking command of the Zabediero forces with a triumphant air, he marched toward the town where the Emir waited, accompanied by the thunderous sound of drums and trumpets echoing across the windswept plains. The column of soldiers stretched far into the distance, their boots raising clouds of dust as they advanced.

QuantumDigitalPublishing.io

Chapter Four

THE TRIUMPHAL ENTRY

TOMSK, founded in 1604, in the heart of the Siberian provinces, is one of the most important towns in Asiatic Russia. Tobolsk, above the sixtieth parallel; Irkutsk, built beyond the hundredth meridian, have seen Tomsk increase at their expense, its influence growing over the centuries.

As mentioned, Tomsk is not the capital of this important province. It is at Omsk that the Governor-General of the province and the official world live, conducting their administrative duties from grand government buildings. But Tomsk is the most considerable town of that territory, with bustling streets and a thriving marketplace. The country being rich, the town is so likewise, for it is in the center of fruitful mines that yield gold, silver, and precious stones in abundance. In the luxury of its houses, its arrangements, and its equipages, it might rival the greatest European capitals. Ornate mansions and elegant shops line the wide streets; these would not look out of place in Moscow or St. Petersburg. It is a city of millionaires, enriched by the spade and pickax, and though it has not the honor of being the home of the Czar's representative, it can boast of including in the first rank of its notables the chief of the merchants of the town, the principal grantees of the imperial government's mines, whose influence extends far beyond the city's boundaries.

But the millionaires have left now, and except for the crouching poor, the town stood empty to the hordes of Feofar-Khan. At four o'clock the Emir made his entry into the square, greeted by a flourish of trumpets, the rolling sound of the big drums, salvoes of artillery and musketry. The echoes of martial music bounced off the abandoned mansions, a mocking reminder of the city's former grandeur.

Feofar mounted his favorite horse, which carried on its head an aigrette of diamonds. The Emir still wore his uniform, its gold braiding glinting in the afternoon sun, the medals on his chest clinking with each movement. A many staff accompanied him, and beside him walked the Khans of Khokhand and Koundouge and the grand dignitaries of the Khanats, their silk robes rustling as they strode forward with measured steps, their faces stern with conquest.

At the same moment, the chief of Feofar's wives, the queen (if that title applies to the Bokharan sultana), appeared on the terrace. But, queen or slave, this woman of Persian origin was beautiful, her presence commanding immediate attention from all who beheld her. Contrary to the Mahometan custom, and no doubt by some caprice of the Emir, she had her face uncovered, revealing features that seemed carved from the finest alabaster. Her hair, divided into four plaits, fell over her dazzling white shoulders, concealed by a veil of silk worked in gold, which fell from the back of a cap studded with gems of the highest value. The intricate embroidery of the veil caught the sunlight, creating a ethereal halo around her form. Under her blue-silk petticoat, fell the "zirdjameh" of silken gauze, and above the sash lay the "pirahn," each layer of fabric moving with fluid grace as she walked. Jewels adorned her from head to toe; gold beads strung on silver threads, chaplets of turquoises from the famed Elbourz mines, and necklaces of cornelians, agates, emeralds, opals, and sapphires—her dress appeared to be crafted of precious stones. Her neck, arms, hands, waist, and feet sparkled with thousands of diamonds, worth countless millions of roubles, reflecting every ray of the afternoon sun.

The Emir and the Khans dismounted, as did the dignitaries who escorted them. All entered a magnificent tent erected on the center of the first terrace, its billowing silk panels adorned with intricate golden embroidery that caught the waning daylight. As usual, they placed the Koran on a decorated mahogany pedestal before the tent.

Feofar's lieutenant did not make them wait, and before five o'clock the trumpets announced his arrival with a piercing blast that echoed across the terrace. With practiced military precision, Ivan Ogareff, nicknamed "the Scarred Cheek," dismounted before the Emir's tent in his distinctive Tartar officer's uniform, complete with medals and braiding. A party of soldiers from the Zabediero camp accompanied him. They lined the sides of the square, reserving a space for the sports, marked by colorful pennants fluttering in the breeze. A large scar, cut across the traitor's face, was visible; the puckered flesh recalled a violent past encounter.

Ogareff presented his principal officers to the Emir, who, without departing from the coldness which composed the main part of his dignity, received them in a way which satisfied them they stood well in the good graces of their chief. His calculating eyes moved from one face to another, measuring each man's worth with the detached assessment of one accustomed to command.

At least so thought Harry Blount and Alcide Jolivet, the two inseparables, now associated together in the chase after news. After leaving Zabediero, they had proceeded to Tomsk, pushing their horses hard through the rugged terrain. The plan they had agreed upon was to leave the Tartars as soon as possible, and to join a Russian regiment, and, if they could, to go with them to Irkutsk. All that they had seen of the invasion, its burnings, its pillages, its murders, the charred remains of villages and the haunted eyes of survivors, had sickened them, and they longed to be among the ranks of the Siberian army. Jolivet had told his companion that he could not leave Tomsk without making a sketch of the triumphal entry of the Tartar troops, if it was only to satisfy his cousin's curiosity, though his hands trembled at the thought of documenting more devastation; but the same evening they both intended to take the road to Irkutsk, and being well mounted on fresh horses gained at considerable expense, hoped to distance the Emir's scouts who patrolled the surrounding countryside.

Alcide and Blount mingled therefore in the crowd, to lose no detail of a festival which ought to supply them with a hundred excellent lines for an article. They admired the magnificence of Feofar-Khan, his wives adorned in silk and precious gems, his officers in their gleaming armor, his guards with their curved sabers, and all the Eastern pomp, of which the ceremonies of Europe can give not the least idea. But they turned away with disgust when Ivan Ogareff presented himself before the Emir, his traitorous smirk concealed beneath a show of deference, and waited with some impatience for the amusements to begin.

"You see, my dear Blount," said Alcide, adjusting his collar in the sweltering heat, "we have come too soon, like honest citizens who like to get their money's worth. All this is before the curtain rises, it would have been better to arrive only for the ballet."

"What ballet?" asked Blount, wiping his brow with a handkerchief.

"The compulsory ballet, to be sure. But see, the curtain is going to rise." Alcide Jolivet spoke as if he had been at the Opera, and taking his glass from its case, he prepared, with the air of a connoisseur, "to examine the first act of Feofar's company." His attempt at levity masked the unease they both felt at being present for such a grotesque display of conquest.

A painful ceremony was to precede the sports. In fact, the triumph of the vanquisher could not be complete without the public humiliation of the vanquished. Soldiers whipped several hundred prisoners, forcing them forward with bent backs and exhausted faces. They would march past Feofar-Khan and his allies before being crammed with their companions into the dark, suffocating prisons in the town.

In the first ranks of these prisoners figured Michael Strogoff, his head held high despite his circumstances. As Ogareff had ordered, a file of soldiers who kept their rifles trained on him with particular vigilance guarded him. His mother and Nadia were there also, forced to witness whatever was to come.

The old Siberian, although energetic enough when her own safety was in question, was pale, her weathered hands trembling as she watched her son. She expected some terrible scene. The Emir had brought her son before him for good reason. She therefore trembled for him, knowing the cruel nature of their captors. Ivan Ogareff wouldn't forgive being whipped, and his revenge would be merciless. No doubt, the captors would inflict some frightful punishment, familiar to Central Asian barbarians, on Michael. Ogareff had protected him against the soldiers because he well knew what would happen by reserving him for the justice of the Emir, savoring and expecting his revenge like a fine wine.

The mother and son could not speak together since the terrible scene in the camp at Zabediero. Marfa longed to ask her son's pardon for the harm she had done him, for she reproached herself with not having commanded her maternal feelings. If she had restrained herself in that Omsk post-house, encountering him, Michael would have passed unrecognized, and she would have avoided all these misfortunes. The weight of this guilt pressed heavily upon her heart with each passing hour.

Michael thought that if his mother was there, Ogareff had brought her to make her suffer by witnessing his punishment, or perhaps Ogareff had reserved a frightful death for her. The thought of his mother being forced to witness whatever torments awaited him was more unbearable than any physical pain he might endure. His imagination conjured up horrific scenarios, each more terrible than the last, as he contemplated their fate.

As to Nadia, she only asked herself how she could save them both, how come to the aid of son and mother. As yet she could only wonder, but she felt she must above everything avoid drawing attention upon herself, that she must conceal herself, make herself insignificant. Perhaps she might at least gnaw through the meshes which imprisoned the lion. At any rate, if given an opportunity, she would seize it and sacrifice herself for Marfa Strogoff's son. Her heart raced with determination even as her mind struggled to form a concrete plan of action.

In the meantime the greater part of the prisoners were passing before the Emir, and as they passed each had to prostrate himself, with his forehead in the dust, in token of servitude. Slavery begins by humiliation. When the unfortunate people were too slow in bending, the rough guards threw them to the ground, their bodies making dull thuds against the hard earth. Some cried out in pain, while others remained eerily silent, their spirits already broken by their circumstances.

Alcide Jolivet and his companion could not witness such a sight without feeling indignant. Their hands clenched at their sides as they watched the degrading spectacle unfold before them.

"It is cowardly, let us go," said Alcide, his voice tight with contained anger.

"No," answered Blount, though his face had grown pale; "we must see it all."

"See it all!, ah!" cried Alcide grasping his companion's arm with such force that Blount winced.

"What is the matter with you?" asked the latter.

"Look, Blount; it is she!"

"What she?"

"The sister of our traveling companion, alone, and a prisoner! We must save her," Jolivet exclaimed, his voice trembling with desperate urgency.

"Calm yourself," replied Blount, placing a restraining hand on his colleague's shoulder. "Any interference on our part in behalf of the young girl would be worse than useless. We would only bring more suffering upon her."

Alcide Jolivet, who had been about to rush forward with reckless determination, stopped in his tracks, his muscles still tense with the desire to act. Nadia, who had not perceived them, her features being half hidden by her disheveled dark hair, passed in her turn before the Emir without attracting his attention, her steps measured.

However, after Nadia came Marfa Strogoff; and as she did not throw herself in the dust like the others, the guards pushed her with the butts of their rifles. She fell with a painful cry.

Her son struggled so violently that the soldiers who were guarding him could hardly hold him back, their faces reddening with effort. But the old woman rose, her dignity intact despite her trembling limbs, and they were about to drag her on, when Ogareff interposed, raising his hand and saying, "Let that woman stay!"

As to Nadia, she regained the crowd of prisoners, melting into their midst like a shadow. Ivan Ogareff had taken no notice of her, his attention focused elsewhere.

Michael was then led before the Emir, and there he remained standing, his bearing proud and defiant, without casting down his eyes.

"Your forehead to the ground!" cried Ogareff, his voice cutting through the tense silence.

"No!" answered Michael, the single word ringing with unmistakable resolve.

Two soldiers endeavored to make him bend, grabbing his shoulders, but they were themselves laid on the ground by a powerful buffet from the young man's fist, the blow sending them sprawling in the dust.

Ogareff approached Michael with deliberate steps, his face contorted with rage. "You shall die!" he said, his hand moving to the hilt of his sword.

"I can die," answered Michael, standing even straighter despite his bonds; "but your traitor's face, Ivan, will not the less carry forever the infamous brand of the knout." His words rang through the courtyard, ensuring all present heard the accusation.

At this reply Ivan Ogareff became livid, the blood draining from his features until his skin took on an almost ghostly pallor. His fingers twitched at his sides, containing his fury.

"Who is this prisoner?" asked the Emir, in a tone of voice terrible from its very calmness. His dark eyes moved between the two men, studying their mutual hatred with cold interest.

"A Russian spy," answered Ogareff, his voice dripping with venom. In asserting that Michael was a spy he knew the sentence pronounced against him would be terrible. A slight, cruel smile played at the corners of his mouth as he spoke.

The Emir made a sign at which all the crowd bent low their heads, their foreheads touching the dusty ground in complete submission. Then he pointed with his hand to the Koran, which was brought him by a robed attendant on a silk cushion. He opened the sacred book with measured reverence and placed his finger on one of its pages, his expression unreadable as stone.

It was chance, or rather, according to the deeply-held beliefs of these Orientals, God Himself who was about to decide the fate of Michael Strogoff. The people of Central Asia give the name of "fal" to this ancient and sacred practice. After having interpreted the sense of the verse touched by the judge's finger, they apply the sentence whatever it may be, accepting it as divine will made manifest.

The Emir had let his finger rest on the page of the Koran, the weight of destiny hanging heavy in the air. The chief of the Ulemas then approached with measured steps, his robes rustling in the tense silence, and read in a loud, resonant voice a verse which ended with these ominous words, "And he will no more see the things of this earth."

"Russian spy!" exclaimed Feofar-Kahn in a voice trembling with fury, his eyes blazing with a mix of triumph and rage. "You see what is going on in the Tartar camp. Then look while you may, for these moments shall be your last with sight." His words cut through the air like a blade, carrying both judgment and menace.

QuantumDigitalPublishing.io
Book II – Chapter V

Chapter Five

LOOK WHILE YOU MAY!

Michael stood before the Emir's throne at the base of the terrace, his arms restrained behind him by thick iron chains that bit into his wrists. His mother, broken by both mental and physical anguish, had collapsed to the ground, her weathered hands covering her face, unable to watch or listen to what was unfolding in this cruel spectacle.

"Observe while you still can," Feofar-Khan declared, extending his arm toward Michael with a flourish of his jewel-encrusted sleeve. Ivan Ogareff, well-versed in Tartar traditions, understood the grave implications of these words, as evidenced by the brief cruel smile that crossed his face before he took his position beside Feofar-Khan. His hand rested on the hilt of his sword, a gesture of casual dominance.

The sound of a trumpet pierced the air, its harsh brass notes echoing off the stone walls and signaling the start of the entertainment. "The ballet is about to begin," Alcide remarked to Blount with bitter irony in his voice, "though these barbarians, unlike us, present it before the major performance." His fingers drummed against his thigh as he watched the scene unfold.

A group of dancers flowed into the clearing in front of the Emir's pavilion. Michael, following his orders, observed it all, his trained eyes missing no detail of the spectacle before him. The performance featured an exotic blend of Tartar musical instruments: the doutare, a guitar with an elongated neck that produced haunting melodies; the kobize, resembling a violoncello with its deep, mournful tones; and the tschibyzga, a long flute made of reed that whistled like desert winds. The deep voices of singers merged with the sounds of wind instruments, tom-toms, and tambourines, creating a hypnotic rhythm that seemed to pulse through the ground itself. Above them all, an unusual aerial symphony played out as a dozen kites, each with strings attached to their centers, hummed in the wind like celestial harps, their silk surfaces catching the late afternoon light.

The dancers took the stage, all of Persian descent and now free to perform as they chose, having once been in bondage. These artists had held official roles in Teheran's court ceremonies, where they had danced for shahs and princes, but when the new ruling dynasty came to power, they faced exile and scorn, forcing them to pursue their art elsewhere among less discriminating audiences. They displayed their heritage through traditional Persian attire, their costumes shimmering with abundant jewels that caught and scattered light with every movement. Their ears were decorated with small, gem-encrusted golden triangles that tinkled as they moved, while their necks and ankles were covered with silver bands marked with dark patterns that spoke of ancient traditions and forgotten stories.

The dancers moved with elegant precision, performing both solo and ensemble pieces. While their faces remained visible, they draped delicate veils over their heads, creating an effect like mist passing across their luminous eyes, reminiscent of clouds drifting past stars. Several of these Persian performers wore pearl-decorated leather belts with small triangle-shaped pouches attached. These ornate pouches, adorned with gold filigree and tiny bells that chimed with each step, contained elongated strips of crimson silk inscribed with Koranic verses. The performers would stretch these bands between them, creating a passage beneath which other dancers would weave, their movements fluid like water flowing through ancient stone channels. As each dancer passed under a particular verse, they would either bow down to touch the ground or leap skyward, acting out the sacred text's instructions as if seeking to join the heavenly beautiful, pure, and eternal companions in Mohammed's paradise, their gestures infused with both reverence and yearning.

What grabbed Alcide's attention was the surprising lack of energy among the Persian dancers. Instead of displaying their usual passionate nature, they moved with an unexpected restraint, as if holding something back beneath their practiced smiles. Unlike the passionate Egyptians, their movements were flowing and elegant, like willow branches in a soft breeze.

As the performance concluded, a harsh voice cut through the air like a whip crack:

"Watch while you still can!"

These words, echoing the Emir's command, came from a tall, lean Tartar who served as Feofar-Khan's executioner. His angular features were as sharp as the impressive curved Damascus blade he wielded behind Michael. The weapon was one of those masterpieces crafted by the renowned weaponsmiths of Karschi and Hissar, its surface rippling with the distinctive water-pattern that marked its superior quality.

The guards behind him, their faces illuminated by its orange glow carried a tripod holding. Instead of smoke, a subtle haze enveloped the dish, created by burning some fragrant resinous material he had scattered across the top, filling the air with an exotic, almost narcotic sweetness.

Following the Persian performers came another group of dancers that Michael knew all too well. The reporters seemed to recognize them too, as Blount remarked to his colleague with a knowing grimace, "Those are the Tsiganes from Nijni-Novgorod."

"Indeed they are," Alcide replied, his voice tinged with suspicion. "I suspect their talents for observation earn them more than their dancing skills. Those women's eyes miss nothing, and their ears catch every whisper."

By all indications, Alcide Jolivet was correct in his assessment that these performers were working as the Emir's spies, gathering intelligence through their innocent entertainment at celebrations and gatherings across the region.

In the front row stood Sangarre, a Tsigane woman in her exotic and striking attire, layers of colored silks adorned with jingling coins and intricate embroidery that caught the lamplight enhanced whose extraordinary beauty.

Though motionless like a statue among the dancers, Sangarre's presence commanded attention, her dark eyes scanning the crowd with predatory intensity. Around her, the other performers moved in steps that blended dance traditions from their ancestral journey - incorporating movements from Turkey, Bohemia, Egypt, Italy, and Spain. The rhythmic clash of cymbals worn on their arms and the resonant beats of finger-played "daires" tambourines, the hypnotic music building accompanied their passionate performance to a feverish crescendo as their bare feet traced ancient patterns across the floor.

Sangarre, holding one of those tambourines which she played between her hands with practiced grace, encouraged this group of wild dancers with subtle nods and piercing glances. A young Romani boy, about fifteen years old, stepped forward from the shadows. He held a "doutare" (a traditional string instrument) which he played by plucking the strings with his fingernails, creating haunting melodies that seemed to float on the night air. He sang, his voice carrying both youth's sweetness and an ancient sorrow. During each verse, with its unique rhythm and plaintive tone, a female dancer would position herself next to him and stand motionless, listening, as if carved from stone. But whenever the chorus came from the young singer's lips, she would resume her dance with renewed vigor, filling his ears with the sound of her tambourine and the clash of her cymbals, her feet moving in perfect time. After the final chorus, the rest of the dancers encircled the Romani boy in their spiraling dance, their movements growing wild and mesmerizing.

Gold coins cascaded from the Emir and his entourage like metallic rain, showering down from officials of every rank who sat on cushioned divans around the performance space. The pieces clinked against the dancers' cymbals with musical precision, mixing with the fading notes of doutares and tambourines in a symphony of wealth and excess.

"They spend like thieves," Alcide whispered to his companion, his voice tinged with both admiration and disgust.

A hush descended, broken only when the executioner placed his calloused hand on Michael's shoulder and repeated those ominous words, each utterance more chilling than the last, his breath visible in the cooling air.

"Look while you may," he intoned, the words carrying across the clearing like a death knell.

The executioner had sheathed his blade, Alcide noted with keen interest, the polished steel disappearing into worn leather with practiced ease. The man's movements were deliberate, almost ceremonial in their precision.

Dusk was settling in as the sun vanished beyond the horizon, its last rays painting the clouds in bruised purples and deep crimsons. Twilight crept across the landscape, while the cedar and pine forest transformed into an impenetrable wall of darkness, the ancient trees seeming to lean inward, witnesses to what was about to unfold. In the distance, the Tom's waters merged with the gathering gloom, becoming indistinguishable from the encroaching night, its surface now black as pitch, reflecting neither stars nor the last remnants of day.

A multitude of torch-bearing slaves, numbering in the hundreds, flooded into the square, their flickering lights creating an undulating sea of flame that cast wild, dancing shadows across the stone. With Sangarre at their head, her dark eyes flashing with fierce pride, the Tsiganes and Persians emerged once more before the Emir's throne, performing their different dance styles in striking contrast to one another. The Tsiganes moved with passionate abandon while the Persians maintained their elegant precision. The Tartar musicians played with even fiercer intensity, their wild melodies intertwining with the singers' deep, throaty calls that seemed to emerge from some ancient place. Above, the grounded kites took flight again, each one carrying a multicolored lantern that swayed and bobbed in the night air, their harp strings resonating more powerfully in the breeze as they soared through the illuminated night sky, creating an ethereal chorus high above the revelry below.

The scene intensified as a unit of Tartar soldiers joined the festivities, their ornate uniforms gleaming with gold thread and polished metal in the torchlight. They merged into the frenzied dances, launching into a remarkable display that spoke of both military discipline and savage joy. Armed warriors moved across the ground wielding unsheathed sabers and elongated pistols, their boots striking the earth in perfect rhythm as they performed intricate steps while discharging their weapons into the air. Each thunderous shot triggered a cascade of percussion, the deep rumble of tambourines, the low growl of daires, large drums and the sharp twang of doutares two string guitars resonating in response, building to a crescendo that seemed to make the very air vibrate with sound and fury.

A spectacular display unfolded as the dancers moved with their arms dusted in metallic-based pigments, creating streams of crimson, emerald, and azure light in the traditional Chinese style. The performers appeared to dance within their own personal fireworks show, their fingertips trailing ghostly ribbons of light through the night air. While reminiscent of ancient military dances performed among bare blades, this Tartar spectacle took on an even more magical quality as colored flames twisted like serpents above the dancers, making their costumes appear trimmed with living fire. The scene transformed into a dazzling array of sparks, shifting and recombining with each graceful movement of the performers, creating ephemeral patterns that hung suspended in the darkness before dissolving into stardust.

The Parisian journalist, despite his presumed immunity to theatrical spectacles given how far modern stagecraft had advanced, found himself impressed. Alcide Jolivet made a subtle nod of approval, the gesture that, back in Paris between Boulevard Montmartre and La Madeleine, would have translated to "Quite impressive indeed." His practiced cynicism forgotten, he leaned forward to better observe the mesmerizing display before him.

In an instant, responding to a signal that cut through the night like a blade, the fantasia's lights extinguished all at once. The dancing stopped, and the performers vanished from sight as if they had never existed, leaving only ghostly afterimages dancing in viewers' vision. As the ceremony concluded, only torches remained to illuminate the plateau that moments before had blazed with spectacular brightness, their steady flames now seeming somehow mundane compared to the magical display that had preceded them.

At the Emir's imperious gesture, Michael was dragged to the center of the square, his chains rattling against the cobblestones.

"Blount," Alcide asked his associate in a low voice, his face ashen, "will you stay to witness how this ends?"

"Absolutely not," Blount responded with a shudder, already turning away from the grim scene unfolding before them.

"I doubt the Daily Telegraph subscribers are interested in reading about an execution done in the Tartar style?" Alcide's attempt at professional detachment masked his revulsion.

"Only your own readers!" Blount's voice cracked.

"What a shame," Alcide remarked, observing Michael's proud bearing even in chains. "Such a brave warrior deserved to die in combat!"

"Is there any way we could rescue him?" Blount inquired, his hands clenching into helpless fists.

"None whatsoever!" The finality in Alcide's tone left no room for hope.

The journalists reflected on Michael's past kindness to them, now understanding the hardships he had endured while staying true to his mission. Surrounded by the merciless Tartars, they found themselves powerless to help him. Unable to bear the thought of witnessing the torment awaiting their unfortunate friend, they retreated to the town, their footsteps heavy with regret. Within the hour, they had set out for Irkutsk, their horses pushing hard through the gathering dusk, determined to join their Russian allies in what Alcide had already dubbed "the campaign of revenge."

Meanwhile, Michael stood defiant, meeting the Emir's imperious gaze without flinching. His face showed nothing but contempt when he looked at Ivan Ogareff. Though prepared to face death, he remained unwavering, without displaying even the slightest trace of fear. His shoulders were squared, his bearing that of a soldier facing his destiny with honor intact.

The crowd gathered in anticipation around the square, including Feofar-Khan's personal guards, for whom executions were another form of entertainment. They would soon disperse to seek their pleasures in drink once their morbid curiosity was satisfied. Some were already placing wagers on how long the prisoner would maintain his composure, their coarse laughter echoing across the stone courtyard.

With a gesture from the Emir, the guards forced Michael forward until he stood at the terrace's base. His boots scraped against the rough ground as they shoved him into position. With icy contempt, Feofar addressed him, "You sought to observe our movements, Russian spy."

Fate, cruel in its twist, had in store for Michael not death, but the permanent darkness of blindness; a punishment perhaps more devastating than death itself. His fate was sealed: he would be robbed of his sight. For a courier whose very mission depended on his ability to see, whose duty required him to witness and report, this sentence was precise in its cruelty.

Yet upon hearing the Emir's brutal decree, Michael's spirit remained unbroken. He stood motionless, his eyes wide, as if trying to burn every image into his memory. He knew better than to beg for mercy from these merciless men, such an act would be beneath him. The thought never crossed his mind. Instead, his thoughts dwelled on his failed mission, on his beloved mother, and on Nadia, whose face he would never again behold. Still, he maintained his composure, refusing to let his inner turmoil show. Then, a powerful urge for retribution seized him. "Ivan," he declared in a voice cold as steel, "Ivan the Traitor, my last gaze shall be reserved for you!"

He shrugged his shoulders, a smirk playing across his weathered face, but Michael refused to face him during the blinding. Instead, his mother Marfa stood before him, her lined face a map of worry and determination.

"Mother!" he exclaimed, his voice cracking with emotion. "Yes, let my last sight be of you, not this villain! Stay where you are, I want to gaze upon your beloved face one last time before darkness takes me forever... Let me remember every detail, every line that tells the story of your love and sacrifice."

The elderly woman approached, her steps measured and dignified despite the trembling of her hands. Her eyes, brimming with unshed tears, locked onto her son's face with fierce maternal pride.

"Remove her!" Ivan commanded, his voice sharp with irritation. His hand slashed through the air in an imperious gesture that brooked no argument.

Two guards moved to grab her, but she backed away with surprising agility for her age, maintaining her position several steps from Michael. Her weathered hands trembled but remained raised in a protective gesture.

The executioner emerged from the shadows, his face impassive beneath his hood as he brandished a glowing white saber he had just retrieved from the chafing-dish. Steam rose from the blade in the cool air, its heat visible in waves. His intention was obvious, to blind Michael using the brutal Tartar method of passing a heated blade before the eyes, a punishment designed to inflict maximum suffering while preserving life.

Michael remained still as stone, offering no resistance against his bonds. In these last moments of sight, his gaze fixed on his mother, drinking in her image with desperate intensity as if trying to burn her features into his memory forever. His entire existence concentrated into this last look, memorizing every line of her face, every silver strand of hair.

Marfa Strogoff stood with arms outstretched toward her son, her eyes wide with horror at the impending brutality. Her lips moved in silent prayer as the blazing blade swept across Michael's field of vision with a terrible hiss.

A heart-wrenching scream pierced the air, echoing off the stone walls of the square as his elderly mother collapsed unconscious, her body crumpling like a marionette with cut strings. Michael Strogoff had been blinded, his world forever darkened by the searing metal.

The Emir and his entourage withdrew from the square with measured steps, satisfied with the day's cruel spectacle, leaving only Ivan Ogareff and the torch bearers behind in the growing shadows. The flickering flames cast grotesque shapes across the cobblestones as evening approached. Would this villain seek to further torment his victim with one last act of cruelty, or was the day's barbarism complete?

Ivan Ogareff approached Michael with deliberate slowness, his boots scraping against the rough cobblestones with each calculated step. Sensing his enemy's presence, Michael straightened his posture, his jaw clenched despite the lingering agony from the heated blade. With theatrical flourish, Ogareff retrieved the Imperial letter from his pocket and unfolded it, the parchment crackling in the evening air. In a display of savage mockery, he held the document before Michael's blinded eyes, sneering, "Read it now, Michael Strogoff. Read it and deliver its contents to Irkutsk. I, Ivan Ogareff, am the true Courier of the Czar."

Having delivered his cruel taunt, the traitor tucked the letter into his breast pocket with a satisfied pat. Without a backward glance, he strode away from the square, the torch bearers following in his wake, their shadows dancing across the weathered stone walls.

In the desolate square, Michael stood mere steps from where his mother lay lifeless, the evening chill settling around them like a shroud. The sounds of revelry and celebration echoed from afar, while Tomsk blazed with light and festivity, its revelry a stark contrast to the darkness that now defined his world.

Listening in the empty silence, his other senses already beginning to sharpen, Michael inched his way toward where his mother had collapsed. His hands found her form, trembling as they traced her familiar features, and he lowered himself close, pressing his face near hers to detect any flutter of life. His lips moved in hushed words, a mixture of prayer and plea.

Whether Marfa lived still and could hear her son's whispered voice remained uncertain - she gave no response, no sign, not even the faintest breath against his cheek. Michael pressed a kiss to her forehead and silver hair before rising, his heart heavy with a grief he dared not yet embrace. Cautiously, he began making his way toward the square's edge, his foot testing each step, his hand reaching out for guidance in the darkness that had become his world.

In that moment, Nadia appeared, emerging from the shadows like a guardian angel. She moved toward her companion, using a knife to slice through the bonds restraining Michael's arms, her movements quick and precise. Being blind, he couldn't know who had freed him, as Nadia worked in silence, her presence known only through the sawing motion at his wrists and the gradual loosening of his bonds.

Only when finished did she speak, her voice thick with emotion: "Brother!"

"Nadia!" Michael whispered her name twice, relief flooding through him at the sound of her familiar voice.

"Come, brother," Nadia said, taking his arm with gentle determination. "While your eyes rest, use mine. I shall guide you to Irkutsk, through every step and every obstacle that lies ahead."

Chapter Six

A FRIEND ON THE HIGHWAY

HALF an hour afterwards, Michael and Nadia had left Tomsk.

In the chaos of that night, many prisoners managed to slip away from their Tartar captors, both officers and soldiers. The celebrations of their victory had led to reckless indulgence, with wine and spirits flowing through the camp. Among those who escaped was Nadia, who was captured but broke free when her guard stumbled away to join a rowdy gathering. She made her way back to the square just as Michael was being brought before the Emir, her heart pounding with each cautious step. Hidden within the crowd, pressed between weather-worn peasants and merchants, she witnessed the horrific scene in its entirety. She remained composed, not uttering a single sound when the burning blade passed before her companion's eyes, though her fingernails dug deep crescents into her palms. Through sheer force of will, she stayed still and silent, even as those around her gasped and turned away. When the elderly Siberian woman collapsed unconscious, Nadia's heart stopped, the sound of the woman's fall echoing in her ears like thunder. But a sudden flash of purpose renewed her determination, cutting through her horror like a blade through darkness. She made a solemn vow to herself: "I shall become his eyes and guide him," the promise burning in her chest as fiercely as her desire for revenge.

After Ogareff left, Nadia pressed herself against the cold stone walls, melting into the shadows and waiting with the patience of a hunter until the last echoes of footsteps faded from the square. Michael remained alone, a figure of tragic isolation, dismissed by passersby who now regarded him as nothing more than a pitiful blind man. Her throat tightened as she watched him crawl to his unconscious mother, press a tender farewell kiss to her weathered forehead, then rise to his feet.

Moments later, their hands found each other in silent understanding, and together they descended the treacherous incline. Following the high, craggy banks of the Tom River to the town's periphery, fortune smiled upon them as they discovered a crumbling section of the perimeter wall, just wide enough to slip through.

The vast expanse before them offered only one route eastward, the well-worn road to Irkutsk stretching into the distance. There could be no confusion about direction, no possibility of wrong turns in this desolate landscape. Time pressed heavily upon them, for they knew that once the Emir's scouts shook off their drunken stupor the next day, they would swarm across the steppes like locusts, choking off all escape routes. Their head start was paramount. It seemed almost inconceivable how Nadia endured that punishing night march between August 16th and 17th. What hidden wellspring of strength sustained her through such an ordeal? How did her feet, torn and weeping blood from the merciless pace, continue their relentless forward motion? The feat bordered on miraculous. Yet the truth, when dawn broke the following morning, twelve hours after their desperate flight from Tomsk, she and Michael had reached Semilowskoe, having conquered an extraordinary thirty-five miles of harsh terrain.

Michael remained silent. Rather than Nadia holding onto him, he was the one who kept a firm grip on her hand throughout the night. Yet thanks to her gentle, trembling guidance, he had maintained his usual walking pace, navigating the treacherous terrain without serious mishap.

They found Semilowskoe deserted, with most of its residents having fled. Only two or three houses showed any signs of life, thin wisps of smoke curling from their chimneys into the morning air. The townspeople had loaded all their valuables and necessities into wagons and departed, leaving behind an eerie stillness that hung over the empty streets. Despite their desire to press on, Nadia needed to stop for a while. Both travelers needed to eat and rest their weary bodies, their strength depleted from the grueling journey.

The girl guided her companion through the town until they reached its outskirts, their footsteps echoing in the abandoned lanes. They discovered an abandoned dwelling with its entrance ajar, the door creaking in the morning breeze. Inside, a weathered wooden bench occupied the center of the room, positioned near the tall stove common to all homes in Siberia. The air was stale and thick with dust, but it offered welcome shelter. Without exchanging words, they took their seats, their exhausted bodies grateful for the respite.

Nadia studied her companion's features with unprecedented intensity, taking in every line and shadow of his face. Her gaze held something deeper than mere thankfulness or compassion, something that made her heart ache with unspoken emotion. Had Michael been able to see her expression, he would have recognized in those gentle, sorrowful eyes an infinite well of loyalty and affection, a devotion that transcended their dire circumstances.

The scorched eyelids of the sightless man drooped halfway, concealing his eyes. His pupils had grown large, while the once-bright blue of his iris had deepened to a darker shade. Though his eyebrows and lashes were singed, his piercing gaze appeared unchanged to observers.

Michael extended his hands outward, his fingers trembling in the dim light.

"Nadia, are you there?" he called out, his voice betraying a hint of vulnerability.

"I'm right here beside you," she answered with gentle reassurance. "And I won't leave your side, Michael. Not now, not ever."

When Nadia spoke his name for the first time, Michael's body tensed. A shiver ran through him as he realized she now knew everything about his identity, his mission, his true purpose, everything he had fought to keep hidden.

"Nadia," he said, his voice tight with emotion, "we must part ways!"

"Part ways? What do you mean, Michael?" Her voice quavered with disbelief and hurt.

"I can't hold you back from your journey! Your father is expecting you in Irkutsk! You need to get to him!" His words came out, almost desperately, as if trying to convince himself as much as her.

"My father would never forgive me if I abandoned you now, not after everything you've done for me!" she declared with fierce determination, her loyalty clear in every word.

"Think of your father, Nadia, only your father!" Michael insisted, his hands clenching at his sides. "He needs you safe, whole!"

"You need me more than he does right now, Michael," Nadia responded, taking a step closer to him. "Are you giving up on reaching Irkutsk?"

"Never!" Michael exclaimed, his voice filled with unwavering determination, echoing against the walls. "Not while breath remains in my body!"

"But you don't have the letter anymore!" Her words hung heavy in the air between them.

"The letter Ivan Ogareff stole from me! No matter, Nadia! They branded me a spy, so a spy I shall become!" His jaw set with grim resolve. "I'll journey to Irkutsk and report everything I've witnessed, everything I've heard. I swear this sacred oath! One day, I shall confront that traitor face to face! But I must reach Irkutsk before he does, before more damage is done."

"Yet you speak of parting ways, Michael?" She touched his arm.

"Nadia, they've stripped me of everything!" His voice cracked with raw anguish. "My dignity, my purpose, my very sight!"

"I still have some roubles, and my sight remains!" Her voice grew stronger with each word. "Let me be your eyes, Michael. I'll guide you to places you cannot reach alone! Together we are stronger than apart."

"How will we travel?" He asked, uncertainty creeping into his voice.

"By foot," she answered, her chin lifted with determination.

"How will we survive?" His fingers brushed against the empty coin purse at his belt.

"We'll beg if we must," she declared without shame. "Whatever it takes."

"Then let us depart, Nadia." He extended his hand, seeking hers.

"Yes, Michael, let's go." She clasped his hand, their fingers intertwining with shared purpose.

Having endured hardships together, the young pair stopped referring to each other as siblings. Their shared troubles had strengthened their bond into something deeper, more profound than mere family ties. Following a brief rest of sixty minutes beneath the shade of a gnarled oak tree, they ventured out into the dusty afternoon. While in town, Nadia had got some tchornekhleb (a bread made from barley) and meod (a Russian honey drink) from sympathetic merchants. She'd gained these without payment, having relied on charity and the kindness of strangers, though the shame of begging still burned in her cheeks. These modest provisions helped ease Michael's hunger and quench his thirst after their long journey. Nadia ensured he received most their meager supplies, watching him with careful attention. He consumed the bread she offered and drank from the container she raised to his mouth with trembling hands.

"Have you taken your share, Nadia?" he questioned repeatedly.

"I have, Michael," the young woman would answer each time, forcing warmth into her voice to mask her deception, though she was surviving on the remnants he didn't consume, her own stomach growling in protest.

Michael and Nadia departed from Semilowskoe and resumed their challenging journey toward Irkutsk. Nadia displayed remarkable endurance in the face of exhaustion, her feet blistered and aching with each determined step forward. If Michael had seen her condition, the pallor of her skin, the dark circles beneath her eyes, the way she sometimes stumbled, he might have lost his resolve to continue. However, Nadia remained silent about her struggles, swallowing her discomfort, and Michael, hearing no complaints, maintained a relentless pace he couldn't help but sustain. What drove him? Was he still hoping to stay ahead of the Tartars? His situation was dire, traveling on foot, without money, and blind. If he were to lose Nadia, his sole guide and anchor in this darkness, his only option would be to collapse beside the road and meet a tragic end. Yet, if through sheer determination he could reach Krasnoiarsk, there might still be hope. The governor there, once Michael revealed his identity, would provide the means for him to complete his vital journey to Irkutsk.

Michael walked, deep in contemplation, his fingers intertwined with Nadia's. Their connection transcended mere physical touch, it was a lifeline of mutual trust and dependency that made words seem unnecessary in the vast Siberian wilderness. Michael would request, "Talk to me, Nadia," seeking reassurance in the gentle melody of her voice.

"What need is there, Michael? Our thoughts are already one," she would respond, masking the exhaustion in her voice, her fingers tightening around his.

Yet there were moments when her strength would falter, her heart appearing to skip a beat, her legs growing unsteady, her arms falling limp at her sides as she lagged behind. The harsh Siberian terrain seemed to drain what little energy remained in her weary body. At such times, Michael would halt, turning his sightless gaze toward her as if willing himself to see through the darkness that enveloped him. His chest would rise with deep emotion, and then, offering her even greater support than before, he would press onward with renewed determination, drawing from some hidden reserve of strength.

While trudging through their endless hardships, fate smiled upon them that day with something that promised to lighten their burden. After two hours of walking from Semilowskoe, their boots heavy with mud and their clothes damp with sweat, Michael came to an abrupt halt, his head tilted slightly as he listened.

"Can you see anyone on the path?" he asked, his voice barely above a whisper.

"Not a living soul," Nadia answered, scanning the desolate landscape before them.

"I think I hear something approaching from behind. We'll need to conceal ourselves if it's the Tartars. Keep your eyes sharp!" His grip on her hand tightened as he spoke.

"One moment, Michael!" Nadia called out, stepping back to where the road curved rightward, her eyes searching for any suitable hiding place among the scattered rocks and sparse vegetation.

Michael Strogoff stood in silence, straining his ears to listen, his body tense and alert like a hunter tracking prey.

Nadia quickly returned with news: "There's a cart coming. A young man's driving it," she reported, out of breath from her brief reconnaissance.

"Is he by himself?"

"Yes, alone. No other travelers that I can see for miles."

For a moment, Michael considered his options. Should he seek cover, or attempt to secure passage in the approaching transport, if not for himself, then at least for his companion? He felt strong enough to grasp the wagon and push it along if needed, as his legs remained sturdy. However, he worried about Nadia, who was forced to walk since their Obi crossing eight days ago, and must be reaching her limits. The harsh journey had taken its toll on them both, but she had shown remarkable resilience. He remained still, watching, his hand resting on his belt.

The wagon soon reached the intersection, its wooden wheels creaking with each rotation. It was an old, weathered wagon, a kibitka, as locals called it, with room for three passengers. While kibitkas required three horses for pulling, this one had just a single steed, a long-haired Mongolian horse with an long tail. This breed was well-known for its exceptional endurance and bravery, perfectly suited to the harsh conditions of the steppes. The animal's muscular frame and alert ears suggested it was still in its prime, despite the rather decrepit state of the vehicle it pulled.

A young Russian man was guiding the vehicle, accompanied by a shaggy-coated Siberian hunting dog that trotted alongside. His calm, friendly face, weathered by the elements but still youthful, put Nadia at ease. He moved, careful not to push his horse too hard on the uneven terrain. Looking at his relaxed demeanor and easy posture on the driver's bench, one would never guess he was traveling on a path that Tartars could overrun at any moment.

Nadia, still holding Michael's hand, stepped aside onto a patch of trampled grass to let the kibitka pass. The driver brought his vehicle to a halt with a gentle tug of the reins, and smiled at the young girl, the corners of his eyes crinkling with genuine kindness.

"Where might you be heading like this?" he asked with genuine curiosity, his eyes wide and sincere beneath the brim of his well-worn fur cap.

When Michael heard the man speak, something stirred in his memory, he knew that voice from somewhere, like a half-forgotten tune. A wave of relief washed over him as he placed the familiar sound, his worried expression softening, tension draining from his shoulders.

"And just where might you be headed?" the young fellow asked again, directing his question to Michael, leaning forward on his perch.

"Our destination is Irkutsk," Michael answered, his voice steady despite their circumstances.

"Oh! my good man, you realize there are countless kilometers between here and Irkutsk?" the driver exclaimed, gesturing at the vast landscape before them.

"I'm well aware," Michael replied with quiet determination.

"And you plan to walk?" The incredulity in his voice was unmistakable.

"Yes, walk."

"You perhaps, but what about the young lady?" He glanced at Nadia.

"She's my sister," Michael stated, deciding it prudent to maintain this description of Nadia, his tone leaving no room for discussion.

"Your sister, you say! Well, take my word for it, she'll never manage the journey to Irkutsk!" The driver shook his head in disbelief, his weathered face creasing with concern.

"My friend," said Michael as he moved closer, his voice dropping to an urgent whisper, "we've been stripped of everything by the Tartars. I don't have even a single copeck for you, but please, take my sister in your cart. I'll walk alongside it, I'll run if I must, and won't slow you down at all!" His words carried the weight of desperate sincerity.

"No, brother!" Nadia burst out, her voice trembling with emotion as she grabbed Michael's arm. "I won't do it! Please, sir ,my brother cannot see!" The words tumbled out before she could stop them, her protective instinct overriding their careful pretense.

"He's blind?" the young man asked, deeply affected by this revelation.

"The Tartars burned his eyes!" Nadia cried, raising her hands in a pleading gesture, tears threatening to spill down her cheeks.

"Burned his eyes! Oh, you poor soul! Listen, I'm headed to Krasnoiarsk. Why don't both of you ride in my kibitka? We can squeeze together, and there's room for all three of us. My dog won't mind walking, and though we won't travel fast since I'm careful with my horse, we'll get there enough," he offered, his voice full of genuine compassion.

"Tell me your name, friend," Michael requested, turning his face toward the sound of the young man's voice.

"I'm Nicholas Pigassof," he replied.

"That's a name I'll carry with me always," Michael responded with heartfelt gratitude.

"Climb in, dear blind friend. Your sister can sit next to you in the back of the cart, while I'll take the front to steer. We've lined the bottom with fresh birch bark and straw, it's quite cozy, like a bird's nest. Move aside, Serko!" Nicholas called to his faithful companion.

The dog obeyed, jumping down with a soft thud. He was a Siberian breed with gray fur, medium-sized with a friendly, pattable head, and devoted to his master. His intelligent eyes watched the newcomers with gentle curiosity as they prepared to board the cart.

Soon after, Michael and Nadia settled into the kibitka. Michael reached out, searching for Pigassof's hands. "Ah, you want to shake hands!" Nicholas said. "Here they are, my friend, hold them as long as you like. They're rough and calloused, but honest working hands."

The carriage continued forward, with Nicholas's horse maintaining a steady pace with no whip. The animal seemed to know the route by heart, its hooves striking a familiar rhythm against the packed earth. While Michael's journey wasn't moving any faster, at least Nadia could rest a bit in relative comfort.

The young girl was so exhausted that the gentle rocking of the carriage soon lulled her to sleep, a deep slumber that showed just how drained she was. Her head drooped until it rested against Michael's shoulder. Together, Michael and Nicholas carefully arranged her on the straw bedding, making sure she was secure and wouldn't roll with the cart's movement. Nicholas felt great sympathy for her condition, and though Michael shed no tears, it was only because the hot iron that had blinded him had dried up his ability to cry.

"Such a lovely girl," Nicholas commented, glancing back at his passengers. "She reminds me of my daughter at that age."

"Indeed," Michael replied, his face turned toward where Nadia lay sleeping.

"These dear ones try to show such strength, little father. They're brave souls, but in the end, they're still delicate creatures. Have you traveled from afar? Your clothes suggest quite a journey."

"A very long way."

"You poor souls! The burning of your eyes, it must have caused terrible pain! I can not imagine such suffering."

"Yes, terrible," Michael responded, turning toward Nicholas's voice as if he could still see him, his scarred face twitching at the memory.

"Didn't you cry?"

"I did." The words came out clipped and raw.

"I would have cried too. Imagine never being able to see your loved ones again. Though they can still see you, maybe that's something to hold onto! A small blessing in such dark times."

"Yes, maybe it is." Michael paused, his head tilted. "Listen, my friend," he went on, his voice taking on an intent quality, "are you sure we haven't met somewhere before?"

"You, sir? Never."

"Your voice sounds familiar to me." Michael leaned forward, his unseeing eyes searching.

"Well!" Nicholas said with a smile, adjusting his grip on the reins, "he recognizes my voice! Perhaps you're asking to figure out where I'm from. I'm from Kolyvan."

"Kolyvan?" Michael echoed, his face brightening with recognition. "Then that's where I met you, weren't you working at the telegraph office?"

"Could be," Nicholas answered, his tone neutral. "I was employed there. I handled the telegraph messages."

"And you remained at your station until the very end?"

"Well, that's when you need to be there!" Nicholas declared with unwavering conviction.

"I remember the day when a Brit and a Frenchman were arguing, waving roubles around, fighting for a spot at your window. The Englishman was sending some verses." Michael's voice carried a hint of amusement at the memory.

"That might have happened, but I can't recall it," Nicholas replied with practiced indifference.

"Really? You don't remember?"

"I never read the messages I transmit. Since I'm supposed to forget them anyway, it's easier to not know them." Nicholas's words came out clipped and precise, like a well-rehearsed response.

The response revealed much about Nicholas Pigassof's nature, his disciplined loyalty to duty and careful discretion. The kibitka continued its journey at a steady rhythm, with Michael wishing they could go a little faster. However, both Nicholas and his horse were set in their ways, following a routine they had no desire to change. Their pattern was consistent: two hours of travel followed by one hour of rest, continuing this way through day and night. During these breaks, the horse would graze in whatever patch of grass it could find, while the travelers shared meals alongside the loyal Serko, who always seemed to know when mealtime approached. Their kibitka carried enough provisions to feed twenty people, packed into every available space, and Nicholas, with characteristic generosity, shared his supplies with his two guests, whom he assumed were siblings traveling together through circumstance.

Refreshed after resting for a day, Nadia found her strength returning, the color coming back to her cheeks and her appetite improving with each meal. Nicholas tended to her needs with great care and attention, offering extra blankets during the frosty nights and ensuring she had the most comfortable spot in the kibitka. Though their progress was unhurried, they advanced and under good conditions, the weather remaining mild for their journey. During the night drives, Nicholas would drift off to sleep, his loud and steady snoring revealing his untroubled mind, his head nodding with each breath and the motion of the cart. In these moments, one might have caught glimpses of Michael's hand reaching for the reins, urging the horse to pick up speed, confusing Serko, who remained silent about these occurrences, though his intelligent eyes followed each subtle movement. Whenever Nicholas stirred from his slumber, the pace would return to its usual amble, but by then the kibitka had already covered several additional miles, their progress hastened under the cover of darkness.

On their journey, the travelers crossed several rivers and passed through many settlements in Siberia. They traversed the Ichirnsk River and moved through a series of villages including Ichisnokoe, Berikylokoe, and Kuskoe, each one more desolate than the last, with shuttered windows and abandoned market squares. Their path then led them across the Marunsk River and its namesake village, followed by Bogostowskoe. They reached the Ichoula, a small stream marking the boundary between Western and Eastern Siberia, its waters running clear and swift between moss-covered banks. The landscape alternated between vast, empty moors stretching to the horizon, where the wind whispered through the tall grass, and dense fir forests that seemed to go on forever, their dark branches creaking in the breeze. The entire region was deserted, with most villages standing empty, their wooden houses creaking in the wind. Local peasants had retreated beyond the Yenisei River, believing its wide waters might block the advancing Tartar forces, taking with them whatever possessions they could carry on their backs or load onto carts.

The kibitka arrived in Atchinsk on August 22nd, having covered two hundred and fifty miles from Tomsk, the wheels worn and muddy from the difficult terrain. They still needed to traverse another eighty miles to reach Krasnoiarsk, a journey that would take them through even more challenging territory as summer waned into early autumn.

The journey had been uneventful, though the constant rocking of the kibitka over uneven ground tested their endurance. Throughout their six days together, Nicholas maintained his characteristic composure, while Michael and Nadia remained anxious, their thoughts drifting to the inevitable moment when their fellow traveler would part ways with them.

Through Nicholas and the young girl's descriptions, Michael experienced the landscape they journeyed across. They took turns painting verbal pictures of their surroundings, allowing him to envision whether they were passing through dense forests or open plains, if there huts dotting the steppe, or if any Siberians ere visible nearby. Nicholas, talkative by nature, kept up a constant stream of commentary, describing everything from the way morning dew glistened on tall grass to the patterns of migrating birds overhead, and his unique perspective on things often brought smiles to his companions' faces. During these long hours of shared observation, the three travelers grew more comfortable with one another, and on one such conversation, Michael inquired about the weather.

"It's fair for now, little father," Nicholas replied, tugging at his thick wool collar, "though we'll be feeling winter's first bite soon enough. Perhaps these conditions will drive the Tartars to seek winter shelter during the harsh months ahead, when the steppes become treacherous with ice and snow."

Michael gave a skeptical shake of his head, his jaw tightening almost imperceptibly.

"Don't you agree, little father?" Nicholas pressed, leaning forward in his seat. "Do you think they'll advance toward Irkutsk despite the coming cold?"

"I'm afraid they will," Michael replied, his voice carrying a weight of certainty.

"Yes... you're right; they have that villainous man with them who won't let them dawdle. Have you heard of Ivan Ogareff?" Nicholas's cheerful face darkened at the name.

"I have."

"You know betraying one's homeland is unforgivable! To turn against Mother Russia herself!"

"Yes... it's unforgivable..." Michael responded, striving to maintain his composure while his fingers clenched against his knee.

"Little father," Nicholas continued, studying his companion's face with growing curiosity, "you seem rather calm when Ivan Ogareff name is mentioned. As a Russian, your blood should boil at the mere sound of his name."

"Trust me, friend, my hatred for him runs deeper than yours ever could," Michael said, each word measured and heavy with an intensity that silenced his talkative companion.

"That's impossible," Nicholas objected, his voice rising with indignation. "No, it can't be! When I think of Ivan Ogareff and the damage he's inflicting on our holy Russia, I become so enraged that if I ever got my hands on him," His fists clenched, knuckles whitening with the force of his emotion.

"If you got your hands on him, friend?" Michael's tone was soft, almost inviting.

"I believe I would kill him." Nicholas declared, chest puffing with patriotic fervor.

"And I know I would," Michael replied with quiet certainty, his words carrying the weight of steel and absolute conviction.

Chapter Seven

THE PASSAGE OF THE YENISEI

As darkness descended on August 25th, Krasnoiarsk appeared on the horizon, its scattered lights twinkling like distant stars. Eight days had passed since leaving Tomsk, the journey marked by caution and weariness. The journey could have been quicker, but Nicholas's lack of rest had prevented them from pushing their horse harder, the animal already showing signs of fatigue from the constant travel. Under different circumstances, another driver and fresh mounts could have covered the same distance in just sixty hours across the Siberian terrain.

The threat of Tartars had subsided, giving them a brief respite from constant vigilance. The road behind their kibitka remained clear, with not a single scout in sight across the vast steppes. This unusual calm suggested something significant had prevented the Emir's forces from advancing toward Irkutsk, though the reason remained uncertain. Recent events had taken an unexpected turn in the region's volatile political landscape. A assembled Russian force from Yeniseisk had attempted to reclaim Tomsk but, finding themselves outnumbered against the massive Tartar army, were forced to withdraw in anarchy. Feofar-Khan commanded a formidable army of two hundred and fifty thousand men, combining his own battle-hardened troops with those from the Khanats of Khokhand and Koun-douze, creating an overwhelming force that swept through the territory. Reinforcements: Without reinforcements from the west, the Russian government lacked the forces in Siberia to counter the threat and halt the invasion. Irkutsk's very existence is threatened, as the Tartar army might march on the city at any moment. On August 22nd: Although isolated from recent news, Michael was unaware that the battle of Tomsk had occurred This explained why the Emir's advance forces hadn't reached Krasnoiarsk by the 25th, giving them this temporary window of safety.

Despite being unaware of what had transpired since he left, Michael Strogoff took comfort in knowing he had a lead of several days over the Tartars, giving him reasonable confidence he would reach Irkutsk before them, even though the city lay another six hundred miles ahead through challenging terrain and unpredictable weather.

In Krasnoiarsk, a town of twelve thousand inhabitants nestled along the Yenisei River, Michael expected securing new transportation. As Nicholas Pigassof planned to remain there, Michael would need to find both a replacement guide and a faster vehicle, one better suited to the tough roads ahead. He was confident that, after presenting himself to the town's governor and verifying his status as the Czar's Courier, he could arrange swift passage to Irkutsk. He intended to bid farewell to the helpful Nicholas Pigassof and depart with Nadia, whom he was determined to deliver to her father, no matter the obstacles they might face. Though Nicholas had stopped in Krasnoiarsk, he had specified this was contingent on finding work there that would allow him to serve the government as faithfully as before. True to his conscientious nature, having stayed at his Kolyvan post until the very end despite mounting dangers, he now sought another government position where he could be of use. "I cannot accept wages I haven't earned," was his principle, a motto that had guided him throughout his years of service.

The traveler decided that if Krasnoiarsk, likely still connected to Irkutsk by telegraph, didn't need his help, he would journey onward to Oudinsk or even Siberia's capital. Should he choose the latter destination, he would continue accompanying the siblings. Indeed, they could hope to find someone more reliable or devoted to their cause, especially given the perilous nature of their journey through the harsh Siberian wilderness.

Their horse-drawn carriage was now half a mile from Krasnoiarsk. Wooden crosses, markers common near the town's entrance, dotted both sides of the road, their weathered forms casting long shadows in the fading light. As evening settled in at seven o'clock, the silhouettes of churches and houses perched on the Yenisei's elevated banks stood against the darkening sky, their forms mirrored in the river's dusky waters below. The last rays of sunlight painted the scene in muted shades of purple and gold.

"What's our location?" Michael asked his sister, leaning forward to peer through the gathering gloom.

"About half a mile before we reach the first buildings," Nadia answered, her voice tinged with both weariness and anticipation.

"Could everyone be sleeping?" Michael wondered aloud. "I can't hear a single sound." The unusual stillness made him uneasy, as even the smallest towns buzzed with some activity at this hour.

"I don't see any lights at all," Nadia said, scanning the horizon intently, "not even smoke rising from chimneys. At this time of year, they should at least have fires burning for warmth."

"What an odd town!" Nicholas remarked from his perch on the driver's seat. "It's silent, and apparently they all turn in early! Even the dogs are quiet, which is most unusual."

A sense of dread crept into Michael's heart, settling like a cold weight in his chest. He hadn't told Nadia that he'd pinned all his hopes on Krasnoiarsk, where he'd expected to find what he needed to complete their journey. The supplies they carried wouldn't last forever, and winter was approaching fast. He was worried that, once again, his expectations would prove false.

Nadia sensed his thoughts, though she couldn't understand why he remained so determined to reach Irkutsk after someone stole the Imperial letter. When she mentioned this to him one day during their arduous journey, he stated, "I made a vow to reach Irkutsk," in a tone that brooked no further discussion.

However, to complete his mission, he needed to secure faster transportation once they reached Krasnoiarsk. Their current pace was far too slow. "My friend," he called out to Nicholas, shifting in his seat, "what's causing our delay?"

"I'm trying not to disturb the townspeople with my carriage's racket!" Nicholas replied with forced cheerfulness, then gave a gentle snap of his whip to urge his horse forward along the darkening road.

The desolate High Street of Krasnoiarsk lay before them. Once dubbed the "Northern Athens" by Madame de Bourboulon, the city now stood eerily empty of its Athenian character. Silence now fell on the once elegant, wide, pristine streets, devoid of carriage sounds. Impressive in their architectural splendor, the grand wooden buildings cast shadows over deserted walkways where no footsteps fell. Siberian beauties in Parisian fashions were missing from the beautiful park carved from a birch forest to the Yenisei's banks. No longer did the cathedral's mighty bell ring, nor did church chimes fill the air. This once-vibrant city had transformed into a ghost town, stripped of all signs of life. Even the marketplace, bustling with merchants hawking their wares and housewives haggling over prices, stood abandoned, its wooden stalls collecting dust.

Prior to the telegraph lines being cut, the Czar's office had transmitted its final directive to Krasnoiarsk. Everyone, from the governor and military forces to ordinary citizens, were commanded to abandon the city, taking with them any valuable or useful items that might aid the Tartar forces. They were to seek sanctuary in Irkutsk. This evacuation order extended to all settlements in the province, as the Russian government's strategy was to leave nothing but empty land for the advancing enemy. The unquestioning obedience to the orders explains why Krasnoiarsk now stands deserted. Windows were shuttered, doors were locked, and even the city's archives and administrative documents had been carefully packed away and transported eastward, leaving behind nothing but hollow buildings and memories of better days.

The trio, Michael Strogoff, Nadia, and Nicholas, tiptoed through the empty town streets, their shadows stretching long against the abandoned buildings in the fading light. A sense of numbness had overtaken them, and their footsteps echoed against the cobblestones, the only sounds breaking the eerie silence of the abandoned city. Though Michael kept his emotions hidden behind his stoic expression, inside he seethed with frustration at his continued streak of misfortune and his thwarted plans, each setback feeling like another obstacle in his urgent mission.

"Oh, what terrible luck!" Nicholas lamented, gesturing at the shuttered shops and vacant houses. "How can I find work in such a desolate place? Not a soul remains to employ me!"

"You should continue traveling with us," Nadia suggested, her voice gentle but firm. "It would be unwise to stay here alone."

"Yes, I suppose I must!" Nicholas agreed, brightening somewhat at the prospect. "I expect the telegraph line between Oudinsk and Irkutsk is still functioning. At least there's that hope. So then, shall we get going, little father?"

"We should wait until tomorrow," Michael suggested, his face turned away as if listening to distant sounds.

"Indeed," Nicholas agreed. "We'll need daylight to navigate the Yenisei crossing! The river can be treacherous even in the best conditions!"

"To see!" Nadia whispered under her breath, thinking of her sightless companion with a pang of sympathy.

Nicholas caught her words and turned to Michael, his expression falling as realization dawned. "I apologize, little father," he said, embarrassed. "How thoughtless of me, day or night makes no difference to you, does it? I sometimes forget about your... condition."

"Please, friend, don't blame yourself," Michael responded, his hand moving to cover his eyes, fingers brushing against the rough fabric that concealed them. "With you guiding me, I can manage just fine. The darkness has been my companion for so long now. Take some hours to rest now. Nadia needs sleep too. We'll resume our journey tomorrow!"

Finding shelter proved easy for Michael and his companions. The first dwelling they entered stood vacant, like all the neighboring homes, its wooden door creaking in the night wind. Inside, they discovered only scattered piles of leaves, brittle and brown, that rustled beneath their feet. Their horse, having no better options, made do with this meager sustenance, pawing at the floor for better morsels. The group still had supplies remaining in their kibitka, allowing everyone a portion of food, simple fare of dried meat and hard bread that they shared in companionable silence. Later, after kneeling in prayer before a small icon of the Panaghia mounted on the wall, its lamp still casting a weak glow that flickered against the weathered timber walls, Nicholas and the young woman drifted off to sleep while Michael kept vigil, unable to find rest himself. His acute hearing picked up every subtle sound of the night, the whisper of wind through cracks, settling old wood, and the steady breathing of his sleeping companions.

At first light on August 26th, the carriage made its way through birch forests, heading for the Yenisei's shores. Michael's mind was troubled. The river posed a significant challenge, if the Tartars' advance had prompted the destruction of all vessels, as he suspected, how would they manage to cross? He was well acquainted with the river Yenisei's formidable nature: its vast expanse and powerful currents. Even under normal circumstances, using designed ferries for passengers, carriages, and horses, the crossing consumed three hours, with boats struggling to reach the far bank. Now, with no ferry service available, the question loomed: how could they transport the kibitka across these waters?

The first rays of dawn were appearing as their horse-drawn cart arrived at the elevated left shoreline, where a broad pathway through the park ended. From their position, thirty meters above the Yenisei River, they had a commanding view of its expansive flow. The cool morning air carried the distant sound of rushing water and the earthy scent of damp soil and river vegetation. Their horse stamped, steam rising from its flanks in the crisp morning air.

"Can you spot any vessels?" inquired Michael, his eyes darting from side to side, a futile habit, given his blindness. His fingers gripped the wooden seat, knuckles white with tension as he strained his other senses to compensate for his lack of sight.

"The morning's still too dim, brother," Nadia answered, squinting into the grayness. "There's a heavy mist hanging over everything, the river isn't visible yet. The fog's so thick it looks like a white blanket draped across the water."

"Though I can hear its rushing waters," Michael noted, his head tilted slightly as he focused on the sound. "The current seems stronger than usual today."

A thunderous roar emerged from within the dense fog as the swollen waters cascaded below, sending occasional spray into the air that merged with the morning mist. The three companions stood waiting for the misty veil to lift, knowing the sun would soon break through and scatter the morning vapors, its warmth already beginning to penetrate the gloom.

"What's happening?" Michael inquired, his fingers drumming against his knee.

"The fog is drifting away," Nadia answered, her voice carrying a note of relief. "It won't be long before everything clears."

"Can you see the water's surface yet?"

"Not yet." She leaned forward, straining her eyes.

"Just wait a moment, little father," Nicholas said, placing a reassuring hand on Michael's shoulder. "This will all vanish soon. Look, there's a breeze coming! It's pushing the fog away. I can already make out trees on the hills across from us. The mist is dissolving, floating off into nothing. The sun's warm rays are burning through all this haze. Oh, what a magnificent sight this is! Such a shame you cannot witness this beautiful scene, my poor friend!".

Michael scanned the horizon before turning to his companion, his face etched with concern. "Do you see a boat?"

"I see nothing of the sort," Nicholas replied, shaking his head.

"Look carefully, my friend, check both banks, as far as you can see," Michael urged, his voice carrying a note of desperate hope. "A raft, perhaps? Even a small canoe?"

Nicholas and Nadia leaned forward, clutching the bushes along the cliff's edge as they peered down at the waters below, their fingers digging into the coarse bark. Their vantage point offered a sweeping view, the wind tugging at their clothes as they searched. Here, the Yenisei River sprawled to nearly a mile wide, splitting into two channels of different sizes where the current rushed through, its waters churning and frothing around submerged rocks. Several islands dotted the space between these channels, lush with alders, willows, and poplars, like green vessels anchored in the flowing water, their leaves dancing in the breeze. Beyond: Rising beyond, the eastern shore showed forested hills wearing a purple crown in the light, each ridge distinct against the sky. Stretching in both directions, the mighty Yenisei presented a magnificent panorama extending fifty miles into the distance, where water and sky appeared to merge in a hazy embrace.

No watercraft were present in the area; the riverbanks were empty where boats usually gathered. Following instructions from military command, every vessel had been removed or demolished, leaving only weathered posts and frayed ropes swaying in the wind. The Tartars could not advance toward Irkutsk unless they brought materials to construct a pontoon bridge, as the Yenisei River formed an impassable barrier, its rushing waters a natural defense line.

"Wait," Michael said, his eyes scanning the distant shoreline. "I recall a small dock upstream, near the edges of Krasnoiarsk where vessels dock. Let's explore the riverbank in that direction, perhaps we'll find an overlooked boat."

Nadia grasped Michael's hand, her fingers tightening with renewed hope, leading them along the suggested route. She hoped to find a vessel, whether a boat or barge, substantial enough to transport either their kibitka or at least themselves across the churning waters. Michael stood ready to brave the crossing at a moment's notice, his determined expression matching the urgency of their mission. After twenty minutes of hurried walking along the rocky shoreline, dodging fallen branches and scrambling over moss-covered stones, the trio arrived at a small quay, where buildings lined both sides down to the water, creating what appeared to be a village extension beyond Krasnoiarsk proper, its wooden structures weathered by years of river mist and seasonal storms.

Their hearts sank at the sight before them. The shoreline stood deserted, no boats, no barges at the modest wharf, not even enough materials to construct a raft capable of bearing three passengers. When Michael questioned Nicholas about their options, the latter's response crushed their hopes: he deemed the crossing impossible under these circumstances, gesturing at the barren stretch of weathered planks and empty moorings.

"We'll make it across!" Michael declared, his voice carrying over the rush of the river waters with unwavering conviction.

They continued their thorough search. The group inspected the deserted houses along the shoreline, all abandoned just like the rest of Krasnoiarsk. The doors needed a gentle push to open, their hinges creaking from disuse and exposure to the elements. These were the dwellings of poor folk, stripped bare save for the occasional broken piece of furniture or tattered scrap of cloth. Nicholas explored one cottage, while Nadia ventured into another, their footsteps echoing through the empty rooms. Even Michael moved about, feeling his way through different houses, hoping to discover something useful among the scattered debris and abandoned belongings.

After Nicholas and Nadia had unsuccessfully searched their respective cottages and were ready to abandon their efforts, their spirits dampened by each empty dwelling, they heard Michael calling out to them. They rushed to the riverbank, their boots clattering against the worn wooden planks, and spotted him standing in a doorway, his silhouette framed by the dim interior of yet another fisherman's home.

"Quick, over here!" he called, waving them forward with urgency. Nicholas and Nadia hurried toward him and followed him inside the cottage, ducking beneath the low doorframe into the musty interior.

"What's all this?" Michael inquired, gesturing toward a pile of items stacked in the corner near a weathered wooden table.

"Those are containers made of leather," Nicholas replied, running his hand over the smooth, well-oiled surface of the nearest one.

"Are they filled?"

"Indeed, filled with koumyss. How fortunate we've found them to supplement our supplies!" Nicholas lifted one to test its weight.

Koumyss, a beverage produced from either mare's or camel's milk through a process of fermentation, provides substantial nourishment and can even produce intoxicating effects. Nicholas and his fellow travelers were quite pleased with their find, knowing how valuable such provisions could be on their journey.

"Keep one," Michael instructed, his voice firm with decision, "but drain the rest."

"Right away, little father." Nicholas began moving the containers into a more organized arrangement.

"These will be useful for crossing the Yenisei." Michael's fingers traced the leather's seams.

"What about the raft?"

"The kibitka will serve as our raft, it's lightweight enough to stay afloat. Plus, we can use these containers to help keep both it and the horse buoyant. The leather will provide extra flotation when we need it most."

"That's clever thinking, little father!" Nicholas said. "With God's blessing, we'll make it across... though we might not manage a straight path, given how swift the current runs! The spring melt makes the waters treacherous."

"What does it matter?" Michael replied, running his hand along the cart's wooden frame. "Once we're across, we can find the way to Irkutsk from the other bank. The road is well-marked on that side."

"Let's get to work then," Nicholas said, emptying the bottles with practiced efficiency.

They kept one bottle of koumyss, but used the rest, sealing in the air, to create a flotation device. Working in the fading daylight, they secured two bottles to each side of the horse to help it stay afloat. The animal shifted as they worked, but Nicholas's gentle words kept it calm. They attached two more bottles to the shafts to keep them level with the cart's body, which had now become a makeshift raft. They completed the task quickly, double-checking each knot and seal.

"Are you frightened, Nadia?" Michael asked, noticing her intent study of the rushing water.

"No, brother," the girl answered, lifting her chin with quiet determination.

"And you, friend?"

"Me?" Nicholas exclaimed, his weather-worn face breaking into a broad grin. "Why, this is like a dream come true, floating along in a cart! We Siberians can make a boat out of anything!"

The riverbank's muddy shore, smoothed by seasons of flowing water, was ideal for easing the kibitka into the water. Cautiously, the horse pulled the vehicle forward until it floated, Serko paddling alongside, creating small ripples.

They wisely removed their footwear and securing it in the cart, the three travelers sat in the kibitka as the water lapped around them; however, thanks to floating bottles, it only reached their ankles. Beneath them, the wooden planks creaked with each gentle wave. Michael handled the reins with steady hands, following Nicholas's guidance to steer the horse at a careful angle, avoiding overexertion against the river's flow. With effort, the animal's powerful muscles strained to maintain its course, avoiding a direct fight against the current. Initially, the journey downstream was smooth, the morning sun glinting off the water, and within minutes they passed Krasnoiarsk's waterfront, where a few early risers watched their unusual passage. Carried northward by the current, landfall became certain well below the town, a fact of little concern given their intended destination. Despite their makeshift vessel, the crossing would have been straightforward had the current remained steady. However, many whirlpools dotted the river's surface like hungry mouths, and despite Michael's best efforts to navigate between them, one of these swirling vortexes caught hold of the kibitka.

The small vehicle was in grave peril. Instead of drifting along, it now spun in circles, tilting toward the whirlpool's heart, reminiscent of a circus performer's calculated rotations. Their steed struggled to keep its nostrils above the churning waters, fighting against the very real threat of drowning, its eyes wide with terror as it thrashed against the merciless pull. Even Serko, the faithful dog, was forced to scramble into the carriage for safety, his wet fur pressed against the wooden planks as he whimpered.

Michael understood all too well the dire situation they faced. He could feel their vessel being pulled inward along an ever-tightening spiral, with no apparent means of escape. The wooden frame creaked with each rotation, water sloshing over the sides and pooling around their feet. How desperately he wished for his sight in that moment, to better navigate this treacherous trap, but such wishes were futile. Beside him, Nadia remained wordless, her hands gripping the cart's edges with white-knuckled intensity as their transport tilted ever more steeply toward the vortex's consuming center. The roar of the water grew louder with each passing second, drowning out even the panicked breathing of their horse.

Was Nicholas blind to the dire circumstances? Did his calm demeanor stem from stoic composure, fearless bravery, or mere apathy toward danger? Perhaps he viewed life as the Eastern philosophers did, as a brief stay at an inn, where one must check out on the sixth day, regardless of desire. Whatever the reason, his cheerful expression remained unwavering, his rosy cheeks still bearing that persistent smile, even as death itself seemed to beckon from the depths below.

The kibitka swirled in the churning waters, its horse spent, foam flecking from its quivering muzzle as it fought against the inexorable pull. Michael sprang into action, his movements decisive and purposeful. Shedding any restrictive clothing, letting his heavy coat and boots fall where they may, he plunged into the water and seized the panicked horse's bridle with iron determination. The icy current bit into his flesh, but he paid it no mind. With tremendous effort, his muscles straining against the relentless force of the water, he guided the animal free from the deadly whirlpool's grip. Once back in the main current, the kibitka resumed its downstream journey, water streaming from its wooden sides.

"Victory!" Nicholas cried out, throwing his arms wide as if embracing their salvation.

After two hours of grueling navigation from the dock, their battered vehicle had made it across the river's treacherous main channel, landing on a welcoming island over six miles downstream from where they began, the wooden kibitka creaking in protest as it dragged against the gravelly shore.

Once there, the horse, sides heaving and nostrils flaring, pulled the cart up the steep riverbank, and they allowed their valiant steed an hour to recover its strength. During this respite, they dried their sodden clothes and shared what remained of their provisions. After crossing the island beneath a canopy of stunning silver birch trees, their branches swaying in the afternoon breeze, they reached the bank of the Yenisei's narrower branch.

This crossing proved far less challenging; the river's second channel lacked the dangerous whirlpools of the first, though the water still churned with considerable force around them. However, the swift current still pushed them off course, carrying them five miles downstream before they could reach the far shore, the horse's hooves at last finding purchase on solid ground. They had drifted eleven miles from their original starting point, the journey having carved a great arc through the mighty river's expanse.

As the travelers crossed these vast Siberian rivers, still unbridged and formidable barriers to easy travel, each crossing had brought its share of troubles for Michael Strogoff. The Tartars had attacked their boat on the Irtych while he traveled with Nadia, the memory of bullets whistling past their heads still fresh in his mind. During the Obi crossing, he had escaped pursuing horsemen after his horse was shot, forced to abandon the dying animal and swim the final distance through the frigid waters. By comparison, their passage over the Yenisei had been uneventful, though no less demanding of their strength and determination.

"It wouldn't have been half as exciting," Nicholas declared as they stepped onto the river's far bank, wringing water from his sodden sleeves, "if it hadn't been such a challenge."

"What we found challenging," Michael Strogoff replied, scanning the distant shore they'd left behind, "may prove impossible for the Tartars to accomplish. Even the most skilled horsemen must respect nature's obstacles."

QuantumDigitalPublishing.io
Michael Strogoff or, The Courier of the Czar
Book II – Chapter VIII

Chapter Eight

A HARE CROSSES THE ROAD

The messenger Michael Strogoff had reason to believe his path to Irkutsk would be unobstructed. He had outpaced the Tartar forces, who remained held up in Tomsk, and by the time the Emir's troops reached Krasnoiarsk, they would discover only an empty town. Since there was no way to cross between the shores of the Yenisei River, it would take several days to construct a pontoon bridge, a challenging task to accomplish in the best of conditions, let alone during a military campaign. For the first time since his confrontation with Ivan Ogareff in Omsk, the Czar's courier felt his anxiety ease, and he thought his journey might continue without further impediments, though experience had taught him to remain vigilant.

The stretch of road linking Krasnoiarsk to Irkutsk was well-maintained, standing out as the finest section of the entire route. Travelers enjoyed smoother passage here, with majestic trees providing welcome shade from the scorching sun that had tormented them across the steppes. In places, vast forests of pine and cedar stretched for a hundred miles, their branches swaying in the mountain breeze. Though no longer the boundless horizon of the steppe, a baron dessert, this fertile region lay vacant, its silence broken only by the occasional cry of a distant bird. They encountered nothing but abandoned settlements along their way, their wooden houses standing like silent sentinels. The Siberian farmers were gone, leaving behind a desolate landscape, not by nature's hand, but by imperial decree that had commanded their evacuation ahead of the advancing invasion.

The weather was pleasant, though the nighttime chill lingered in the morning air, slow to dissipate even as the sun climbed higher. As September approached, daylight hours grew shorter in this elevated region, the sun setting earlier each evening and rising later each dawn. The autumn season here was brief, despite being at the same latitude as Edinburgh and Copenhagen, around the fifty-fifth parallel, where fall stretched for months. Winter seemed to arrive almost without warning in this part of Siberia, descending like a heavy curtain across the landscape. Extreme temperatures characterized these harsh Asiatic Russian winters; sometimes the mercury plunged to an astounding 42 degrees below zero, a temperature even the hardiest locals found unbearable.

The group enjoyed favorable weather as they traveled, with no storms or rain to impede their progress. The clear skies and moderate temperatures made their journey almost pleasant. Both Nadia and Michael had regained their strength since departing from Tomsk, their previous exhaustion fading away as their bodies adjusted to the rigors of constant travel.

Nicholas Pigassof was thriving, feeling better than ever before. His cheeks had taken on a healthy ruddy glow, and his step had become more vigorous with each passing day. He viewed their journey not as a hardship but as an enjoyable expedition, a welcome use of his mandatory time off. The fresh mountain air and daily exercise had done wonders for his constitution, and he often hummed as they walked.

"I must say," he declared, "this beats spending twelve hours daily hunched over a stool, operating that telegraph machine! My back feels ten years younger already!"

The duo had convinced Nicholas to push his horse harder. Michael had achieved this by telling Nicholas that he and Nadia were rushing to reunite with their father, who was in exile in Irkutsk. While they needed to be careful not to exhaust the horse, especially since finding a replacement might prove impossible in these remote regions, they could still maintain a decent pace. By allowing the horse to rest every ten miles, they could cover forty miles within a day. The horse was well-suited for such a journey, being from a hardy breed known for its endurance in the harsh Siberian climate, and the route offered plenty of lush grass for grazing, ensuring the animal stayed well-nourished throughout their trek. Given these favorable conditions, they felt justified in asking the horse to increase its speed without risking its health.

Nicholas accepted all their reasons with enthusiastic understanding. The situation of the two young people about to join their father in exile touched him. He had seen nothing so moving in all his years of service. Smiling at Nadia, his eyes crinkling with genuine emotion, he said, "Oh, what joy Mr. Korpanoff will feel when he sees you, when he opens his arms to embrace you! If I make it to Irkutsk, which seems now, would you allow me to witness that reunion? You will, won't you? It would warm my heart to see such a happy moment."

Then, suddenly slapping his forehead with a sharp crack that startled them both, he added, "But oh! I forgot! What sorrow he'll feel when he discovers his poor son is blind! Ah! Such is life, joy and sadness always mixed, like light and shadow on a summer's day!"

Consequently, as a result, the kibitka's wheels turned over the rough terrain, now traveling faster, nearly eight miles per hour, according to Michael's careful calculations. Sensing: Sensing their passengers' urgency, the horses maintained a brisk pace despite the challenging road conditions.

Arriving: In the early hours of September 4th, just as dawn broke over the horizon, the carriage arrived at Biriousensk, having crossed the small Biriousa River whose waters flowed beneath. Nicholas was relieved by this arrival, as he had noticed their food supplies dwindling to low levels over the past few days. Luckily, he discovered several "pogatchas", traditional cakes made with fat from sheep, baking in an oven, their rich aroma filling the air, along with a considerable amount of cooked rice. This lucky find came at just the right time, as they needed to replace the koumyss, a fermented drink they had stocked up on while in Krasnoiarsk, which had run out during their journey.

The group resumed their travels later that day, following their brief stop. They were now within three hundred miles of Irkutsk. The Tartar advance forces remained unseen. Michael Strogoff felt optimistic that he would face no further interruptions and could reach the Grand Duke within eight to ten days at most, assuming the roads remained passable and weather favorable.

Just as they were departing Biriousinsk, a hare darted across their path in front of the kibitka, its brown fur a blur against the dusty road. "Ah!" Nicholas called out, jerking back on the reins.

"What's wrong?" Michael asked, reacting with the heightened awareness typical of a sightless person responding to unexpected sounds. His hands gripped the side of the cart.

"Did you notice that?" Nicholas asked, his cheerful expression turning gloomy, the color draining from his rosy face. He added, "Oh, but of course you couldn't have seen it, and that's probably for the best, my friend!"

"I saw nothing," Nadia said, glancing around with confusion at Nicholas's sudden change in demeanor.

"That's fortunate! Very fortunate! But I, I saw it!" Nicholas's voice trembled with genuine concern.

"What did you see?" Michael inquired, his sightless face turned toward the driver's voice.

"A hare ran across our path!" Nicholas replied, crossing himself with his free hand.

According to Russian folklore, a hare crossing one's path is considered an omen of impending misfortune, a sign that dark forces were at work. Being as superstitious as most Russians, those who spent their lives on the road, Nicholas brought the kibitka to a halt and muttered a quick prayer under his breath.

Michael could sense his companion's unease, though he didn't share the same superstitious concerns. "You needn't worry," he said, a gentle smile crossing his face. "Such omens only have the power we give them."

"Perhaps you and she have nothing to worry about, little father," Nicholas replied, his fingers still gripping the reins, "but I do! My grandmother always said a crossing hare means the devil himself is watching."

"Whatever happens is meant to be," he added with resigned determination, then urged his horse forward with a soft click of his tongue. Despite his gloomy predictions and frequent backward glances, they made it through the day without incident, though Nicholas remained quiet.

The kibitka came to a stop at noon on September 6th in Alsalevok village. Like the surrounding countryside, the village was completely abandoned, with only the whisper of wind through empty doorways and the occasional creak of shutters to break the eerie silence. While there, Nadia discovered two sturdy hunting knives with sharp blades, the kind used by Siberian hunters for skinning game and survival in the wilderness, lying on a doorstep. She kept one knife for herself and gave the other to Michael, who tucked it away in his clothing, both recognizing that such tools might prove invaluable on their journey.

The gloomy mood still clung to Nicholas. The bad omen had shaken him far more deeply than anyone might have expected. Once known for his constant chatter, unable to stay quiet for even thirty minutes, he now sank into prolonged silences that Nadia struggled to break. Their kibitka raced along the road at full speed, yes, full speed! Nicholas had abandoned his usual careful treatment of the horse, now sharing Michael's urgent desire to reach their destination. Despite his fatalistic nature and acceptance of fate, he wouldn't feel safe until Irkutsk's walls protected them. His reaction wasn't unusual among Russians, many would have shared his fears, and some would have even turned back after seeing a hare cross their path.

As they traveled onward, his keen observations, which Nadia relayed to Michael, suggested their hardships weren't over yet. While the natural resources around Krasnoiarsk had remained untouched, the woodlands they now encountered showed clear signs of destruction by fire and blade, showing that a substantial military force had moved through the area. Charred stumps dotted the landscape where healthy trees had once stood, and deep ruts carved into the earth spoke of heavy wagons and artillery pieces being dragged through. Even the underbrush had been stripped away in places, likely used for campfires by an army on the move. Nicholas's experienced eye could read these signs like a book, and the story they told made him pull his coat tighter around himself despite the mild temperature.

When they reached a point twenty miles from Nijni-Oudinsk, the unmistakable evidence of recent destruction pointed to the Tartar forces. The damage went beyond mere trampled fields and felled trees. The scattered homesteads along their route stood empty, some destroyed, others charred by fire. Their walls bore the telltale pockmarks of bullet impacts, and broken window frames gaped like hollow eyes beneath scorched eaves. Household belongings lay strewn across muddy yards, testament to hasty departures or violent looting.

Tension gripped Michael as the evidence became undeniable. Fresh tracks confirmed Tartar riders had indeed traversed this route, yet these couldn't be from Emir's forces, such a group would have been spotted. This raised alarming questions: what unknown raiders had appeared, and through which hidden steppe trails had they connected with the main Irkutsk road? The Czar's messenger now faced the daunting prospect of confronting mysterious new adversaries. His military training told him these raiders were skilled in stealth operations, moving swiftly and striking without warning, a far more dangerous proposition than facing conventional forces in open combat.

The fearful thoughts remained locked in his mind, as he chose not to burden Nicholas and Nadia with his concerns. His determination to press forward remained steadfast until they encountered a impassable barrier. As they continued their journey the following day, signs of recent military movement became clear. Wisps of smoke rose on the distant horizon, dark plumes that stained the otherwise clear Siberian sky. They guided the kibitka forward with great caution, every creak of the wooden wheels setting their nerves on edge. They passed through abandoned villages where several houses still smoldered, the fires set within the past twenty-four hours. The acrid smell of burnt timber and thatch hung heavy in the air, while scattered belongings in the dirt told of hasty departures.

Finally, on September 8th, their progress came to an abrupt halt when the horse refused to move another step, its ears pinned back and nostrils flaring with obvious distress. Serko's fierce barking pierced the air, the dog's hackles raised as he faced the road ahead with uncharacteristic aggression.

"What's wrong?" Michael called out, his hand instinctively moving to his belt as he scanned the surroundings for danger.

"There's a dead body!" Nicholas shouted back, jumping down from the kibitka. It was the corpse of a peasant, disfigured and already lifeless, his simple homespun clothing stained dark with blood. Nicholas made the sign of the cross, muttering a quick prayer under his breath. With Michael's help, he gripped the body under the arms and moved it to the roadside, laying it beneath a scraggly bush. He wished he could give the poor soul a proper burial to protect it from the wild animals of the steppe, but Michael wouldn't allow them to spare the time.

"We must go, my friend!" he urged, his voice tight with contained urgency. "We can't afford even an hour's delay!" And with that, they drove the kibitka onward, the wheels crunching over scattered stones.

During their journey toward Nijni-Oudinsk, Nicholas and his companions encountered a grim scene, the road was littered with dozens of victims, their bodies scattered across the landscape in groups of twenty or more, some still clutching makeshift weapons or lying over fallen loved ones.

They had no choice but to continue along this route until it became too dangerous to proceed without risking capture by the invading forces. Though the path grew treacherous, with deep ruts and debris making travel difficult, they couldn't deviate from it. Each village they passed through showed escalating signs of destruction and bloodshed, with evidence of recent violence still fresh, doors hanging from hinges, wells fouled, livestock scattered and dead. Gathering any details about what had transpired proved futile, not a single survivor remained who could recount the tragic events that had unfolded, leaving only the silent testimony of the devastation around them.

As the day drew toward late afternoon, around four o'clock, Nicholas spotted the distinctive high steeples of Nijni-Oudinsk's churches piercing the sky. Strange wisps of vapor, not natural clouds, swirled around the towers, their shifting patterns casting eerie shadows across the landscape below.

Nicholas and Nadia studied the scene before sharing their findings with Michael, their eyes straining to make sense of the unsettling sight before them. They faced a crucial decision. A deserted town would offer safe passage, but if the Tartars had somehow seized control, an unexpected yet possible scenario given recent events, they would need to avoid Nijni-Oudinsk at all costs. The risks of encountering enemy forces in such a confined space were too great to ignore.

"Move forward with caution," Michael Strogoff commanded, his voice tight with tension, "but keep moving!"

After traveling about a mile across rough terrain, they stopped abruptly, the horses stamping nervously beneath them.

"Look!" Nadia cried out, her face pale with dawning horror. "Those aren't clouds, it's smoke! Brother, the town is on fire!" The dark plumes now visible against the afternoon sky left little doubt about the grim situation that awaited them ahead.

The terrible truth was undeniable. Bright flashes pierced through the thickening haze as it billowed skyward, casting an eerie orange glow across the landscape. But who was responsible for this destruction? Could it be the Tartars? Or perhaps Russian forces following the Grand Duke's commands? Was this part of the Czar's strategy to deny the Emir's army any shelter, burning everything from Krasnoiarsk to the Yenisei River? Michael wrestled with what action to take, his jaw clenched tight as he weighed their dwindling options.

Uncertain at first, he evaluated the situation, scanning the horizon for any sign of movement. Though traversing the unpaved steppe would pose significant challenges, with its treacherous terrain and lack of water sources, he concluded it was preferable to risking another Tartar capture. Just as he prepared to suggest leaving the road to Nicholas, a gunshot cracked through the air from their right, shattering the tense silence. A bullet whizzed past, striking the kibitka's horse in the head, killing it instantly. The animal crumpled without a sound, its weight causing the carriage to lurch violently.

Before they could react or even cry out in alarm, about twelve mounted warriors surrounded them, their weapons drawn and faces obscured by dark cloth wrappings. In mere moments, Michael, Nadia, and Nicholas found themselves captive, their hands bound with coarse rope as they were taken toward the burning town of Nijni-Oudinsk, the acrid smoke growing thicker with each step.

Despite this second assault, Michael maintained his composure. His blindness made self-defense impossible, but even with functioning eyesight, he wouldn't have fought back. Such resistance would have meant certain death for him and his fellow travelers. Though his vision failed him, his hearing remained sharp, allowing him to comprehend the attackers' conversation, their voices carrying through the smoke-laden air.

Their speech patterns revealed them to be Tartar soldiers, their harsh consonants and distinctive inflections unmistakable to Michael's trained ear. Their discussion made it clear they were scouts advancing ahead of the major invasion force, gathering intelligence about the territory's defenses and population centers.

From the current discussion and fragments of dialogue he caught afterwards, Michael gathered the following information: the Emir, who was held up somewhere past the Yenisei River, dealing with logistical challenges of moving his massive army did not command the soldiers. Instead, they belonged to a separate third division, comprising of Tartars from the Khokland and Koondooz territories, fierce warriors known for their skilled horsemanship and ruthless efficiency. This force met up with Feofar's main army somewhere near Irkutsk, creating a pincer movement that would make defending the city impossible.

The invading column, acting on Ogareff's guidance, had taken a route along the Altai Mountains' base to ensure successful conquest of the Eastern provinces. As they advanced, they left destruction in their wake, burning villages and destroying infrastructure, reaching the upper Yenisei River. Understanding the Czar's defensive measures at Krasnoiarsk, they deployed a fleet of boats to help Feofar's forces cross the river and continue their march toward Irkutsk. The crossing took several days, with local fishing vessels commandeered to ferry troops and supplies. After establishing this crossing, the column moved downstream along the Yenisei valley until intersecting the main road near Alsalevsk. From this small settlement onward, they unleashed a devastating campaign of destruction, characteristic of Tartar military tactics, burning crops, poisoning wells, and leaving nothing behind that could sustain pursuit or resistance. The town of Nijni-Oudinsk fell to their onslaught after a day of fighting, and now fifty thousand Tartar warriors had positioned themselves outside Irkutsk, their campfires dotting the landscape like malevolent stars as they awaited reinforcement from the Emir's approaching army.

The situation had grown dire for this remote region of Eastern Siberia and the small group of soldiers protecting its principal city, their resources already stretched thin by the harsh winter and dwindling supplies.

One might expect Michael to have fallen into despair given these circumstances. Yet remarkably, his resolve remained unshaken, and he repeated only one phrase with determination: "I will get there!" His voice carried the same steadfast conviction it had held since departing Moscow, despite the mounting obstacles.

The small group reached Nijni-Oudinsk thirty minutes after fleeing from the Tartar cavalry's assault. Michael Strogoff led the way, accompanied by Nadia and Nicholas, while their loyal canine companion trailed behind at a distance, whimpering at the acrid smoke filling the air. With the town engulfed in flames and the last raiders preparing to depart, remaining there was impossible. The wooden buildings crackled and spat embers into the darkening sky as they burned. The captors forced their prisoners onto horseback and departed, their rough handling betraying their nervousness about lingering too long. Nicholas maintained his characteristic resignation, his weathered face showing accepting a man long accustomed to life's hardships, while Nadia's confidence in Michael remained unwavering, her eyes fixed on him with complete trust. Michael himself appeared detached, though he stayed vigilant for any chance to break free, his muscles tense beneath the ropes that bound him.

The Tartar soldiers discovered one prisoner was sightless, and their cruel nature drove them to mock their helpless captive. As they rode, Michael's horse, lacking guidance, veered off course, disrupting the formation. This behavior prompted the soldiers to heap abuse and harsh treatment upon Michael, causing Nadia deep anguish and filling Nicholas with rage. Yet, they could not intervene, unable to communicate in Tartar, and their pleas for mercy went unheeded. The soldiers soon devised an even crueler torment, deciding to switch Michael's mount for a blind horse. Their motivation became clear when Michael caught their whispered suspicion: "Maybe this Russian isn't really blind!"

Forced onto the horse, Michael had the reins thrust into his grasp. The mob drove the animal into a frenzied gallop through a barrage of whips, stones, and shouts. Like its rider, the horse was blind, careening into trees and veering off the path. These violent collisions and tumbles could have proven fatal. The soldiers' raucous laughter echoed through the wilderness as both beast and man struggled to maintain their balance, the horse's hooves slipping on loose rocks and roots. Michael gripped the saddle with his knees, his face betraying no emotion despite the blood trickling from fresh cuts on his face and arms. The blind horse's terrified whinnies pierced the air as it stumbled forward, guided only by the cruel shouts and threatening weapons of their tormentors.

Yet Michael remained stoic, never uttering a sound of protest. When his mount fell, he waited for it to rise again, his face an expressionless mask despite the fresh bruises forming on his body. Others would haul the horse back to its feet, cursing and shoving as they did so, eager to resume their cruel sport. Watching this barbaric display, Nicholas struggled to help his companion but was kept down and beaten for his attempts to intervene, his captors' fists leaving him doubled over in pain.

The entertainment would have continued, much to the Tartars' delight, if not for a tragic turn of events. On September 10th, the sightless steed bolted, its hooves thundering against the rocky ground as it charged toward a deep chasm, perhaps thirty or forty feet in depth, that lay beside the path, its jagged walls promising certain doom.

When Nicholas attempted to pursue, others restrained him, their iron grips leaving bruises on his arms. With no one to guide it, the horse plunged into the pit, its terrified scream echoing off the canyon walls as it took its rider down to the bottom. Nicholas and Nadia released an anguished scream, their voices joining the horse's dying cry as they feared their companion had met his death.

On rushing to help him, they discovered Michael had leaped clear of the saddle at the last possible moment and was unharmed, though his poor horse lay with two broken legs, its sides heaving with labored breaths, beyond saving. They abandoned the animal to a slow death, its agony unrelieved in the cold shadow of the ravine, while Tartar riders bound Michael with rough rope to a saddle and forced him to continue on foot across the treacherous terrain.

Yet still he uttered no word of protest or complaint. He kept pace, not needing the rope that bound him, his face set in grim determination as his boots found purchase on the uneven ground. He remained true to his nature as "the Man of Iron", just as General Kissoff had described him to the Czar!

As darkness fell on September 11th, the military group made its way through Chibarlinskoe village, its weathered wooden houses casting long shadows in the dying light. What happened there would prove fateful. The Tartar cavalry, who had stopped to rest, were drunk on fermented mare's milk and local spirits as they prepared to resume their journey, their raucous laughter echoing through the village streets. Until that moment, Nadia had been fortunate to receive decent treatment from the soldiers, but now one of them, emboldened by drink, subjected her to harassment.

Though Michael couldn't witness the offensive act or identify the perpetrator, Nicholas observed everything from his position among the guards, his hands clenching into fists at the sight. Without hesitation or apparent forethought, Nicholas approached the offender with deadly purpose in his stride. Before the man could react or defend himself, Nicholas grabbed a pistol from the soldier's holster and fired into his chest, the report of the shot shattering the evening's quiet.

Upon hearing the report echo through the evening air, the commanding officer rushed to the scene, his boots kicking up dust as he ran. Though the soldiers were ready to kill Nicholas on the spot, their rifles already raised and fingers on triggers, their officer signaled otherwise with a sharp wave of his hand. Following his command, they bound Nicholas with rough rope, draped him over a horse's back like a sack of grain, and the entire unit departed at full gallop, their hoofbeats thundering into the growing darkness.

Michael, who had been gradually chewing through his bonds throughout the chaotic scene, felt the fibers give way when the horse lurched forward over uneven ground. His captor, dulled by drink and focused on the commotion ahead, continued riding without noticing his prisoner's escape into the shadows of the roadside brush.

In the aftermath, Michael and Nadia remained behind, finding themselves alone on the deserted road, with only the settling dust and the distant sound of retreating horses to mark the violent events that had just transpired.

© 01/01/2025
QuantumDigitalPublishing.io

Chapter Nine

IN THE STEPPE

Michael and Nadia had regained their freedom, much like during their earlier trek from Perm to the Irtych riverbanks. Yet their current circumstances differed from before. Their previous journey was comfortable, they'd traveled in a well-appointed tarantass with fresh, reliable post-horses that had carried them swiftly to their destination. Now they were forced to walk, with no possibility of finding alternative transportation. They had no money or supplies, unsure of where their next meal would come from, and still faced a daunting journey of three hundred miles. Also, Michael now relied on Nadia's eyesight to navigate their way, his own vision still clouded by the effects of his injury.

They had just lost the friend who fate had brought to them, and they worried about what might become of him. The memory of Nicholas's sacrifice weighed heavily on their hearts, adding to the burden of their arduous journey. The late summer sun beat down mercilessly as Michael lay on the ground, concealed beneath the roadside thickets, his clothes dusty and worn from their travels. At his side stood Nadia, silent and ready, her keen eyes scanning the horizon for any sign of danger or pursuit. Her hand rested near Michael's shoulder as she awaited his signal to resume their journey, knowing each step forward would test their resilience and determination.

The time was ten o'clock, and a chill had settled over the land. Over three hours had passed since the sun had set, leaving only starlight to pierce the oppressive darkness. Not a single dwelling could be seen in any direction across the desolate landscape. The final Tartar rider had vanished into the distance, his horse's hoofbeats long since faded into silence. Michael and Nadia found themselves isolated in the vast emptiness.

"What's going to happen to him?" the girl cried out, her voice trembling with emotion. "Dear Nicholas! Meeting us must have sealed his fate!" Michael remained quiet, his shoulders tense with unspoken concern.

"Michael," Nadia persisted, clutching at his sleeve, "have you forgotten how he stood up for you when the Tartars were tormenting you? How he put his life on the line for my sake? For both our sakes?"

Michael kept his silence, the weight of their situation clear in his rigid posture. He sat motionless with his face covered by his hands, as if trying to shut out the world. Was he lost in thought? Though he offered no response, perhaps he was listening to Nadia's words, letting them sink into his troubled conscience.

Indeed, he was hearing her, because when the young girl asked, her voice softening with concern, "Which way should I guide you, Michael?"

"To Irkutsk!" came his answer, resolute despite everything they'd endured.

"Along the main road?"

"Yes, Nadia," he replied, his determination clear in those simple words.

Unwavering in his determination, Michael remained steadfast in his commitment to reach his goal, regardless of circumstances. Taking the main road seemed the most direct route, though it carried obvious risks. They could always veer off into the countryside if Feofar-Khan's advance forces were seen, using the dense forests and rolling terrain for cover.

With their hands clasped together, fingers interlocked for support and guidance, Nadia and Michael began their journey, their footsteps falling into a synchronized rhythm on the well-worn path.

They rested at Joulounov-skoë village the following day, September 13th, after covering twenty miles through difficult terrain. The village lay in ruins, abandoned, with only hollow-eyed windows and scorched walls bearing witness to the recent violence. Throughout the night, Nadia had searched for Nicholas's remains along their path, examining the rubble and the fallen with trembling hands, but her efforts proved futile. Each unidentified body made her heart race until closer inspection revealed it wasn't him. With dread, she wondered if they had taken him to Irkutsk for brutal punishment, a fate perhaps worse than death.

Weak from hunger, their stomachs cramping from two days of minimal sustenance, Nadia discovered a cache of preserved food in one of the abandoned houses, dried meat wrapped in cloth and "soukharis," a type of dehydrated bread that maintains its nutritional value indefinitely because of the drying process. The discovery felt like a minor miracle in their otherwise bleak circumstances.

Together with Michael, she gathered as much as they could physically transport, stuffing their pockets and makeshift sacks with the precious dried provisions. This would sustain them for many days ahead, and water would pose no concern in this region, which was well-irrigated by the various small tributaries flowing into the Angara River, their surfaces glinting like ribbons of silver in the harsh light.

The pair pressed onward, with Michael maintaining a steady, purposeful stride that he tempered only out of consideration for Nadia. Though exhaustion weighed heavily upon her, she forced herself to keep pace, her legs trembling with each step, taking comfort because his blindness concealed her deteriorating condition. Her breath came in ragged gasps she tried to silence.

Yet Michael sensed her struggle, his acute hearing picking up the subtle changes in her breathing and gait. "You're exhausted, dear one.

"I'm fine," came her steadfast reply, though her voice wavered slightly.

"If your strength fails, I'll carry you myself," he insisted, his powerful shoulders squaring with determination.

"Very well, Michael," she conceded, knowing his was no idle offer.

The travelers encountered the small Oka river that day, but found it shallow enough to wade across without trouble. The frigid water numbed their feet as they picked their way between slick stones. Though the sky remained overcast, the weather stayed mild, the dense clouds hanging low over the landscape like a gray wool blanket. While they worried about potential rain making their journey more difficult, only brief showers passed over them, leaving behind the fresh scent of wet earth.

They maintained their previous pace, walking together with joined hands and minimal conversation, each lost in their own thoughts. Nadia remained vigilant, scanning their surroundings, her eyes darting to investigate every rustle in the grass and distant movement. They stopped twice daily to rest, dedicating six hours each night to sleep, though their slumber was often fitful and light. In the occasional hut they passed, Nadia found small portions of mutton, trading what few valuables they could spare. However, contrary to Michael's expectations, the region was devoid of pack animals, all horses and camels had been slaughtered or stolen, leaving behind only empty corrals and abandoned stables. With no choice but to continue on foot, they pressed forward across the vast, tiresome steppe, where the wind whispered through endless waves of golden grass.

Along their path, the third Tartar column had left unmistakable evidence of their march toward Irkutsk. Scattered remains dotted the landscape: lifeless horses, discarded wagons with broken wheels and splintered axles, and most tragically, the bodies of Siberian victims strewn near village entrances, their frozen faces bearing witness to their last moments. Despite her revulsion, Nadia forced herself to witness these grim scenes, knowing they carried valuable lessons about their enemy's movements.

The greatest threat wasn't what lay ahead, but what followed behind them. Ivan Ogareff, leading the Emir's army's advance guard, could appear at any moment, his ruthless reputation preceding him like a dark shadow. By now, the invaders would have seized the boats sent downstream on the lower Yenisei at Krasnoiarsk, commandeering them for their own crossing. With no Russian forces stationed between Krasnoiarsk and Lake Baikal to resist them, the path lay wide open for the invaders to sweep across the defenseless territory. Michael knew it was only a matter of time before Tartar scouts would emerge from the endless grasslands.

During each stop, Nadia would ascend a nearby hill and scan the Western horizon with concern, her hand shielding her eyes from the harsh sun as she searched in vain for any dust clouds that might show approaching horsemen. The ritual had become almost compulsive, performed three or four times during each rest period, though the empty horizon brought both relief and growing dread.

They would then continue their journey, with Michael slowing his pace whenever he noticed Nadia struggling to keep up, her boots dragging in the dusty earth. Their conversation was sparse, focusing on Nicholas, each word measured against the rhythmic crunch of their footsteps. Nadia would reminisce about all the ways their brief companion had helped them during their short time together, from his clever insights to his minor acts of kindness that had made their desperate flight more bearable.

Michael, in his responses, tried to reassure Nadia about Nicholas's fate, despite knowing in his heart that their friend was doomed to die. The weight of this knowledge sat in his chest, making each comforting phrase feel like a betrayal. He couldn't bring himself to share his true beliefs about Nicholas's inevitable death, choosing instead to protect her with gentle lies.

Michael turned to the girl one day and whispered, "Nadia, you never tell me anything about my mother." His voice carried an unusual vulnerability, breaking their unspoken agreement to avoid such tender subjects.

His mother! The subject had always given Nadia pause, making her throat tighten with unspoken grief. Why stir up painful memories that were better left buried in the past? Wasn't his mother, that brave Siberian woman, already gone? Hadn't Michael already bid his last farewell to her lifeless form on the vast Tomsk plains, where the wind had carried away his quiet sobs?

"Please, Nadia," Michael urged, his fingers fidgeting with the hem of his coat. "Tell me about her. It would mean a lot to me."

Finally, Nadia broke her silence on the matter. She revealed everything about her interactions with Marfa, starting from their chance encounter in Omsk. She described how she had felt drawn to the elderly prisoner, not knowing her identity and how warmly Marfa had responded to her. Back then, she knew Michael only as Nicholas Korpanoff, a stranger traveling under an assumed name.

"The man I should have been all along," Michael said, his expression growing darker, shadows deepening around his eyes.

A moment later, he continued, his voice thick with self-reproach, "I've failed to keep my oath, Nadia. I swore I wouldn't see my mother!"

"But you didn't seek her out, Michael," Nadia countered, leaning forward. "It was pure chance that brought you together."

"I swore no matter what happened, I wouldn't reveal myself." His hands clenched into fists at his sides.

"Michael, Michael! How could you not react when they raised the whip against Marfa?" Nadia's voice rose with emotion. "No oath should stop a son from protecting his mother!"

"I broke my oath, Nadia," Michael said, bowing his head in shame. "May God and the Father forgive me!"

"Michael," the girl said, her dark eyes filled with concern, "I need to ask you something. Don't answer if you feel you shouldn't. I won't be upset by anything you say!"

"Go ahead, Nadia." His voice was gentle despite the tension in his shoulders.

"Now that they've taken the Czar's letter from you, why are you still so determined to reach Irkutsk? Most men would have given up by now, after everything we've been through."

Michael squeezed her hand but remained silent, his face a careful mask that revealed nothing of his thoughts.

"Did you know what was in that letter before leaving Moscow?" she pressed, watching his expression intently.

"No, I didn't." The words came out clipped and decisive.

"Are you expecting me to think your only purpose in traveling to Irkutsk is to reunite me with my father, Michael?" Her voice softened with a mix of gratitude and suspicion. "After all these dangers and hardships, there must be more to it than that."

"I won't lie to you, Nadia," Michael responded with solemnity. "It would be dishonest to let you believe that. I'm following where my duties lead me. But think about it, aren't you the one guiding me to Irkutsk now? You've become my eyes, and your hand steers my path. The help I once offered you has been returned many times over. I can't predict if our misfortunes will end, but when the time comes for you to express gratitude for bringing you back to your father, I'll be thanking you in return for helping me reach Irkutsk." His voice carried a weight of unspoken burdens, yet held steady with determination.

"My poor Michael!" Nadia's voice trembled with feeling, her fingers tightening around his. "Please don't talk like that. You haven't answered my question. Tell me, why this desperate rush to reach Irkutsk now?" Her eyes searched his face, hoping to glimpse some revelation in his stoic features.

"I must arrive before Ivan Ogareff does," Michael burst out, his composure cracking. The name seemed to taste bitter on his tongue.

"Even in your condition?" she asked, unable to hide her concern.

"Yes, even now, and I swear I'll make it there!" His jaw clenched with fierce resolve, his entire bearing radiating an iron determination that brooked no argument.

There was something deeper behind Michael's fierce declaration than mere hatred for the traitor. Nadia sensed her companion was holding back, either unable or unwilling to reveal his full motives. His every word seemed measured, as if speaking freely might betray some vital secret.

On the fifteenth of September, after three days of travel, they arrived at Kouitounskoe village. The young woman was in terrible pain. Though her feet were so sore she could barely walk, blisters forming and breaking with each determined step, she persevered through her exhaustion with a single thought driving her forward: "Since he cannot see my suffering, I must continue until I can go no further." She bit her lip to keep from crying out when sharp stones pierced through her worn boots.

This stretch of their journey was free from obstacles and dangers, now that the Tartars had moved on, though it remained grueling. They pressed on like this for three days, sleeping in abandoned barns and subsisting on what meager provisions they could find. Evidence of the third invasion column's swift eastward advance was clear in their wake, the scattered cold ashes and decaying bodies they left behind. Burned-out homesteads dotted the landscape, their blackened timbers reaching toward the sky like accusing fingers, while carrion birds wheeled overhead in ever-watchful circles.

Looking westward, there was no sign of activity; the Emir's vanguard remained absent. Michael pondered the potential causes for this unexpected delay. Could Russian forces be posing a serious threat to Tomsk or Krasnoiarsk? Was there a possibility that the third column had become separated and vulnerable to isolation from the primary force? Such circumstances would benefit the Grand Duke's defense of Irkutsk, any postponement of the invasion improved their chances of resistance. Though Michael entertained these optimistic possibilities, he recognized them as a dream. The Grand Duke's survival rested on his shoulders, and each passing hour brought both opportunity and danger.

Nadia continued her arduous journey, her feet dragging through the dust and debris of the ravaged countryside. Though her spirit remained unbroken, her body was reaching its limits, betrayed by trembling muscles and labored breath. Michael understood this reality all too well. Had he not lost his sight, Nadia would have pleaded with him: "Michael, go on without me! Leave me in a shelter somewhere! Complete your mission to Irkutsk! Find my father and tell him my location! Let him know I'm waiting! You must go now! Don't worry about me, I'll stay hidden from the Tartars! I'll keep myself safe until you both return! Please, Michael, continue on! I cannot take another step!" Her imagined words echoed in his mind with the desperation of exhaustion, though she remained silent beside him.

Nadia had to pause frequently to rest, her legs trembling with each stop. During these breaks, Michael would lift her into his powerful arms without hesitation, cradling her against his chest. Free from worrying about her weariness, he could then press forward at his tireless pace, his feet finding sure purchase on the rough terrain.

They reached Kimilteiskoe on September 18th at ten o'clock at night, the air heavy with autumn's chill. Standing atop a hill, Nadia glimpsed a long luminous streak on the horizon, the Dinka River, its waters reflecting what little moonlight filtered through the clouds. Silent flashes of heat lightning danced across its surface, unaccompanied by thunder, creating an eerily beautiful display. Nadia guided Michael through what remained of the village, their footsteps crunching through layers of destruction. The ashes they found were cold, scattered by recent winds, suggesting the Tartar forces had moved through at least five or six days earlier.

Exhausted, Nadia lowered herself onto a stone bench just outside the village, her muscles aching in protest. "Should we stop here for a while?" Michael suggested, his face turned toward her with concern.

"Night has fallen, Michael," Nadia said, unable to mask the weariness in her voice. "Wouldn't you like to rest for a few hours?"

"I'd prefer to get across the Dinka first," Michael responded, his jaw set with determination. "I want that river between us and the Emir's scouts. But you're exhausted, my dear Nadia! I can hear it in every breath you take."

"Let's go, Michael," Nadia insisted, grabbing his hand and pulling him onward with renewed determination despite her fatigue.

The Dinka river cut across the Irkutsk road about two or three miles ahead, its waters invisible in the darkness but audible as a distant murmur. Encouraged by her companion, the young girl was determined to make this final push forward. The lightning flashes illuminated their path in brief, stark bursts, casting eerie shadows across the terrain. They traversed an endless desert plain, through which the small river meandered like a silver ribbon. The landscape was flat, without a single tree or hill to break its monotony, leaving them exposed under the vast night sky. The air was still, almost unnaturally so, allowing even the faintest noise to carry across vast distances like a whisper in an empty hall.

Michael and Nadia froze, as if rooted to the spot, their breathing shallow and controlled. A dog's bark echoed across the steppe, sharp and clear in the stillness. "Did you hear that?" Nadia whispered, her fingers tightening around Michael's sleeve.

A heart-wrenching cry, the desperate last plea of someone facing death followed the bark. The sound sent chills down their spines, hanging in the air like a ghost's lament.

"Nicholas! Nicholas!" the girl called out, her voice filled with dread, scanning the darkness for any sign of movement. Michael listened, his body tense and alert, and shook his head in response, his expression grim in the intermittent flashes of lightning.

"Hurry, Michael, we must go," Nadia urged, her breath coming in short gasps. Though she had been struggling to walk moments before, a sudden surge of energy now coursed through her veins, driving her forward with desperate determination.

"We've strayed from the path," Michael observed, noticing the change from dusty ground to grass beneath his feet. His boots sank into the softer earth with each step, making their progress more difficult.

"We had to!" Nadia insisted, her voice sharp with urgency. "The sound came from over there, to the right!" She gestured into the darkness, her hand trembling in the air.

Within minutes, they had covered half a mile from the river, their legs burning from the effort. Another bark echoed through the air, fainter this time, but closer. Nadia halted in her tracks, her body going rigid with anticipation.

"Yes!" Michael exclaimed, hope lighting up his features. "That's Serko barking!... He must have followed his master!" His words carried both relief and worry, knowing the loyal dog would never leave Nicholas's side willingly.

"Nicholas!" the girl shouted out, her voice cracking with emotion. No response came, only the whisper of wind through the grass.

Michael strained to hear, cupping his hands behind his ears and turning slowly in place. Nadia scanned the landscape, which lit up with flashes of electric light, but saw nothing beyond the endless waves of prairie grass. Then another sound reached them, a weak voice calling out, "Michael!" The cry was barely more than a whisper on the wind, but it was enough to send their hearts racing.

Suddenly, a blood-covered dog rushed up to Nadia, its fur matted and dark with crimson stains, panting from exertion.

It was Serko! Nicholas had to be nearby! Only he would have whispered Michael's name like that, with such desperate familiarity! But where was he? Nadia found herself too weak to call out again, her throat constricting with fear and exhaustion. Michael, down on the ground, began feeling his way around with his hands, fingers searching through the tall grass and loose soil.

Serko let out another bark, fierce and protective, and rushed at an enormous vulture that had descended from above, its wingspan casting an ominous shadow in the dim light. When Serko charged at it, the bird took flight but then swooped back down to attack the dog, talons extended. Serko jumped up to meet it with unwavering loyalty, but the vulture's mighty beak struck his head with devastating force, sending him crashing to the ground, lifeless, his last act one of protection.

In that moment, Nadia let out a horrified scream that pierced the prairie night. "Look... over there!" she cried out, her trembling finger pointing into the darkness.

A human head protruded from the earth, pale and ghostly in the intermittent flashes of electric light! She had stumbled upon it in the darkness, nearly losing her footing.

Nadia collapsed to her knees beside the buried figure, her hands shaking uncontrollably. It was Nicholas, buried up to his neck in the ground, a cruel Tartar punishment that left victims to perish slowly from thirst or fall prey to wolves and scavenging birds, a fate worse than a quick death.

The victim lay entombed in the earth, enduring unimaginable agony. The soil was packed he couldn't shift an inch, his arms pinned against his sides like a body prepared for burial. Trapped in this earthen prison, this living grave, the poor soul could do nothing but yearn for death's merciful release. His parched throat burned with each labored breath, and the weight of the earth pressed against his chest like an iron vise.

Three days earlier, the Tartars had buried their captive in this cruel fashion. For three endless days, Nicholas had waited for rescue that arrived too late. Vultures had discovered his exposed head at ground level, and his faithful dog had spent hours fighting off these savage scavengers, protecting his master. The ground around him bore evidence of the brutal battle, scattered feathers and deep claw marks in the soil where the loyal animal had stood its ground.

Frantically, Michael carved into the earth with his blade, desperate to free his companion. The frozen soil crumbled beneath his frenzied strikes, each second feeling like an eternity. Nicholas's eyes, which had been shut until that moment, fluttered open, glazed with exhaustion and pain.

Upon seeing Michael and Nadia, a faint smile crossed his lips. "Goodbye, dear friends," he whispered. "I'm thankful to have seen you one last time. Remember me in your prayers." His voice was barely audible, each word a tremendous effort against his depleted strength.

Despite the ground being packed as solid as rock, Michael persisted in his digging, finally managing to extract his friend's body. His hands were raw and bleeding from the effort, but he could not feel the pain. With trembling hands, he checked for a heartbeat... There was one! Faint and irregular, but present beneath his fingers.

Determined to give him a proper resting place rather than leaving him exposed, Michael widened the cruel pit where Nicholas had been buried alive. Now it would serve as his last resting place, though this time with the dignity and respect his friend deserved. Beside him lay the loyal Serko, master and faithful companion united in death, their shared fate a testament to unshakeable loyalty.

A distant sound echoed from the road, half a mile away. Michael Strogoff strained his ears, every muscle tensing as he listened. The unmistakable rhythm of hoofbeats grew clearer, a cavalry unit was approaching the Dinka, their cadence too precise to be ordinary travelers. "Nadia, Nadia!" he whispered, his voice tight with warning.

Nadia rose from her prayers at his call, her face still wet with tears. "Look!" he urged, gesturing toward the road.

"The Tartars," she breathed, her voice quavering with fear.

Indeed, it was the Emir's vanguard, galloping along the Irkutsk road, their weapons glinting in the harsh light.

"They won't stop me from giving him a proper burial," Michael declared, his jaw set with determination as he resumed his solemn task. The approaching danger only made his movements more purposeful, more urgent.

Michael and Nadia knelt beside the freshly dug grave, offering their last prayers for Nicholas. They had just laid his body to rest, his hands folded across his chest, a small wooden cross fashioned from broken branches marking the site. Their hearts were heavy with grief for their loyal companion, whose only crime had been his unwavering dedication to them, a devotion that cost him his life at the hands of their pursuers.

"At least here," Michael murmured as he scattered earth over the grave, his calloused hands trembling, "he'll be safe from the steppe wolves."

His expression hardened as he watched a group of horsemen passing in the distance, their silhouettes dark against the pale sky. With contained anger, he raised his fist toward them, his knuckles white with fury. Turning to his companion, he said, "Come, Nadia. We must move on before they spot us."

Michael was forced to avoid the main road, which had fallen under Tartar control, its dusty length now patrolled by enemy riders. Instead, he had to traverse the steppe and find an alternate route to Irkutsk, picking his way through the wild grass and rocky outcrops. While crossing the Dinka River was no longer necessary, he faced a new challenge, Nadia was immobile but could still use her sight to guide him through the treacherous terrain. Carrying her in his arms, her slight form wrapped in his worn coat, he pressed southwest through the province, always keeping watch for the telltale dust clouds of approaching patrols.

They still had to cover one hundred and forty miles of difficult terrain. Questions plagued them: How would they manage such a distance? Could their bodies withstand the extreme exhaustion? What would sustain them along the journey? How could they scale the formidable Sayansk Mountains? Neither Michael nor Nadia had answers to these daunting questions, but they shared an unspoken determination that drove them forward, one painful step after another.

Yet somehow, through sheer force of will and despite the biting autumn winds that tore at their clothes and the nights spent huddled in whatever shelter they could find, twelve days later, on October 2nd at six in the evening, Michael Strogoff stood before the vast expanse of Lake Baikal. The ancient sea, as the locals called it, stretched out before him like a sheet of hammered steel beneath the darkening sky, its waters disappearing into the misty horizon.

QuantumDigitalPublishing.io
Book II - Chapter X

Chapter Ten

BAIKAL AND ANGARA

Lake Baikal sits at an elevation of 1,700 feet above sea level. This massive body of water stretches approximately 600 miles and spans seventy miles across. Its true depth remains a mystery, though some estimates suggest it plunges more than a mile into Earth's crust. According to Madame de Bourboulon's account, local boatmen insist the lake prefers to be addressed as "Madam Sea", they claim it becomes turbulent if referred to as "Sir Lake," with waves rising as if in protest. A curious local belief persists among Siberians that Russians never drown in its waters, though they offer no explanation for this supposed immunity.

The vast freshwater lake, which receives water from over three hundred rivers and countless mountain streams, lies encircled by majestic volcanic peaks that pierce the clouds like ancient sentinels. Its waters find their sole exit through the Angara River, which flows past Irkutsk before joining the Yenisei River just upstream from Yeniseisk, carving a path through the rugged Siberian landscape. The surrounding mountain range, part of the Toungouzes chain, extends from the greater Altai mountain system, creating a natural amphitheater that cradles the sacred waters.

This region experiences unusual weather patterns, with autumn merging into an early winter, pausing for the traditional transition of seasons. By early October, darkness falls by five in the evening, and nighttime temperatures plummet to freezing point, creating ghostly wisps of steam above the lake's surface. The first snowfall, destined to remain until summer, already covers the peaks of the surrounding mountains, transforming them into white-capped guardians. During the harsh Siberian winter, the lake's surface freezes several feet thick, becoming a solid pathway for caravan sleighs to traverse, their runners creating intricate patterns across the crystalline expanse.

Lake Baikal experiences fierce storms, whether because of the discourteous habit of some people referring to it as "Sir Lake," or perhaps because of natural weather patterns. Like all inland seas, it produces short, choppy waves that pose a serious threat to the various vessels, rafts, prahms, flat bottom boats, and steamboats, that traverse its waters during the summer months. The wind howls across the surface, whipping up whitecaps and sending spray high into the air, while dark clouds gather over the distant shores.

Michael had reached the lake's southwestern shore, bearing Nadia, whose entire being seemed focused through her gaze alone. Yet their situation appeared hopeless in this desolate area, what fate awaited them but death from hunger and exhaustion? And yet, considering the massive four-thousand-mile journey the Czar's courier had undertaken, what remained was modest: forty miles along the lakeshore to reach the Angara River's mouth, then another sixty miles from there to Irkutsk. The total distance of one hundred miles might take a robust individual three days to cover on foot, assuming favorable conditions and sufficient strength to maintain a steady pace.

Was Michael Strogoff destined to face another challenge? The question hung heavy in the crisp air, as ominous as the gathering storm clouds above.

Providence seemed to show mercy, sparing him from further hardship. The area near Lake Baikal's edge, a barren wasteland, teemed with life. Where desolation reigned, roughly fifty people had gathered at the lake's corner, their presence bringing an unexpected vitality to the otherwise stark landscape. Their movements and voices carried across the water, breaking the usual silence of this remote location.

As Michael emerged from the mountain pass carrying Nadia, she spotted the assembled crowd. For one terrifying moment, she feared they'd encountered a Tartar patrol searching the Baikal shoreline, an encounter that would have left them with no escape route. Her anxiety, however, subsided as she made out the familiar shapes of Russian clothing and heard snippets of her native tongue carried on the wind.

With a very weak voice, she said "Russians!" before her strength gave out completely, her eyes falling shut as she slumped against Michael's chest, the exhaustion of their journey overwhelming her.

Their presence hadn't gone unnoticed, several Russians spotted them and came to their aid, guiding the sightless man and young woman to a nearby raft that was anchored at a small inlet. Strong hands helped steady Michael as he made his way across the uneven shoreline, still cradling Nadia.

The vessel was moments away from departure, its wooden planks creaking against their moorings. Its passengers were refugees from various walks of life, brought together by shared circumstance at Lake Baikal, merchants, farmers, and craftsmen alike, their social distinctions erased by common adversity. Having been forced back by Tartar scouts who patrolled the surrounding territories with increasing frequency, they sought sanctuary in Irkutsk. With the invaders controlling both shores of the Angara River, making the journey by land was impossible, too many eyes watched the paths and roads. Their only hope lay in traveling downriver through the heart of the city itself, using the waterway as their path to safety.

The thought of their scheme made Michael's spirits soar, though he masked his excitement, determined to maintain his disguise more carefully than ever. Years of practiced deception had taught him the value of restraining visible emotion, even as his heart raced with anticipation.

The escapees had devised an uncomplicated strategy. They would take advantage of a lake current that flowed along the upper shore toward where the Angara River began. By riding this current, they aimed to reach Lake Baikal's outlet. From there, the Angara's swift waters would carry them toward Irkutsk at eight miles per hour. With luck, they could expect to catch sight of the city in just a day and a half, assuming the weather held and they encountered no unexpected obstacles along the way.

They were forced to build their own watercraft since none could be found. What they created was a basic raft, constructed in the style used for timber transport on Siberian waterways. Using trees from a nearby fir forest on the riverbank, they fashioned a sturdy platform by binding the logs together with flexible willow branches. The resulting craft was spacious enough to carry a hundred passengers, its broad deck reinforced with cross-beams and sealed with pitch gathered from the forest. The craft might have been simple, but it represented their best hope for salvation.

Michael and Nadia were brought aboard the makeshift vessel, helped by several fellow refugees who had witnessed their arrival. The young woman had regained consciousness by then, though she still appeared weak from her ordeal. After they were both given something to eat, a simple meal of dried fish and bread, she made herself comfortable on a cushion of leaves gathered from the surrounding forest and drifted into a profound slumber.

In the bustling town, Michael Strogoff maintained strict silence about the events at Tomsk when questioned by the curious passengers and crew. He presented himself as a resident of Krasnoiarsk, claiming he hadn't reached Irkutsk before Tartar forces occupied the Dinka's left bank. His story, delivered with quiet conviction, seemed to satisfy most inquiries. He suggested that most likely, the main Tartar army had established their position outside the Siberian capital, though he was careful not to provide too many details that might expose his true identity.

Time was of the essence, as the temperature continued to plummet with each passing day. The mercury dipped below freezing during the nighttime hours, creating a crystalline frost that coated the raft's logs each morning, and ice crystals had formed across Lake Baikal's vast surface. While the raft could still navigate the lake without difficulty, cutting through the thin sheets of ice with its sturdy hull, the Angara River posed a potential challenge, as larger ice fragments could obstruct their passage between its shores and damage their vessel.

The raft was released from its moorings at eight o'clock and began drifting with the current near the shoreline. Several strong moujiks guided it using long poles, their muscles straining against the water's pull, while a seasoned Baikal boatman of sixty-five years served as commander. The sun and lake winds had weathered his complexion into deep leather-like creases, and a thick white beard cascaded down his chest like a frozen waterfall. A fur cap worn smooth with age topped his stern countenance, and he wore a long great-coat cinched at the waist that reached his feet, its hem dark with spray. This quiet elder maintained his post at the stern, directing operations through hand signals, his weathered hands moving with practiced precision. The crew's primary task was keeping the vessel within the shore current, fighting against crosswinds and eddies while avoiding any drift toward treacherous open water.

The raft accommodated Russians from every walk of life, their bodies pressed together in uneasy fellowship. Alongside destitute moujiks, women clutching shawls tight against the cold, the elderly with rheumy eyes, and wide-eyed children were several pilgrims caught unaware by the invasion, as well as a handful of monks in rough-spun robes and a priest whose silver cross glinted in the morning light. The pilgrims, each carrying a well-worn staff and a gourd fastened to their belts with fraying rope, sang psalms in mournful tones that echoed across the water. They came from diverse regions: one from Ukraine with his melodious accent, another from the Yellow Sea area with weather-beaten features, and a third from

Finland with ice-blue eyes. The Finnish pilgrim, an elderly man with joints stiffened by countless miles, wore a locked collection box at his waist, much like those found at church entrances, its metal dulled by years of faithful service. He maintained strict devotion to his cause, everything gathered during his hard journeys were meant for others, not himself, a fact clear in his tattered clothing and calloused feet. Such was his commitment that he didn't even possess the key to the box, which would remain sealed until his journey's end, whenever and wherever that might be.

A group of religious men, Monks, journeyed southward from the Empire's northern reaches. Their pilgrimage had begun in Archangel three months earlier, when the first snows had dusted the northern coastline. Along their route, they had made stops at many holy sites: the hallowed isles off Carelia's shoreline, where ancient wooden crosses stood against the wind, the monasteries of Solovetsk and Troitsa with their golden domes gleaming in the sun, the Kiev sanctuaries of Saints Antony and Theodosia, their walls heavy with centuries of prayers, the Kazan monastery, and the Old Believers' shrine, where incense still lingered in the air. Now, dressed in their traditional garments, robes, cowls, and serge clothing worn smooth by constant wear, they were making their way toward Irkutsk, their boots marking the dusty path before them.

The village priest was a simple man, one among the six hundred thousand ordinary clerics scattered throughout the Russian Empire, each serving their communities with quiet dedication. His attire was as humble as the peasants', reflecting his equal social standing with the moujiks, a worn cassock patched at the elbows and mud-spattered boots that had seen many seasons. He tended his own plot of land like any farmer while performing his religious duties, conducting baptisms in the old stone font, joining young couples' hands in marriage beneath tarnished icons, and offering final blessings at graveside funerals. When danger approached, he had sent his wife and children to safety in the Northern provinces, though the parting had torn at his heart. Devoted to his parish, he remained until the last possible moment, continuing to offer comfort and guidance to those who stayed behind, only fleeing when necessary. With the Irkutsk road blocked by the advancing threat, he had made his way to Lake Baikal, following the ancient paths of traders and pilgrims before him.

On the front section of the raft, the priests huddled together, their black robes rustling in the breeze as they offered prayers at steady intervals that pierced the quiet night. After each prayer verse, their voices rang out with "Slava Bogu", Glory to God!, the sacred words carrying across the dark waters like a shield against unseen dangers.

The night passed without incident, though the cold air bit into their bones. Nadia remained in a daze while Michael kept vigil beside her, adjusting the blankets around her shoulders and only drifting into brief, restless sleep. As dawn broke, strong headwinds had slowed their progress, the raft's wooden planks creaking against the current, leaving them still forty miles from where the Angara River emptied into Lake Baikal. They estimated reaching their destination between three and four in the afternoon, but this delay didn't worry them. If anything, they preferred it, knowing that traveling downriver after nightfall would provide better cover for their entry into Irkutsk, when the shadows would help conceal their movements from unfriendly eyes.

The elderly boatman's sole concern centered on ice forming across the water's surface, his weathered face creasing with worry as he studied the river ahead. After a frosty night, ice fragments could be spotted floating westward, their crystalline surfaces catching the early morning light. These particular pieces posed no threat, as they had already moved past the river mouth and couldn't enter the Angara. However, ice chunks from the lake's eastern section might get pulled by currents between the river's banks, creating problems. Such an occurrence could slow their progress or, worse still, form an impassable barrier that would halt the raft, leaving them stranded in dangerous waters.

For this reason, Michael watched the lake's conditions with keen attention, monitoring for any significant accumulation of ice. He turned to Nadia, who had now awakened and sat huddled in her thick wool coat, for updates on the situation, and she reported her observations to him, her breath forming small clouds in the frosty morning air.

The Baikal's surface was witness to remarkable events as the ice blocks drifted. From deep within the lake bed, where nature had created natural artesian wells, spectacular fountains of boiling water burst forth. These powerful streams soared skyward, transforming into clouds of vapor that caught and reflected the sun's rays before condensing in the frigid air, creating halos of crystalline mist that danced above the water's surface. Such an extraordinary display would have captivated any traveler fortunate enough to visit this Siberian lake during more peaceful times, though now it served as both a beautiful distraction and a potential warning sign of changing conditions beneath the surface.

The boatman's keen eyes spotted the Angara's mouth at four o'clock, nestled between towering granite cliffs that cast long shadows across the churning waters. The right bank revealed Livenitchnaia's modest port, with its white-washed church and scattered wooden dwellings perched along the waterfront, their weathered facades telling stories of harsh winters past. More concerning was the sight of ice blocks floating downstream from the East, making their way between the Angara's banks toward Irkutsk, their crystalline surfaces glinting in the wan light. Yet their numbers remained manageable, not enough to impede the raft's progress, and the temperature hadn't dropped to speed up their formation.

With a gentle thud, the vessel reached the small dock and came to a halt against the worn wooden pilings. To conduct needed repairs, the aging ferryman, required an hour's stop. Because: With the raft's logs loosening and their bindings frayed by the constant motion and spray, tighter binding was crucial to withstand the swift Angara River waters which could destroy even the strongest vessel.

Though the weathered boatman hadn't expected picking up any more refugees at Livenitchnaia, two figures emerged from an abandoned dwelling, their desperate movements visible even at a distance, and sprinted toward the shoreline just as the raft contacted the bank, their boots kicking up loose gravel in their haste.

Sitting on the raft, Nadia stared at the coastline. She cried out, but caught herself, grabbing Michael's hand just as he lifted his head, her fingers trembling with urgency against his weathered palm.

"What's wrong, Nadia?" he asked, alert to her distress.

"Look, it's them," she said, her voice barely above a whisper. "The two who traveled with us."

"You mean the French and English travelers we encountered in the Ural mountain passes?" Michael's shoulders tensed as he spoke.

"Yes, that's them," she confirmed, tightening her grip on his hand.

The sudden realization hit Michael, his maintained disguise was in danger of unraveling. When Jolivet and Blount would see him now, they'd recognize him not as Nicholas Korpanoff but as his true identity: Michael Strogoff, the Czar's trusted messenger. The journalists had crossed paths with him twice after parting ways at the Ichim station, first witnessing him publicly whip Ivan Ogareff at Zabediero camp, then present at his sentencing by the Emir in Tomsk. They knew who he was and understood the gravity of his mission, and their presence here threatened to expose everything he'd fought so desperately to protect. His jaw clenched as he considered the implications, knowing that even the slightest recognition could put not just him, but everyone aboard the raft in danger.

Making a swift decision, Michael turned to his companion. "Nadia," he instructed, "when they come aboard, please direct them to me. I must handle this myself."

Having found their way to the port of Livenitchnaia, Blount and Jolivet arrived by the same turn of events that had guided Michael Strogoff there. After witnessing the Tartars' entrance into Tomsk, they had left before seeing the brutal conclusion of the festival, their journalistic duties compelling them to press onward. Thus, they didn't know the Emir had spared their former companion from death, though he had ordered him blinded, a fate they would have considered devastating.

After their successful acquisition of horses, they departed Tomsk that very evening, resolute in their plan to send future correspondence from the Russian military encampment in Eastern Siberia. They pushed forward at a relentless pace toward Irkutsk, determined to outrun Feofar-Khan's forces, stopping only when necessary to rest their mounts. Their strategy would have succeeded if not for the sudden emergence of a third military column advancing northward through the Yenisei valley, its banners marking it as another Tartar contingent. Like Michael before them, they found themselves blocked before reaching the Dinka, forcing them to retreat toward Lake Baikal, their original plans in shambles but their determination undiminished.

After spending three uncertain days at the location, huddled in makeshift shelters and rationing their dwindling supplies, they were relieved when the makeshift vessel showed up through the morning mist. The escapees shared their strategy with the others, outlining each detail of their proposed crossing. There was a real possibility they could slip through under the cover of darkness and make their way into Irkutsk, using the river's natural flow to mask their approach. They determined this was their best option to pursue, despite the considerable dangers that lay ahead.

Without delay, Alcide approached the elderly ferryman and requested passage for himself and his traveling companion, stating he would provide whatever payment was asked for, regardless of the amount. His fingers played with the purse of coins at his belt as he spoke.

"Payment isn't accepted here," the weathered boatman responded, his deep-set eyes reflecting years of hardship on these waters. "The only currency is the risk to one's own life!"

The pair of reporters boarded the vessel, with Nadia observing them settle into positions at the front of the raft, their bodies tense with anticipation. Harry Blount maintained his characteristic English reserve, having spoken a word to her throughout their journey across the Urals, his stern face set like granite against the approaching darkness. Alcide Jolivet appeared more somber than was his custom, his usual wit and charm subdued by the gravity of their situation, and given the current situation, his serious demeanor was quite understandable. His hands gripped the rough wooden railings as he stared ahead into the gathering gloom.

As Jolivet took his position on the raft, he felt someone grasp his arm with urgent fingers. Upon turning, he found himself face-to-face with Nadia, sister to the man who had shed his identity as Nicholas Korpanoff to reveal himself as Michael Strogoff, the Czar's messenger. Just as he was about to cry out in astonishment, he noticed her finger pressed against her lips, signaling for silence, her eyes conveying the gravity of discretion.

"Join us," Nadia called out, her voice controlled to sound casual. Alcide stood up with feigned nonchalance and followed her, gesturing for Blount to come along, his practiced journalist's instincts telling him something momentous was about to unfold.

The correspondents had been startled to find Nadia on the raft, but their astonishment turned to utter shock when they spotted Michael Strogoff, a man they'd believed dead, sitting quietly in the shadows of the raft. Their faces paled at the sight of him, as though seeing a ghost materialize before their eyes.

Michael remained motionless as they approached, his head tilted toward the sound of their footsteps. When Jolivet turned to question Nadia, she explained, her voice thick with emotion, "He cannot see you. The Tartars burned his eyes. My poor brother is blind now." Her hands trembled as she spoke the devastating truth.

Deep sympathy washed over the faces of Blount and his companion as the horror of Michael's fate sank in. They settled beside Michael, clasping his hand in solidarity and waiting for him to speak, the gentle lapping of water against the raft's sides filling the heavy silence between them.

"Gentlemen," Michael whispered, his fingers tightening around their clasped hands, "you must not know my true identity or my mission in Siberia. I need you to keep my secret. Can I trust you with this?"

"I give you my word," Jolivet declared without hesitation, his French accent thick with sincerity.

"I swear on my honor as a gentleman," Blount added, his British resolve clear in every syllable.

"Very well, then." Michael's shoulders relaxed at their pledges.

"Is there any way we can assist you?" Harry Blount inquired, leaning forward. "Perhaps we could help you complete your mission?"

"I must do this alone," Michael responded, his jaw set with determination.

"But those scoundrels have taken your vision," Alcide protested, his voice rising with indignation. "Surely you cannot."

"I have Nadia with me, and her eyes are all I need!" Michael's voice carried an edge of steel that brooked no argument.

Thirty minutes later, the raft departed from Livenitchnaia's small harbor and entered the flowing waters, the wooden planks creaking beneath them as they pushed off from shore. Evening was settling in at five o'clock, with darkness approaching like a heavy curtain drawn across the sky. The night ahead promised to be pitch black and bitter cold, as the temperature had already dropped below freezing, sending shivers through the small group huddled on the craft. A cutting wind swept across the water, carrying with it the first hints of winter's cruel embrace.

Despite their promise to keep Michael's secret, Alcide and Blount remained by his side, speaking in hushed, urgent tones. The blind man pieced together their whispered information with his existing knowledge, forming a clear picture of the situation like assembling fragments of a shattered mirror. The evidence was undeniable, the Tartars had surrounded Irkutsk, with all three military columns now united into an iron ring around the city. Without question, both the Emir and Ivan Ogareff were positioned outside the capital, their forces poised like predators waiting to strike.

Yet a mystery remained, why was the Czar's messenger so desperate to reach the city? The Imperial letter he carried could no longer be delivered to the Grand Duke, and he remained unaware of its contents, the words forever sealed away from his sightless eyes. Like Nadia before them, Alcide Jolivet and Blount found themselves puzzled by this inexplicable urgency that drove the blind man forward despite all odds.

The group maintained silence about earlier events, the only sounds the creaking of the raft and the splash of water against wood, until Jolivet felt compelled to address Michael, his voice carrying a note of genuine remorse. "We should apologize for refusing to shake your hand when we parted ways at Ichim."

"Your reaction was justified, you believed me to be cowardly," Michael responded, his voice carrying no trace of bitterness. "Anyone would have thought the same in those circumstances."

The Frenchman added with satisfaction, rubbing his hands together, "Well, you gave that scoundrel a proper thrashing with the knout. He'll bear those marks for quite some time! I've never seen someone wield that weapon with such precision."

"Not for long," Michael replied, a shadow passing across his face as he turned away.

Within thirty minutes of departing Livenitchnaia, Blount and his fellow traveler learned of the harrowing ordeals that Michael and his companion had endured, the brutal imprisonment, the desperate escapes, and the relentless pursuit across the harsh terrain. They found themselves impressed by his remarkable fortitude, matched only by the young woman's unwavering loyalty through every trial and tribulation. Their assessment of

Michael echoed the Czar's words in Moscow with profound understanding: "Here is a Man!"

The raft navigated between massive ice chunks swept along by the Angara's powerful current, its wooden planks creaking with each impact. The shoreline created an enchanting illusion, though the raft moved swiftly, it seemed to hover motionless while a series of dramatic landscapes paraded past like scenes from a living painting. Towering granite cliffs gave way to untamed gorges where torrents of water thundered down in pristine white cascades. Occasional clearings revealed smoldering villages, their blackened timbers still releasing thin wisps of smoke into the crisp air, followed by dense pine forests aflame, their burning canopies casting an eerie orange glow across the water's surface. While evidence of the Tartars' destruction marked every vista, from scorched earth to abandoned settlements, the warriors themselves remained unseen, having concentrated their forces near Irkutsk.

Throughout the journey, pilgrims' prayers echoed across the water, their murmured supplications mixing with the rush of the river and the crack of shifting ice. The seasoned boatman maintained their course, his weathered hands steady on the steering oar. With practiced skill honed by years on these treacherous waters, he fended off encroaching ice blocks, keeping the raft centered in the Angara's swift current, his eyes scanning ahead for the safest passage through the frozen obstacles.

Chapter Eleven

BETWEEN TWO BANKS

The absolute darkness of night had descended by eight o'clock, just as the earlier sky had predicted. With the moon in its new phase, no lunar light penetrated the blackness, leaving only the faintest glimmer of starlight struggling through gaps in the cloud cover. The riverbanks vanished into invisibility when viewed from the water's center, their familiar contours reduced to formless shadows against an even darker backdrop. Towering cliffs merged with the thick, low clouds above, creating an oppressive ceiling that seemed to press down upon the water's surface. Every so often, an eastern breeze would stir, only to fade away within the confined walls of the Angara valley, leaving behind an eerie stillness broken only by the gentle lapping of the water.

The night's shroud worked to the advantage of those attempting to escape, concealing any movement upon the river's surface from prying eyes. Even with Tartar sentries positioned along both riverbanks, their torches mere pinpricks in the darkness, the raft stood a good chance of slipping by unnoticed in the inky blackness. The attackers had likely left the river unobstructed upstream of Irkutsk, knowing full well no reinforcements would come to the Russians from the province's southern regions, where the rebellion had already severed all lines of communication. Winter itself would soon create an impassable barrier, as frost would bind the ice fragments scattered between the shores, transforming the flowing water into an immobile sheet of white.

The raft drifted in complete stillness, with the pilgrims' once-loud voices now reduced to audible whispers of prayer, too faint to reach the shoreline. The escapees pressed themselves flat against the platform, leaving the raft riding so low it broke the water's surface, the weathered planks creaking beneath their weight. Up front, the aged boatman huddled with his crew, their gnarled hands gripping long poles, focused on fending off the drifting chunks of ice that threatened their passage.

The ice flows proved helpful, provided they didn't block the raft's path. Although a single boat might have been visible even in the dark, the raft's appearance blended with the various sizes of drifting ice chunks, looking like just another shadow among the river's natural obstacles. The loud collisions between ice blocks masked any telling sounds that might have given them away, from the occasional splash of the poles to the suppressed coughs of the freezing passengers.

Frost coated every surface, and delicate crystalline patterns formed along the raft's edges as the bitter cold cut deep. The group of refugees had nothing but flimsy birch branches for protection as they huddled close, sharing what little warmth they could muster, their breath forming small clouds that dissipated in the night air. The temperature had plunged to ten degrees below freezing, and even the gentle breeze, having swept across the snow-covered eastern peaks, seemed to slice through their very bones, numbing fingers and toes despite their desperate attempts to keep moving and maintain circulation.

In the raft's rear, Michael and Nadia endured their mounting misery in silence, their bodies pressed together for whatever meager warmth they could find. Nearby, Jolivet and Blount weathered the harsh embrace of the Siberian winter as best they could, their faces buried deep within the collars of their frost-covered coats. Not a whisper passed between them now. Their dire circumstances consumed their every thought, each person lost in private contemplation of their mortality. They knew that at any moment, their precarious situation could turn deadly.

For a man on the verge of completing his vital task, Michael exhibited remarkable composure, his features set in stone despite the biting cold that threatened to overwhelm them all. His resolute spirit had never wavered, even during the most critical moments, drawing strength from some deep internal well that seemed bottomless. He could almost grasp that precious instant when he would be free to turn his thoughts to his mother, to Nadia, and to his own concerns, like a runner glimpsing the finish line through the fog. Only one last fear now plagued his mind: the possibility that ice might block the raft's passage before reaching Irkutsk. This single worry consumed his thoughts, gnawing at his concentration like a relentless beast, and he stood ready to attempt a daring maneuver if circumstances demanded it, his muscles tense beneath his frozen garments.

Exhausted but revitalized by a brief respite, Nadia's physical strength had returned. Though her hardships had tested her body, they had never once weakened her iron resolve. Her determination, forged in the crucible of their harrowing journey, remained as unshakeable as ever. She felt compelled to stay by Michael's side, knowing he might need her guidance for whatever challenges lay ahead. As they drew closer to Irkutsk, thoughts of her father grew vivid in her mind, each passing moment bringing fresh waves of anticipation and longing. She pictured him within the besieged city, separated from his loved ones, yet fighting the invaders with unwavering patriotic spirit, organizing defenses and rallying the citizens to resist. Just hours separated her from falling into his embrace, where she would deliver her mother's last message, and they would never face separation again. If Wassili Fedor's exile proved permanent, she would share his fate, making a new life in this harsh but beautiful land. Her thoughts then drifted to her loyal companion, her "brother," who had made this reunion possible through countless sacrifices and unwavering dedication. Once the Tartar threat was eliminated, he would journey back to Moscow, and she feared their paths might never cross again, leaving an emptiness in her heart that no future friendship could fill.

Alcide Jolivet and Harry Blount shared an identical thought, this was the stuff of gripping journalism. Both men recognized the raw dramatic power of the scene before them, each crafting how they would shape it into a compelling story. Blount's mind turned to his faithful readers at the Daily Telegraph, while Jolivet pictured his beloved Cousin Madeleine poring over his words, perhaps sharing them with her literary circle in Paris.

Despite their professional detachment, neither could suppress their emotional response to the unfolding events. The weight of history pressed upon them, demanding they serve as more than mere observers but as chroniclers of this pivotal moment.

"All the better!" Jolivet mused to himself, adjusting his worn leather notebook. "One must feel to make others feel! There's a famous line about that somewhere, though it escapes me now." Straining his experienced eye, he tried to penetrate the darkness shrouding the river below, his pencil hovering over the blank page. The night air carried whispers of danger, and his journalistic instincts told him the actual story was yet to unfold.

Brilliant flashes pierced the darkness, transforming the riverbanks into surreal landscapes, sometimes a blazing forest, sometimes the smoldering remains of a village. The Angara River was lit up from shore to shore, the light so intense it seemed to turn night into an unnatural day. Countless ice blocks drifted by like mirrors, each one catching and reflecting the dancing flames in a rainbow of colors as the river's whims carried along them. Among these drifting ice fragments, the raft moved and unnoticed, its occupants crouching low to maintain their shadowy sanctuary.

Yet these illuminated stretches weren't where the real peril lay, for light could reveal as much as it could conceal.

The fugitives faced an unexpected threat, one they couldn't have expected or evaded, lurking beneath the very waters that carried them to safety. Alcide Jolivet discovered it by chance when he dangled his hand into the water from the raft's edge, his journalist's curiosity getting the better of his caution. The current felt thick against his fingers, with an unusual, oily texture that made him recoil. Using both touch and smell, his nostrils flaring at the distinct petroleum scent, Alcide realized with certainty that a layer of liquid naphtha was flowing on the river's surface, creating an invisible but deadly companion to their journey.

This revelation raised alarming questions. Their raft was now gliding across this flammable substance, but where had it come from? They wondered whether this was a natural occurrence on the Angara River or if the Tartars had released it. Could this be part of a sinister plan to set Irkutsk ablaze? The mere thought of a spark igniting this invisible menace made their precarious situation even more treacherous.

Alcide pondered these thoughts, deciding to share this information only with Harry Blount. Together, they kept quiet about this additional threat, not wanting to worry the rest of their group. Their fellow travelers already carried enough burden without the knowledge that they were floating atop a potential inferno.

The terrain of Central Asia is well-documented to be saturated with hydrogen, much like a liquid-filled sponge. Throughout the region, from Bakou's harbor along the Persian border by the Caspian Sea, across Asia Minor, into China along the Yuen-Kiang, and throughout Burma, countless natural oil springs bubble up from beneath the earth's surface. This region mirrors the famous "oil country" found in North America. The phenomenon was so common that local inhabitants had for centuries used these natural seepages for light and heat, treating them as gifts from the earth itself.

A fascinating ritual unfolds at the port of Bakou during certain religious ceremonies, where local fire-worshipers create an extraordinary spectacle.

They pour liquid naphtha onto the Caspian Sea's surface, and because the oil is less dense than water, it floats and spreads across the waves. As darkness falls, they ignite this floating layer of mineral oil, transforming the sea into a breathtaking display of undulating flames that dance and ripple with the evening winds, creating what appears to be an ocean of living fire. The ceremony dates back centuries, and travelers from distant lands often journey to witness this mesmerizing demonstration of nature's raw power harnessed by human hands.

What might be a cause for celebration in Bakou could turn into a catastrophic disaster on the Angara River. A fire, whether started or by accident, could spread across Irkutsk in mere seconds. While there was no risk of careless accidents on the raft itself, the real danger came from fires burning along both sides of the Angara. If even a single burning straw or spark were to land on the water, it could ignite the entire naphtha-filled current, creating an unstoppable inferno that would race downstream with devastating consequences.

Jolivet and Blount's fears were palpable. Their years of journalistic experience had taught them to recognize dangerous situations, and this one made their skin crawl. The situation begged the question: wouldn't it be wiser to seek refuge on the riverbank until the threat passed? "Well," Alcide remarked with certainty, his voice carrying a mix of determination and concealed anxiety, "I can tell you one person who won't be abandoning ship!"

The speaker directed his words of Michael Strogoff, who maintained his characteristic stoic expression despite the implied challenge.

The raft continued drifting between ice floes that were converging around them, the wooden beams creaking with each collision. They had not yet encountered any Tartar scouts, showing they hadn't reached the enemy outposts. Around ten o'clock, Harry Blount spotted several dark shapes moving across the ice, leaping from block to block and drawing nearer, their fluid movements casting eerie shadows in the dim light.

"Tartars!" he thought to himself, his heart racing. He crept over to the elderly boatman and pointed out the mysterious figures, his finger trembling in the cold.

The old man studied them, squinting through the darkness before declaring, "Just wolves! I'd rather face them than Tartars. Still, we'll need to defend ourselves, and be quiet!" His weathered face betrayed both relief and concern.

The group would need to protect themselves from the vicious creatures that prowled the province, driven by their desperate hunger and the bitter cold that had descended upon the region like a merciless blanket. The wolves had detected smelling the raft and would launch their attack, their yellow eyes gleaming with predatory intent from the shoreline. With Tartar outposts likely nearby, the group couldn't risk using their guns. The sound would carry for miles across the frozen landscape. They positioned the women and children in the raft's center, huddled together for warmth and safety, while the men formed a defensive ring around them, clutching poles and knives with white-knuckled grips, ready to fend off the approaching threat. Though the defenders remained silent, the night air resonated with the wolves' haunting howls, a chorus of hunger that echoed across the icy expanse.

Unwilling to stay passive, Michael positioned himself where the ferocious pack was attacking. Armed with his knife, he struck at any wolf that came within range, driving his blade deep into their necks and throats. Jolivet and Blount were active, fighting the creatures with desperate strength. Their fellow travelers fought alongside them with equal valor, jabbing with poles and slashing with whatever weapons they possessed. Despite the eerie silence of the battle, broken only by snarls and the sound of tearing flesh, many of those fleeing suffered serious wounds from the wolves' razor-sharp teeth and powerful jaws.

The conflict showed no signs of ending soon. More wolves kept arriving from the Angara's right shore to join the attack, their bodies slinking across the ice like dark shadows. "This is endless!" exclaimed Alcide as he wielded his blood-covered dagger, his breath coming in ragged gasps in the frigid air.

The ravenous wolves showed no signs of retreat, with fresh packs still pouring across the frozen expanse even thirty minutes into the brutal assault. Fatigue had taken its toll on the desperate survivors, whose resistance was crumbling under the relentless onslaught. Muscles trembled from exhaustion, and movements grew slower with each passing minute. Just as their situation seemed dire, ten massive wolves, their crimson eyes blazing with feral hunger in the blackness, launched themselves onto the raft with bone-jarring force. Jolivet and his companion plunged headlong into combat with the savage creatures, their blades flashing in the dim light, and Michael was moving to join the fray when something unexpected occurred.

The wolves abandoned both the raft, and the frozen river's surface, their claws scrabbling against ice as they fled. Their dark shapes scattered in all directions like leaves in a storm as they retreated to the riverbank, whimpering in clear terror. These predators hunt in darkness with supreme confidence, but now an intense light flooded the entire waterway, turning night into an eerie twilight.

It was: A massive conflagration was the source. The massive bonfire engulfed the small settlement of Poshkavsk, transforming its buildings into towering infernos that reached toward the starless sky. The Tartars had arrived and were completing their destructive mission with methodical efficiency, the orange glow of their torches visible as they moved between structures. From this position, their forces controlled both sides of the river beyond Irkutsk, their campfires dotting the shoreline like malevolent stars. The escapees had now entered the most perilous stretch of their journey, with twenty miles still separating them from the capital city, each one promising new dangers.

Through the darkness, the raft drifted among scattered ice floes, catching glints of distant light that reflected off the frozen surfaces like mirror shards. The escapees lay still on the wooden platform, daring to breathe, knowing that even the slightest movement could reveal their presence to the watchful eyes that lined the shores. Their bodies pressed against the cold planks. They could feel every subtle shift and crack of the ice against their craft.

Behind them, a fast inferno was consuming the town. The wooden buildings, constructed of fir, burned like massive torches, over a hundred and fifty structures ablaze. The air filled with the terrible mixture of crackling flames, collapsing timber, and the fierce cries of the Tartars. Taking advantage of a nearby ice chunk, the elderly boatman guided the raft toward the right bank, putting three to four hundred feet between them and the burning remnants of Poshkavsk, its orange glow casting long shadows across the frozen river.

Terror gripped Jolivet and Blount at the thought of their raft floating on flammable liquid; their knuckles whitened as they gripped the wooden planks below. The burning buildings, transformed into massive furnaces, shot millions of sparks skyward, reaching heights of five to six hundred feet. The flames' reflection made the trees and cliffs along the right bank appear to be ablaze as well, creating an otherworldly scene of double destruction. Just one spark landing on the Angara's surface could ignite the entire river, spreading devastation from shore to shore like wildfire across a summer meadow. Within moments, such an event would spell doom for the raft and everyone aboard, leaving them with no escape from the liquid inferno.

The wind, fortunately, was not blowing in their direction. Coming from the east, it pushed the inferno toward the left side, carrying the deadly shower of sparks away from their vulnerable craft. This gave the escapees a precious chance to avoid the deadly threat, though they remained tense and vigilant. They made it past the burning settlement, their hearts pounding with each yard gained. The fiery glow diminished, the sound of crackling wood subsided to a distant roar, and the flames vanished behind the steep cliffs that emerged at a sharp bend in the river.

Midnight was approaching, bringing with it a bone-chilling cold. Darkness once again provided its protective cover over the raft, wrapping them in its concealing embrace. Though invisible in the blackness, the Tartars moved about near the riverbank, their voices carrying across the water. Their guard posts were marked by blazing fires, creating orange beacons that the raft's crew avoided.

The blocks of ice made navigation treacherous, forcing the crew to maneuver with greater precision through the floating maze. The elderly helmsman rose to his feet, joints creaking in protest, while the moujiks took up their poles again, muscles straining against the current. Their task grew more challenging by the minute as ice continued to clog the waterway, scraping against the raft's wooden planks with ominous groans.

Michael inched forward with Jolivet close behind, both men crawling on their bellies to maintain their balance, straining to catch the urgent exchanges between the old boatman and his crew. Every whispered command could mean the difference between safe passage and disaster.

"Watch the starboard side! She's listing heavy!"

"Ice floes approaching from port, three gigantic masses!"

"Push them away with the hooks! Put your backs into it, brothers!"

“The closing channel will trap us within the hour!”

"If that be the Lord's will," the old man responded, crossing himself with gnarled fingers. "We cannot fight His decisions. We can only accept them with grace."

"Did you catch that?" Alcide whispered.

"Indeed," Michael answered with quiet determination. "But the Lord stands with us! We must keep faith."

Conditions grew dire as the temperature continued to plummet. A halt to the raft's progress would spell disaster. Not only could they not reach Irkutsk, but the ice would soon tear apart their makeshift vessel, forcing them to abandon it. The willow bindings would snap under the relentless pressure, the pine logs would splinter and vanish beneath the frozen crust like matchsticks in a storm, leaving the desperate travelers with nowhere to go but atop the treacherous ice blocks. Come daybreak, the first golden rays would expose their position, and patrolling Tartars would spot them, showing no mercy as they slaughtered them.

Michael made his way back to where Nadia waited, his boots crunching on the frozen deck. Drawing near, he took her hand, feeling its familiar strength despite the biting cold, and asked the same question he always did: "Nadia, are you ready?" And as always, she answered, her breath visible in the frigid air, "I am ready!"

The ice floes continued to impede the raft's progress for several more miles, their jagged edges scraping against the wooden hull. If they reached a narrower section of the river, the ice would create an impassable blockade, crushing them between its merciless jaws. Their speed was already diminishing, each minute bringing fresh anxiety. They faced constant challenges, violent collisions with ice blocks that shuddered through the entire vessel and necessary diversions, sometimes to prevent dangerous impacts that could splinter their craft, other times to navigate through channels that seemed to close as quickly as they appeared. As time passed, the obstacles grew concerning, looming larger and more threatening in the darkness. Time was running out, and their survival hung in the balance.

At 1:30, the raft hit a dense ice barrier, becoming stuck. The drifting ice from behind continued to push against the raft with relentless force, wedging it in place as if it had run aground on some frozen shoal, the creaking of timber growing more ominous with each passing moment.

This section of the Angara River was only half its regular width, causing ice to accumulate and freeze together under increased compression and frigid temperatures. About 500 feet downstream, the river expanded again, where ice chunks broke free from the frozen mass and resumed their journey toward Irkutsk. The ice barrier wouldn't have formed if the riverbanks hadn't constricted the flow, creating a natural bottleneck that trapped both water and ice. However, there was no way to undo what had happened, and those fleeing had to abandon their hopes of reaching their destination, watching as their last chance slipped away.

The stranded group needed whaling tools to cut paths through the frozen expanse, equipment that could have led them to the wider river section, and possible salvation. But without even basic implements to crack the frost-hardened ice, which had become as impenetrable as stone in the bitter cold, they found themselves trapped, their frozen prison growing stronger with each passing minute.

Their dire situation worsened as gunfire erupted from the right riverbank, sending bullets raining down on their makeshift raft. The enemy had spotted them, their muzzle flashes piercing the darkness like angry fireflies. Almost immediately, more shots rang out from the left bank, catching them in a deadly crossfire that echoed across the frozen river. The helpless group now served as targets for Tartar marksmen on both sides, pinned down with nowhere to take cover. Despite the darkness making precise aim difficult, the random barrage struck and wound several members of their party, their cries of pain mixing with the sharp crack of rifles and the dull thud of bullets striking wood and ice.

"Nadia," Michael whispered close to her ear, his breath forming small clouds in the frigid air.

Without a word and prepared for anything, Nadia grasped Michael's hand, her fingers trembling but her grip firm.

"We need to get past their line," he murmured, his lips moving. "Lead the way, but be careful. No one can spot us leaving the raft. One flash of movement could give us away."

Nadia complied. Together they slipped across the ice in the darkness, broken only by brief flashes from gunfire that cast eerie, momentary shadows. Nadia crawled ahead of Michael as bullets rained around them like hailstones, striking the frozen surface with sharp, crystalline cracks. Their hands soon bled from the jagged ice as they scrambled over, leaving faint crimson trails that disappeared into the darkness, but they pressed onward without pause, driven by desperate necessity.

The barrier's far side came into view after ten minutes of grueling travel. The Angara waters resumed their unimpeded flow, creating a constant, muffled rushing sound beneath the ice. Several ice fragments, breaking free from the main floe, drifted downstream toward the town, their edges scraping against the larger ice sheet. Michael's intentions became apparent to Nadia as she observed a particular ice block connected to the floe by just a thin strip rocking with the current.

"Let's go," Nadia urged, her voice barely above a breath. Together, they positioned themselves on the ice chunk, distributing their weight as their combined mass caused it to break free with a soft crack.

The ice block began its journey downstream, rocking with each ripple and swell. As the river expanded before them into a dark ribbon under starlight, their escape route emerged through the frozen landscape. The sounds of gunfire reached their ears in sharp staccato bursts, along with desperate screams and Tartar battle cries that echoed across the ice. These mixed sounds of suffering and savage triumph grew fainter as distance separated them, until only the whisper of water against ice remained.

"Those poor souls!" Nadia whispered, her words forming small clouds in the frigid air.

For thirty minutes, Michael and Nadia drifted on their ice floe, carried by the river's relentless flow. Each crack and groan of the ice beneath them brought fresh fear it might splinter, sending them plunging into the deadly cold waters. The powerful current kept them centered in the river's path like a practiced helmsman, making any diagonal movement unnecessary until they approached Irkutsk's stone quays, their dark shapes looming larger with each passing minute. Michael remained silent, his jaw clenched tight enough to make his temples ache, every sense alert for danger in the surrounding darkness. Never had his goal been close, within reach.

He could feel it in every fiber of his being. Success was within his grasp, separated only by a diminishing stretch of icy water!

The darkened horizon shimmered with twin rows of lights near midnight, where the Angara's shores melded into darkness. Irkutsk's illumination beckoned from the right bank, a constellation of lanterns and torches marking civilization's edge, while the Tartar encampment's fires blazed on the left, their savage orange glow reflecting off the low-hanging clouds.

"Finally," Michael Strogoff whispered, standing half a mile from the city walls.

Nadia's sudden scream cut his relief short, piercing the night like a blade through silk.

The sound made Michael leap to his feet on the unstable ice, sending hairline cracks spider-webbing beneath his boots. He thrust his arm toward the river's course, his face taking on an eerie cast in the strange blue glow that now bathed the waters. As if comprehending the brilliant flames spreading across the water's surface, their otherworldly radiance growing brighter with each passing moment, he cried out in despair, "No! Even the heavens conspire against us!"

QuantumDigitalPublishing.io

Chapter Twelve

IRKUTSK

Serving as Eastern Siberia's capital, Irkutsk boasts a substantial population of thirty thousand residents during peacetime. The city features a prominent hill on the Angara River's right bank, adorned with various churches, an imposing cathedral, and residential buildings scattered in a charming, unplanned fashion. The wooden houses, painted in cheerful colors, stand shoulder to shoulder with more austere stone structures, their weathered facades telling tales of countless Siberian winters.

When viewed from the Siberian highway's vantage point, twenty miles away atop a mountain, the cityscape creates an almost Eastern appearance with its distinctive features: cupolas piercing the sky, bell-towers standing proud, spires as delicate as minarets, and domes resembling rotund Chinese vessels. However, this oriental illusion dissolves once visitors enter the city itself. The broad, European-style streets and familiar Russian architecture reveal Irkutsk's true character as a frontier outpost of western civilization, though one cannot help but notice subtle Asian influences in the decorative details of buildings and the occasional temple rising above the rooftops.

This vibrant city blends Eastern influences, with elements of both Byzantine and Chinese heritage, yet transforms into a European landscape through its modern features. Well-paved streets with proper sidewalks crisscross the city, while a network of canals weaves throughout, their waters reflecting the bustling life above. Towering birch trees line the thoroughfares, their silver-white bark catching the sunlight, and buildings constructed of brick and wood, some reaching multiple stories, dot the cityscape. The streets bustle with various vehicles, from traditional tarantasses to elegant broughams and coaches, their wheels clattering against the cobblestones as they navigate the busy thoroughfares. The sophisticated residents keep up with contemporary culture, even following the latest fashion trends from Paris, their attire a testament to the city's cosmopolitan character.

Irkutsk served as a haven for all Siberians in the province, causing the city to be populated, its neighborhoods teeming with life from dawn until dusk. The city was well-stocked with many provisions, from necessities to exotic luxuries. As a major trading hub connecting China, Central Asia, and Europe, Irkutsk handled countless varieties of goods, its warehouses and markets overflowing with silks, tea, furs, spices, and precious metals. Given these resources, the authorities felt confident in welcoming the peasants from the Angara valley, even though this meant leaving empty land between the city and the advancing invaders, a strategic decision that would test the city's resilience.

The city housed the governor-general of Eastern Siberia, who led the regional administration from an imposing three-story mansion overlooking the central square. Under his authority worked several officials: a civil governor who managed provincial affairs and supervised tax collection, a police chief whose responsibilities were considerable because of the large exile population and frequent disturbances, and a mayor who headed the merchant class and regulated trade matters. The mayor wielded significant influence over the citizenry and possessed considerable wealth, evidenced by his ownership of several prominent businesses and his lavish entertainment of foreign dignitaries.

The military force stationed in Irkutsk comprised two primary units: a 2,000-strong Cossack infantry regiment, known for their fierce loyalty and exceptional horsemanship, and a police contingent distinguished by their silver-trimmed blue uniforms and helmets that gleamed in the winter sun. Because of the unfolding crisis, the Czar's brother had taken refuge within the city walls since the enemy first advanced into the territory, occupying an entire wing of the governor's residence with his personal staff and guard detail.

The Grand Duke embarked on a significant journey through the remote provinces of Central Asia, inspecting military outposts and meeting with local administrators. He traveled through major Siberian cities without royal fanfare, choosing a military style over princely pomp, often sleeping in garrison quarters rather than governors' mansions. With his officers and a battle-hardened Cossack regiment escort, he made his way across the Trans-Baikalcine provinces, enduring bitter winds and treacherous mountain passes. He stopped to visit Nikolaevsk, the easternmost Russian town on the Sea of Okhotsk's shore, where he reviewed the Pacific naval installations and conferred with regional commanders.

As the Grand Duke began his return journey toward Irkutsk from the empire's edges, planning to continue to Moscow, news of the invasion struck like lightning through the telegraph offices. He rushed to reach the capital, pushing his convoy to exhaustion through day and night, arriving mere moments before all contact with Russia was severed. In those final precious minutes, he exchanged a handful of urgent telegrams with St. Petersburg and Moscow, sending his responses before the lines went dead with an ominous silence. With the wires cut and the postal routes blocked, Irkutsk now stood cut off from the outside world, a fortress of Russian authority marooned in a sea of uncertainty.

As news reached Irkutsk of Ichim, Omsk, and Tomsk falling to enemy forces, the Grand Duke resolved to mount a stalwart defense of Siberia's capital city. He approached this grave task with the same remarkable composure and resolve he had showed in previous crises. With reinforcements far off and the scattered Siberian troops too few to halt the advancing Tartar armies, the Duke recognized that an assault on Irkutsk was inevitable. His priority became fortifying the city to withstand an extended siege, as this appeared to be their best hope for survival.

Preparations began when Tomsk was captured by the Tartars. Along with this devastating news, the Grand Duke received word that the Emir of Bokhara and his allied Khans were leading the invasion. However, he remained unaware that their lieutenant was Ivan Ogareff, a Russian officer whom the Grand Duke had demoted, though he had never met the man in person. The Duke ordered strengthening the city's defensive walls, the stockpiling of provisions, and the organization of the civilian population into work brigades. Every able-bodied man was asked to assist in the fortification efforts, while warehouses were filled with grain, salted meats, and other essential supplies that would sustain the population through a prolonged encirclement. Despite the gravity of their situation, the Grand Duke's calm leadership helped maintain order and purpose among the anxious citizens of Irkutsk.

The people living in Irkutsk province had no choice but to flee their communities, abandoning generations-old homesteads and farms in the face of the advancing threat. Those unable to seek shelter in the provincial capital were forced to evacuate to the region beyond Lake Baikal, where they would be looked after from the invaders' destruction, though many faced arduous journeys through difficult terrain. All grain crops and animal feed were gathered and stored within Irkutsk city, which, serving as the last stronghold of Russian authority in the Far East, was reinforced to withstand an extended siege by hostile forces.

In 1611, its founders established Irkutsk where the Irkut and Angara rivers meet, along the Angara's right bank, recognizing the strategic value of this natural confluence. Two wooden drawbridges supported by sturdy piles driven deep into the riverbed, each span engineered to withstand both the region's harsh winters and spring floods linked the city to its suburbs across the water. The left bank offered strong defensive advantages, with its elevated position and obvious lines of sight. When danger threatened, the suburbs were driven out and the bridges demolished, leaving only blackened stumps of the support pillars visible above the water's surface. The Angara's considerable width, combined with its swift current and exposed approaches, made any crossing attempt under the defenders' fire impossible, creating a natural moat that had protected the city through many conflicts.

However, the river could be crossed both upstream and downstream from the city, leaving Irkutsk vulnerable to attack from the east, where no defensive walls had been built up. This oversight had long worried military strategists, who recognized that an determined enemy force might ford the Angara at shallower points and outflank the city's primary defenses.

The citizens threw themselves into strengthening the city's defenses, working around the clock. The Grand Duke watched with pride as his people showed remarkable dedication to the task, knowing their determination would serve them well in the coming battle. Everyone, from military personnel and traders to outcasts and farmers, united in protecting their shared home. Women and children carried stones while craftsmen applied their skills to reinforce weak points. They completed impressive earthen barriers a week ahead of the Tartar forces reaching the Angara River, the fresh-packed soil rising fifteen feet high in places. A water-filled trench was dug between the inner and outer walls, its muddy depths studded with sharpened stakes. Now: Too well-fortified for a swift capture, the city's constructed yet formidable defenses showed the inhabitants' resolve. Surrounding and besieging the city would be the enemy's only option, a prospect testing both sides' endurance in the harsh Siberian climate.

Near Irkutsk, the Tartar force from the Yenisei valley appeared on September 24th. They took control of the abandoned outskirts, where all structures had been flattened to provide clear lines of fire for the Grand Duke's artillery, though these guns were few and modest in size. The Tartars established their encampment along the Angara's banks, their tents and campfires stretching for a mile along the shoreline, awaiting reinforcements from two additional columns under the Emir and his confederates.

On September 25th, these separate forces merged at the Angara camp, their combined numbers darkening the landscape like a vast shadow. Under Feofar-Khan's unified command, the invasion force was now complete, save for the troops left to hold their conquered territories, their garrisons spread thin across the vast Siberian expanse.

The Tartar army, led by Ogareff, found a way around what seemed an impossible crossing of the Angara River near Irkutsk. Several miles upstream, they constructed makeshift bridges using boats requisitioned from nearby fishing villages, lashing the vessels together with heavy ropes and covering them with wooden planks. This ingenious solution allowed a substantial force to cross. The Grand Duke, lacking any field artillery to reach such distances, could do little to stop this maneuver and was required to remain within Irkutsk's walls, watching as enemy forces accumulated on both sides of the river.

After establishing themselves on the river's right bank, the Tartar forces advanced toward the city with methodical precision. Along their approach, they set fire to the governor-general's summer residence, sending plumes of black smoke into the winter sky as an obvious message of their intentions. They surrounded Irkutsk and prepared their positions to begin the siege, establishing a series of fortified camps at strategic points around the city's perimeter.

The frustrated military engineer Ivan Ogareff found his plans thwarted at every turn, his initial confidence eroding with each passing day. Though skilled in conventional siege warfare, he lacked the equipment for swift action, the heavy artillery and siege engines that might have made a decisive difference. His primary goal, to catch Irkutsk off guard, had slipped through his fingers like melting snow. The battle of Tomsk had slowed the Tartar forces' advance, costing them precious time and resources, while Irkutsk's defenders had fortified their positions with surprising speed, transforming the city into a formidable stronghold. These setbacks forced Ogareff to abandon his hopes for a quick victory and instead commit to a lengthy, formal siege of the city, a prospect that pleased neither him nor his restless troops.

The Emir, acting on his counsel, launched two separate attacks to seize the stronghold, though these attempts resulted in heavy casualties. His forces targeted vulnerable sections of the fortifications, but the defenders showed remarkable bravery in beating back both assaults. Leading the defense, the Grand Duke and his commanders displayed exceptional leadership, joining the fight and rallying townspeople and rural folk to defend the walls. Showing admirable dedication, the city and countryside populations fought, forming bucket brigades to fight fires and tending to the wounded under heavy fire.

During their second assault, the Tartars breached one gate, flooding through the opening like a wave of steel and horsehair. A fierce battle erupted along Bolchaia Street, which stretched for two miles beside the Angara River, with fighting that raged from doorway to doorway and rooftop to rooftop. However, the combined forces of Cossacks, police, and local citizens mounted such a formidable defense, using overturned carts as barricades and raining projectiles from upper windows, that they repelled the Tartar invaders, forcing them to retreat in disarray back through the shattered gate.

Unable to take the city by force, Ivan Ogareff devised a cunning strategy. His scheme involved infiltrating the town, gaining the Grand Duke's trust, and then, at the opportune moment, betraying the city by opening its gates to the besieging army. This would also allow him to exact his revenge against the Czar's brother. His companion, the Tsigane woman Sangarre who had followed him to the Angara, encouraged him to proceed with this treacherous plan, whispering dark promises of glory and retribution in his ear during their clandestine meetings beneath the city walls.

Time was of the essence. The Russian forces stationed in Yakutsk were marching toward Irkutsk, gathering their strength along the Lena River's upper reaches. They would reach the city within six days, which meant Ogareff had to ensure Irkutsk's betrayal before then. He could not afford to wait any longer. The winter winds were growing fiercer, and each passing hour brought the possibility that the vigilant defenders who scrutinized every newcomer with increasing suspicion might discover his true identity.

On the evening of October 2nd, military leaders convened for a strategic meeting in the governor-general's palace's grand salon. Overlooking: Overlooking the river below, the palace stood at the end of Bolchaia Street. From the palace windows: The Tartar encampment was visible, and longer-range artillery could have made the palace impossible for the attackers to occupy. Thousands of enemy campfires flickered across the darkening landscape, like malevolent fireflies.

In the meeting chamber, several dignitaries had assembled: the Grand Duke, General Voranzoff, the city governor, the merchant guild leader, and various military officers. They gathered to discuss and evaluate different strategic options. Maps and dispatches littered the massive oak table, and servants moved around the room's perimeter, keeping the oil lamps burning bright against the encroaching night.

"Ladies and gentlemen," the Grand Duke addressed the group, his stern face illuminated by lamplight, "you're all aware of our current predicament. I remain confident that we can maintain our position until reinforcements arrive from Yakutsk. Once they join us, we'll be capable of repelling these savage invaders, and I assure you, they'll pay a heavy price for daring to encroach upon Muscovite soil." His words carried the weight of imperial authority, though the shadows under his eyes betrayed nights of restless planning and concern.

"Your Grace," General Voranzoff responded, his weathered hand resting on the hilt of his saber, "I can guarantee that every citizen of Irkutsk stands ready to support our cause."

"Correct, general," the Grand Duke responded, adjusting the gold-braided collar of his uniform, "and I respect their patriotic spirit. Thankfully, they've been spared from the ravages of disease and starvation so far, and I'm hopeful they'll continue to avoid such hardships. But what impresses me is their remarkable bravery defending the walls. Their dedication has not gone unnoticed. Note my words, honored merchant, and please convey this message to them."

"On behalf of our town, I express our gratitude, Your Highness," the merchant leader replied, bowing as he spoke. His silk robes rustled in the lamplight. "If I may inquire, what is the latest we can expect the relief forces to arrive?"

"Only six days, your Highness," the Grand Duke responded with renewed vigor. "A courageous and resourceful courier entered the city this morning, having braved the enemy lines under cover of darkness. He informed me that General Kisselef is leading fifty thousand Russian troops, advancing across the frozen landscape. They reached Kirensk along the Lena River two days ago, and neither ice nor snow will slow their progress. These fifty thousand capable soldiers, well-armed and determined, will strike the Tartars from the side, bringing us swift liberation."

"We stand prepared to follow your commands whenever your Highness orders an attack."

"Excellent," the Grand Duke answered, a glimmer of satisfaction crossing his features. "Once we spot the relief forces' vanguard on the ridges, we'll destroy these trespassers who dare besiege our city."

The Grand Duke turned to General Voranzoff, his military bearing clear in every movement. "Tomorrow we shall inspect the fortifications on the right bank," he declared. "The Angara is carrying ice floes now, and once it freezes, the Tartars might attempt a crossing. We must ensure every defensive position is secure."

"Your Highness, if I may observe?" ventured the merchant leader, stepping forward with assuring one who knew the region's waters.

"Please proceed."

"I have witnessed the Angara during temperatures of thirty and even forty degrees below zero," the merchant explained, gesturing toward the sound of rushing water beyond the walls. "Even then, ice continues to flow without the river freezing solid. This occurs because of the river's powerful current, which never sleeps, even in winter's harshest grip. Therefore, I can assure Your Highness that if the Tartars have no alternative means of crossing, they will never enter Irkutsk by the frozen river. Nature herself stands as our guardian."

The governor-general nodded in agreement, his weathered features reflecting years of frontier service.

"That's indeed fortunate," the Grand Duke replied, stroking his chin. "Still, we must remain prepared for anything that might happen. The Tartars are known for their resourcefulness."

Turning to face the police chief, who stood at rigid attention near the chamber door, he inquired, "Do you have anything to report?"

"Yes, Your Highness," the police chief responded, stepping forward and producing a folded document from his uniform pocket. "I've received a petition that was sent to you through my office."

"Who sent it?"

"It comes from the Siberian exiles, there are five hundred of them in town, as Your Highness is aware. They've been most eager to make their voices heard."

The political exiles scattered across the province had gathered in Irkutsk as soon as the invasion began. Following orders, they left their villages where they had worked in various roles, as doctors, professors at the Gymnasium, instructors at the Japanese School, and teachers at the School of Navigation, to assemble in the town. Many had brought valuable skills and knowledge with them, despite their status as exiles. Both the Czar and the Grand Duke had faith in their patriotism, providing them with weapons and equipment, and these exiles had proven their valor beyond doubt, fighting with determining men seeking redemption.

"What request do the exiles make?" the Grand Duke inquired, leaning forward in his ornate chair.

"Your Highness," the head of police responded, bowing, "they wish to form their own special unit and be located at the forefront of the first offensive. They're eager to prove themselves."

"Indeed," the Grand Duke replied, his voice thick with unconcealed emotion, rising to his feet as he spoke, "these exiles are Russians, and they have every right to defend their homeland! They've suffered enough for their past deeds."

"I can assure Your Highness with confidence," the governor-general stated, straightening his military jacket, "these men will prove to be among your finest troops. Their dedication is unmatched."

"They'll need someone to lead them," the Grand Duke responded, pacing across the polished floor. "Who do you have in mind?"

"The men would like to propose," the police chief interjected, exchanging glances with the governor-general, "one of their own who has proven himself in battle. He's shown exceptional courage under fire."

"Russian, is he?" the Grand Duke's eyes narrowed with interest.

"Indeed, from our Baltic territories. A man of considerable military experience."

"Tell me his name."

"Wassili Fedor, Your Highness. He's earned the respect of every man in the unit."

In the harsh city of Irkutsk, Dr. Wassili Fedor, Nadia's father, served both as a physician and a patriot. Beyond his medical duties, he channeled his energy into strengthening the city's defenses, often working late into the frigid Siberian nights to organize patrols and fortifications. His influence extended to fellow exiles, whom he united for their common survival, creating an informal network of support that stretched throughout the city's snow-laden streets. These displaced citizens had caught the Grand Duke's attention through their remarkable dedication, sacrificing their lives in various battles for their beloved Russia, from street skirmishes to full-scale defensive operations against rebel forces.

Though Wassili Fedor's courage earned him recognition multiple times, during the brutal winter siege, he remained humble, never seeking rewards or special treatment, preferring instead to tend to his patients and maintain his modest practice. When the exiles formed their own military unit, they selected him as their leader, a decision made without his knowledge while he was away treating wounded soldiers at the eastern garrison.

Upon hearing this name from the police chief, the Grand Duke showed his familiarity with it, a slight smile of recognition crossing his weathered face.

"Yes," General Voranzoff confirmed, adjusting his medal-laden uniform, "Wassili Fedor has proven himself both worthy and brave. He's always commanded considerable respect among his fellow men. Even the most hardened veterans seek his counsel."

"How much time has he spent in Irkutsk?" the Duke inquired, drumming his fingers on the polished surface of his desk.

"Two years now, Your Excellency, without incident," the chief responded with certainty.

"And his behavior?"

"His behavior," the police chief replied, straightening his posture, "shows complete adherence to the special regulations that bind him. He has never once given us cause for concern."

"General," the Grand Duke declared with sudden decisiveness, "I want you to bring him before me at once. This matter requires my personal attention."

The Grand Duke's commands were carried out, and within thirty minutes, Fedor stood before him in the ornate chamber. A towering figure in his forties, the Duke possessed a solemn, melancholic expression that seemed etched into his features. His life story could be captured in one word, struggle, as he had battled and endured hardships throughout his years, from military campaigns to political upheavals and personal losses. Looking at his face, one could see where his daughter Nadia Fedor had inherited her looks, as their features were similar, from the sharp eyes to the proud set of their jaw.

The Tartar offensive had dealt him a devastating emotional blow and crushed a father's dreams while he remained stranded eight thousand miles away from his hometown. The distance felt like an insurmountable chasm, made worse by the cruelty of timing. He had received word through correspondence about his wife's passing, the letters bearing tear-stained edges and words of consolation that brought little comfort. Along with this heartbreaking news came word his daughter had secured governmental permission to reunite with him in Irkutsk. Nadia was set to depart from Riga on July 10th, carrying with her his last hopes for family connection. With the invasion beginning on July 15th, and if Nadia had crossed the border by then, her fate among the invading forces remained unknown. One can only imagine the distressed father's torment, having received no word about his daughter since that time, each passing day adding additional weights to his already heavy heart.

Wassili Fedor stepped into the Grand Duke's chamber, made his obeisance with the practiced grace of a man who understood ceremony, and stood awaiting the Duke's words, his weathered face betraying none of his inner turmoil.

"Wassili Fedor," the Grand Duke began, his voice carrying the gravity of command that filled the ornate chamber, "your fellow exiles have requested permission to create an elite fighting unit. They understand that joining this corps means they must be prepared to fight until none remain standing? This is not a decision to be made, nor a commitment that allows for half-measures."

"They understand this, your Grace," Fedor answered, his voice steady despite the weight of what he represented.

"They have chosen you to lead them," the Grand Duke stated, studying Fedor's weathered features with keen interest.

"Me, your Highness?" Fedor's composure wavered for just a moment, betraying his surprise.

"Will you accept command of these men?" The question hung in the air between them, heavy with significance.

"If it serves Russia, then yes." The words came without hesitation, born of years of unwavering loyalty.

The Grand Duke addressed Captain Fedor, his voice carrying the full authority of his station. "You are no longer an exile."

"I am grateful, your Highness," Fedor replied, choosing his words. "But may I lead those who still bear that burden?"

"None bear it any longer!" declared the Czar's brother, rising from his seat with sudden vigor. In that moment, he had pardoned all of Fedor's fellow exiles, transforming them from outcasts to fellow soldiers with a single proclamation that echoed off the chamber's gilded walls.

Overwhelmed with emotion he could no longer conceal, Wassili Fedor clasped the Grand Duke's extended hand before taking his leave, his steps lighter than they had been in years as he withdrew from the chamber.

After Fedor's departure, the Grand Duke turned to his officers with a knowing smile, his gold-trimmed uniform catching the lamplight. "The Czar will approve these pardons. After all, we require heroes to protect Siberia's capital, and I have just created some. Men fight harder when they have something to prove, and to preserve."

This merciful act of pardoning the Irkutsk exiles proved both just and wise, transforming condemned men into loyal defenders when the city needed them most.

The darkness had fallen, wrapping the city in its winter shroud. The flames from the Tartar encampment glowed through the palace windows like malevolent eyes, visible across the Angara River where they cast dancing reflections on the water. Ice chunks floated downstream with hollow scraping sounds, with some becoming trapped against the old bridge supports while others rushed past in the current, their edges gleaming in the firelight. As the trader had noted, The Angara would struggle to freeze. This meant Irkutsk's defenders needn't worry about an assault from that direction, though the open water provided little comfort given their other vulnerabilities. As the clock struck ten with deep, resonant tones, the Grand Duke prepared to send his officers away and head to his chambers, when a commotion erupted outside the palace, shouting voices and hurried footsteps.

The door burst open moments later with a bang that echoed through the chamber, and an aide-de-camp hurried in, his boots leaving wet tracks on the polished floor as he made his way to the Grand Duke.

"Your Highness," he announced, out of breath, "a messenger has arrived from the Czar!"

Chapter Thirteen

THE CZAR'S COURIER

The council members all lurched forward at once, their chairs scraping against the wooden floor. A messenger had arrived from the Czar in Irkutsk! The very notion sent ripples of excitement through the chamber. Had the officers considered how unlikely this was, given the Tartar blockades and treacherous conditions, they would have doubted the news.

"This messenger!" the Grand Duke cried, rushing toward his aide-de-camp with such haste that his ceremonial sword clattered against his hip.

Into the room stumbled a man who looked spent, his breathing labored and irregular. He wore a Siberian peasant's garments, now in tatters and pierced with bullet holes that told silent stories of narrow escapes. A traditional Muscovite cap sat atop his head, dusted with the grime of long travel, and his face bore the mark of a fresh scar healed, pink and raw against his weathered skin. His exhausted appearance and ruined shoes, held together by crude repairs, suggested he had traveled far by foot across the harsh terrain.

"Are you His Highness the Grand Duke?" he inquired, his voice hoarse but steady.

The Grand Duke approached him, studying the mysterious arrival with keen interest. "Are you serving as the Czar's courier?" he questioned.

"Indeed, your Highness,".

"From where do you come?"

"Moscow, your Highness,".

"When did you depart Moscow?"

"The fifteenth of July,".

"What shall I call you?"

"Michael Strogoff," the man declared, yet something in his bearing suggested there was nothing simple about him at all.

This was, in truth, Ivan Ogareff, who had assumed the identity of the man he believed he had rendered helpless. Not a soul in Irkutsk, including the Grand Duke himself, could recognize him, and he saw no need to disguise his appearance. Having the means to verify his false identity, he knew his claim would go unchallenged. He had come, driven by an unwavering determination, to expedite the invasion's goal through acts of betrayal and murder. His lips curved into the faintest of smiles, knowing how perfectly his deception had already taken root.

The Grand Duke dismissed his officers after Ogareff's response, leaving just himself and the impersonator of Michael Strogoff in the chamber. The heavy oak doors closed with a resonant thud, the sound echoing off the stone walls.

For several moments, the Grand Duke studied Ivan Ogareff before asking, "Were you present in Moscow on July 15th?" His piercing gaze sought any sign of deception, any crack in the courier's composure.

"Indeed, your Highness. The previous evening, on the 14th, I had observed His Majesty the Czar at the New Palace." Ogareff's voice remained steady, each word measured and delivered with practiced confidence.

"Do you carry correspondence from the Czar?"

"I do. Here it is," Ogareff replied, reaching into his weather-worn coat with deliberate movements.

Ivan Ogareff presented the Imperial message to the Grand Duke. Ivan Ogareff had compressed the paper until it was tiny, folding and refolding it countless times into a tight square no larger than a copper coin.

"Was it delivered to you in this condition?"

“No, your Highness. I had to destroy the outer envelope to conceal it from the Emir’s men.

"Did the Tartars capture you?"

"Indeed, your Highness. The rebels held me captive for quite some time," Ogareff explained, his face showing measured distress. "That's why my journey took seventy-nine days, departing Moscow on July 15th, as stated in the letter, I didn't reach Irkutsk until October 2nd.

With deliberate movements, the Grand Duke examined the letter, unfolding it. With each crease releasing its secret, the paper crackled. There was his brother's handwriting, the Czar's signature preceded by the official imperial formula, the ink still dark against the weathered paper. The letter's authenticity was beyond question, as was the courier's identity. Though the Grand Duke had harbored some suspicions about Ogareff's face, noting something familiar yet disconcerting in his features, he maintained a neutral expression, and his doubts soon melted away like morning frost under the sun.

After a long moment of silence, the Grand Duke studied the letter with careful deliberation, absorbing every word, his fingers tracing the lines of text. "Tell me, Michael Strogoff, are you familiar with what this letter contains?" he inquired, his voice measured and controlled.

"Indeed, your Highness," Michael replied, standing at rigid attention. "I memorized it in case I needed to destroy the physical letter to keep it from the Tartars. That way, I could still deliver its message to you without fail, even under the most dire circumstances."

"And you understand this letter commands us to fight to the death rather than surrender the town?" The Grand Duke's eyes narrowed as he spoke.

"I do, your Highness," Michael confirmed, his jaw set with determination.

"Are you aware it tells me about the troop movements organized to halt the invasion?" The Grand Duke's fingers drummed on the paper.

"Indeed, your Highness, but their efforts have proven futile." Michael's voice carried a hint of regret.

"Explain yourself."

"Feofar-Khan's soldiers now control Ichim, Omsk, Tomsk, and many other major Siberian cities."

"But there was resistance? Did our Cossacks not engage the Tartars?" The Grand Duke leaned forward, his expression intense.

"Frequently, your Highness," Michael responded.

"And they suffered a defeat?"

"Their numbers were too few to stand against the enemy. Our brave soldiers fought valiantly, but they were overwhelmed."

"Where did these battles occur?" The Grand Duke's fingers tightened on the letter's edge.

"At Kolyvan and at Tomsk." Though Ogareff had spoken until this point, he now added, hoping to demoralize Irkutsk's defenders by magnifying the defeats, "And a third time near Krasnoiarsk." His voice carried just the right note of regret and military professionalism.

The Grand Duke pressed his lips together so tightly that no words escaped, his knuckles white against the paper he held. "Tell me about this recent clash."

"With respect, your Highness," Ogareff replied, bowing his head in deference, "it was more than a clash, it was a full-scale battle."

"A battle?" The Duke's voice carried both disbelief and dread.

"Our forces numbered twenty thousand Russians, drawn from the frontier regions and Tobolsk province. We faced an army of one hundred and fifty thousand Tartars. Despite fighting, we were overwhelmed." Ogareff's hands moved in subtle gestures as he painted the scene. "The field ran red that day."

"You dare lie to me!" the Grand Duke burst out, his fury contained. He half-rose from his chair, trembling with rage.

Ivan Ogareff maintained his cool demeanor, not flinching from the Duke's outburst. "Every word is accurate, your Highness. I witnessed the battle of Krasnoiarsk myself, it's where I was taken." His eyes met the Duke's, the perfect picture of a devoted officer delivering painful news.

The Grand Duke regained his composure, sinking back into his chair with measured control, and with a subtle gesture of his hand, showed that he accepted Ogareff's account. "When did this battle of Krasnoiarsk occur?" he inquired, his voice now steady and deliberate.

"September second, Your Highness, just as the sun was rising," Ogareff replied without hesitation.

"Have all the Tartar forces gathered in this location?" The Duke's fingers drummed on the arm of his chair.

"Yes, every one of them. They've merged their position along the river-bank."

"What's your assessment of their numbers?"

"I'd say around four hundred thousand soldiers, well-armed and ready for battle," Ogareff stated with calculated precision.

Once again, Ogareff inflated the size of the Tartar forces, continuing his pattern of deception. His practiced eyes observed any sign that the Duke doubted his words.

"Should I expect any reinforcements from the western provinces?" the Grand Duke inquired, leaning forward in his seat.

"Not until winter ends, Your Highness. The passes are already becoming treacherous with early snow."

"Listen, Michael Strogoff." The Grand Duke's voice took on a steely edge of determination. "Even if these savages numbered six hundred thousand, and even without support from either eastern or western regions, I shall never surrender Irkutsk! This city will stand against any force they dare bring against us!"

Ogareff's sinister gaze narrowed, a shadow of malice flickering across his features. He mused that the Czar's brother did not know the true consequences of betrayal, nor how close that betrayal lurked.

The Grand Duke, being strung, struggled to maintain his composure upon hearing such catastrophic intelligence. His fingers drummed against his thigh as he paced around the chamber while Ogareff watched him, like a predator eyeing its marked prey. Pausing at the frost-rimmed windows, the Duke observed the flickering fires of the Tartar encampment dotting the darkness like malevolent stars and listened to the sound of ice chunks breaking apart in the Angara River with thunderous cracks.

Fifteen minutes passed in tense silence before he spoke again, the only sounds heard were the crackle of the hearth and his boots against the wooden floor. Picking up the letter once more, its paper now crumpled from his repeated handling, he studied a particular section and said, "You know this letter warns me about a traitor I should guard against?"

"Yes, your Highness," Ogareff replied, his voice measured.

"He intends to infiltrate Irkutsk disguised, win my trust, and then hand the town over to the Tartars." The Duke's voice carried a mixture of disgust and disbelief.

"I am aware of this, your Highness. I also know that Ivan Ogareff has made a personal vow of vengeance against the Czar's brother." Ogareff's words carried just the right note of concerned loyalty.

"For what reason?" The Duke's brow furrowed.

"From what I understand, the Grand Duke had sentenced the officer to a degrading punishment that left him forever marked with shame," Ogareff responded, his own face a masterpiece of sympathetic concern.

"Indeed, I recall that. It only proves that this scoundrel, who later turned against his homeland and led these savage invaders, deserved such punishment. Such men have no honor, only self-interest."

"His Majesty the Czar," Ogareff stated, his voice carrying the weight of imperial authority, "was especially concerned that you be warned of Ivan Ogareff's murderous schemes against you. He feared for your safety above all else."

"Yes, the letter mentions this," the Duke replied, touching the document on his desk.

"His Majesty spoke to me about it, instructing me to be watchful of this traitor. He emphasized the gravity of the situation."

"Have you encountered him?" The Duke leaned forward.

"Yes, your Highness, following the battle at Krasnoiarsk. Had he realized I carried a letter for your Highness exposing his plans, I wouldn't have escaped unharmed. The fighting was fierce that day."

"Not at all, you would have perished!" the Grand Duke declared, pounding his fist on the desk. "Tell me, how did you manage your escape?"

"I plunged into the Irtych River," came the response, delivered with just the right mix of modesty and pride. "The current carried me far from danger."

"And your entry into Irkutsk?"

"During an evening raid against a Tartar force. I joined the town's defenders, revealed my identity, and was escorted to your Highness. The soldiers recognized the urgency of my mission."

"Well done, Michael Strogoff," the Grand Duke commended, his weathered face brightening with relief. "You've showed great courage and dedication in your perilous mission. Such loyalty to the Czar and Empire won't go unrewarded. I won't forget this. Is there anything you wish to request?"

"Only to fight by your Highness's side," Ogareff answered with calculated humility.

"Granted, Strogoff. From this day forward, you'll serve on my personal staff and live in the palace. Your rooms will be prepared at once."

"And if Ivan Ogareff should appear before your Highness using a false name, as he intends?" he pressed, feigning concern.

"With your help, we shall expose him, for you know his face. He will die under the knout, (a **harsh, heavy whip**) like the traitor he is. You may go!"

Ogareff offered a precise military salute, mindful of his supposed position as a captain of the Czar's couriers, and withdrew with measured steps through the ornate palace doors.

Ogareff's treacherous scheme had unfolded, exceeding even his own expectations. Having earned complete trust from the Grand Duke through his masterful performance, he now stood poised to betray that confidence at the moment of his choosing. His position within the palace itself gave him intimate access to the town's defensive strategies, fortification plans, and troop movements. With such privileged information at his disposal, he controlled Irkutsk's fate. That not a soul in the city could recognize him or expose his true identity made his deception complete, a perfect disguise that would ensure his victory. With everything aligned to his advantage and the pieces of his plot falling into place, he determined to begin his plan, while fortune still favored his deception.

The situation grew more dire by the hour. They had to seize the town before Russian forces could arrive from the North and East, an event that would occur within days. If the Tartars captured Irkutsk, dislodging them would prove difficult. Even if they were forced to retreat, they would ensure the city's complete destruction first, and would not leave before the Grand Duke had been killed at Feofar-Khan's command.

At the break of dawn, Ivan Ogareff made his rounds of the fortifications, where soldiers, officers, and townspeople greeted him with enthusiasm. They saw this supposed messenger from the Czar as their vital connection to the empire they served. His presence alone seemed to lift their spirits, though each warm welcome only fueled his contempt for their blind trust.

With unwavering confidence, Ogareff spun elaborate tales about his fictional journey. True to his calculating nature, he steered conversations toward the dire military situation, embellishing both the Tartar victories and their army's size, just as he had done when deceiving the Grand Duke.

He insisted that any reinforcements, if they arrived at all, would prove inadequate. He planted seeds of doubt, suggesting that any battle near Irkutsk's walls would end in disaster, much like the devastating defeats at Kolyvan, Tomsk, and Krasnoiarsk. With each retelling, he added subtle details that made his fabrications more convincing, watching with satisfaction as worry lines deepened on the faces of his listeners. His words spread through the garrison like poison, weakening the resolve of even the most stalwart defenders.

Ogareff measured his suggestive remarks, allowing them to penetrate the thoughts of Irkutsk's defenders. He maintained an air of reluctance when responding to questions, emphasizing that they must battle until their last breath and destroy the town before surrendering. His voice would drop to near whispers during these conversations, as if sharing painful truths that weighed heavily upon his conscience.

These deceptive claims would have caused greater damage if possible, but both the military forces and citizens of Irkutsk possessed too strong a sense of national pride to be swayed. Among all those confined within this isolated city at the edge of Asia, whether soldier or civilian, merchant or laborer, nobleman or peasant, not one considered the possibility of surrender. The Russians held nothing but absolute disdain for these invading barbarians, their contempt clear in every stern face and resolute gesture. Even the children played at defending imaginary walls, mimicking their parents' unwavering determination to protect their homeland at any cost.

At first, no one suspected Ivan Ogareff's villainous role; everyone believed he was the Czar's courier rather than a traitor. After reaching Irkutsk, Ogareff developed a close relationship with Wassili Fedor, one of the city's most valiant defenders. Worry about his daughter Nadia consumed Wassili Fedor. According to her last letter from Riga, she had planned to leave Russia, but her fate remained unknown. Had she traversed the provinces now overrun by invaders, or had she been captured? Wassili found his only solace in fighting the Tartars, though such opportunities were too rare for his liking. The evening of the false courier's arrival, Wassili visited the governor-general's palace. There, he confided in Ogareff about Nadia's departure from European Russia and expressed his deep concerns for her safety. Though Ogareff had encountered Nadia in Ichim when she was with Michael Strogoff, he had paid her no more attention than the two reporters also present at the post-house. Thus, he could offer Wassili no information about his daughter.

His face a masterpiece of practiced sympathy, Ogareff listened to the worried father's words. Behind his concerned expression, however, his calculating mind was already searching for ways to use this information to his advantage. He leaned forward in his chair, maintaining the perfect image of an attentive friend and loyal servant of the Czar.

"When did your daughter depart from Russian soil?" Ogareff inquired.

"Around the same period you did," Fedor responded, his weathered hands clutching the edge of the table.

"I departed from Moscow on July 15th," Ogareff stated with careful precision.

"That's when Nadia must have left Moscow too. Her letter stated this," Wassili said, pulling a crumpled piece of paper from his pocket as if to verify the date once more.

"She was still in Moscow on July 15th?" Ogareff's voice carried a note of calculated curiosity.

"Indeed, she was there on that specific date," Wassili confirmed, his eyes clouding with worry as he remembered.

"Then it would have been impossible for her, No, wait, I'm getting my dates confused." Ogareff furrowed his brow in an feigned display of mental calculation. "it seems quite that your daughter crossed the border, and your only remaining hope is that she might have halted her journey upon hearing about the Tartar invasion!" His voice carried just the right mixture of concern and encouragement to appear genuine.

The father dropped his head in despair, his weathered hands trembling at his sides! He was well aware of Nadia's determined nature, that unwavering spirit she'd inherited from her mother, and knew without doubt she would have embarked on her journey regardless of circumstances. Ivan Ogareff's cruel act was needless, a calculated twist of the knife. A single word from him could have put Fedor's mind at ease, could have lifted the crushing weight from the old man's shoulders. Even though Nadia had crossed the border under the conditions we know about, Fedor could have calculated that she was looked after by comparing two crucial dates: when his daughter would have reached Nijni-Novgorod, and when the travel ban was announced. This simple math would have shown him that Nadia had avoided the invasion's dangers and remained, albeit, within the Empire's European territory, protected by the very restrictions meant to contain the populace.

Ogareff, true to his cruel nature and indifferent to others' pain, could have uttered that crushing word, could have granted this small mercy to a suffering father. Yet he held his tongue, savoring the anguish he had cultivated. Fedor walked away with shattered hopes, his shoulders slumped and steps unsteady, this final meeting having extinguished his last glimmer of optimism like a candle snuffed out in a dark room.

Over October 3rd and 4th, the Grand Duke questioned the man claiming to be Michael Strogoff, pressing him to recount everything he'd learned in the New Palace's Imperial Cabinet. Ogareff, having prepared for such interrogation, answered without a moment's pause. He emphasized how the Czar's government had been caught entirely off-guard by the invasion, explaining that the rebels had planned their uprising in absolute secrecy. Before Moscow even received word of the attack, he detailed how the Tartars had seized control of the Obi line. The Russian provinces, he stressed, were unprepared, lacking the troops and resources for effective resistance against the Siberian invaders.

In the shadows of Irkutsk, Ivan Ogareff moved through the city, examining its defenses. His treacherous eyes focused on the Bolchaia Gate, which he intended to betray to the enemy. He scrutinized every detail of the fortifications, noting their vulnerabilities with calculated precision. Under the guise of strengthening the city's protection, he walked the ramparts daily, mapping each weakness and identifying the optimal points where the Tartar forces could breach the walls. The guards, believing him to be their savior, shared additional information about patrol schedules and ammunition stores, aiding in their own destruction.

As evening fell, he visited the glacis of the gate, (the **gentle, sloping embankment fortified** in front of the gate) pacing along its length, his footsteps echoing against the stone fortifications. He felt secure in his observations, knowing the nearest enemy positions were at least a mile from the city walls, hidden behind the rolling terrain. Yet his solitude was not complete, while he believed himself unobserved, a shadow detached itself from the darkness beyond the earthworks, moving with feline grace. It was Sangarre, who had risked death to contact Ogareff, her dark cloak making her invisible against the twilight sky.

For 48 hours, those under siege experienced a calmness that was unusual, given how the Tartars had behaved since beginning their blockade, with their previous relentless assaults and provocations. These orders came from Ogareff, who orchestrated every detail of the deception. As Feofar-Khan's second-in-command, he wanted to pause all forceful attempts to capture the city, knowing that patience would serve his treachery better than brute force. His strategy was to wait for the defenders' vigilance to weaken, counting on human nature's tendency to relax when danger appears to recede. Meanwhile, thousands of Tartar soldiers remained stationed at strategic positions, prepared to storm the gate, their weapons ready and their horses saddled. Ogareff expected the defenders would abandon their posts, lulled into complacency by the false peace, allowing his forces to launch their attack when he gave the signal, a signal already arranged and awaiting only his command.

He knew he had to act without delay. Everything needed to be finished before the Russian forces arrived at Irkutsk. Ogareff had made his preparations, and as night fell, he arranged for a message to be dropped from the fortifications into Sangarre's waiting hands. The parchment, weighted with a small stone and sealed with wax, contained his last instructions for coordinating the assault.

The time was set. In the dead of night, between October 5th and 6th, at precisely two in the morning, Ivan Ogareff would execute his plan to surrender Irkutsk to the enemy. The darkness would mask his treachery, and the late hour would ensure most of the city's defenders were drowsy at their posts, their reactions dulled by exhaustion and the false sense of security that had settled over the fortifications.

Chapter Fourteen

THE NIGHT OF THE FIFTH OF OCTOBER

The strategy devised by Ivan Ogareff was carefully planned, and barring any unexpected complications, he was sure of its success. The crucial element was ensuring the Bolchaia Gate remained either unprotected or defended when he surrendered it. To achieve this, the defenders' attention needed to be diverted elsewhere in the city. He had coordinated this diversionary tactic with the Emir, spending countless hours refining every detail until it was flawless.

The diversion would unfold upstream and downstream along the Irkutsk riverbank. While mounting serious assaults at these locations, they would also stage a mock attempt to cross the Angara from the opposite shore. This multi-pronged approach would leave the Bolchaia Gate vulnerable, especially since the Tartar forces on that side had withdrawn, giving impressing a retreat. The defenders would have no choice but to spread their forces thin, as Ogareff had calculated.

The autumn day of October 5th marked a critical turning point. Within just twenty-four hours, the Emir would seize control of Eastern Siberia's capital, while Ivan Ogareff would capture the Grand Duke himself. Anticipation hung heavy in the air as the conspirators completed their preparations, knowing Irkutsk's fate would be decided by tomorrow.

The Angara camp buzzed with unusual activity throughout the day. Those watching from the palace windows could observe significant military preparations across the river. Tartar forces streamed toward the camp, bolstering the Emir's army with each passing hour. This military display, staged to intimidate those under siege, unfolded before their watchful eyes, with the glint of weapons and armor visible even at a distance.

The menacing warning came from Ogareff, who alerted the Grand Duke about an imminent assault. According to his intelligence, enemy forces planned to strike from positions above and below the town. Based on this information, he advised the Duke to bolster defenses at these vulnerable points, emphasizing the gravity of the threat with chosen words and grave expressions. Following a strategic meeting in the palace war room, military commanders issued directives to focus their defensive efforts along the Angara's banks and at the town's extremities, where earthen fortifications guarded the river. Redeploying troops began, with soldiers hurrying through the streets to their new positions as the afternoon shadows lengthened across Irkutsk.

Ogareff's plan aligned with his intentions. While he expected some defenders would remain at the Bolchaia Gate, he counted on their numbers being minimal. His strategy was twofold: create such a significant diversion that the Grand Duke would have no choice but to commit all his forces to counter it, and unleash a catastrophe so terrible that it would shatter the morale of those under siege. A cruel smile played across his face as he contemplated the chaos that would soon unfold.

The people and soldiers of Irkutsk remained vigilant throughout the day, their nerves taut with anticipation. They had implemented defensive measures to guard against attacks on unthreatened areas, fortifying walls and establishing new observation posts at strategic points. The Grand Duke and General Voranzoff made their rounds, reinforcing positions through their directives and offering words of encouragement to boost troop morale. Under Wassili Fedor's command, forces held the northern section of the town, ready to respond wherever the threat was most severe, with scouts positioned at regular intervals to relay signals at the first sign of enemy movement. They positioned their limited artillery to defend the Angara's right bank, rationing their precious ammunition for maximum effect. These preparations, executed in good time following Ivan Ogareff's timely warning, offered reasonable hope of withstanding the impending assault. Should they repel the Tartars, the discouraged attackers would postpone further attempts on the town for some days. Meanwhile, reinforcements dispatched to aid the Grand Duke could arrive at any moment, their approach watched for by lookouts stationed in the highest towers. Irkutsk's fate hung in the balance, with the lives of thousands resting on the outcome of the coming battle.

The sun had risen at 5:40 AM and set at 5:40 PM, spending eleven hours traversing the sky. As dusk settled in, it would wage a two-hour battle with nightfall before complete darkness enveloped the landscape. With cloudy skies and no moon in sight, the intense darkness would work to Ivan Ogareff's advantage, providing ideal cover for his forces to maneuver undetected.

The bitter cold of recent days had heralded the onset of Siberia's harsh winter, and tonight's frost was biting, with temperatures plummeting well below freezing. Along the Angara's banks, Russian soldiers maintained their concealed positions without fires for warmth, enduring the brutal temperature while their breath formed frozen clouds in the air. In the river below them, massive ice chunks drifted with the current, a steady procession that had continued throughout the day between the shorelines, their grinding and cracking creating an eerie symphony in the growing darkness.

The Grand Duke and his commanders viewed this development as helpful, studying the river's conditions from their elevated position in the town. If the Angara's channel remained blocked, crossing would be impossible. The Tartars could not deploy either rafts or boats through the treacherous maze of ice. Even crossing on ice was out of the question, as the thin, newly-formed ice sheet couldn't support the weight of an attacking force without shattering into deadly fragments that would plunge soldiers into the freezing waters below.

While this situation seemed to benefit Irkutsk's defenders, Ogareff showed no signs of concern. Being a traitor, he knew the Tartars did not intend to cross the Angara, and their activities there were a diversionary tactic, designed to draw attention away from their true objectives.

As evening approached ten o'clock, the river's condition underwent an unexpected transformation, much to the amazement and misfortune of those under siege. The impassable waterway became navigable, as if nature itself had conspired against the city's defense. The Angara's channel had cleared; where countless ice blocks had been drifting by for days, now only five or six remained between the shores, bobbing in the dark waters. Upon noticing this striking change, Russian officers informed the Grand Duke, theorizing that the ice had likely accumulated at a narrow section of the Angara upstream, creating a natural dam that trapped the deadly flow of ice fragments.

The Russians knew they were exposed. With the Angara crossing now accessible to the enemy forces, they had every reason to maintain heightened vigilance. Guards doubled their patrols along the riverbank, torches were lit to better monitor the water's surface, and soldiers stood ready at their posts, knowing that each passing moment could bring an assault from across the cleared channel.

Midnight struck without incident. Silence reigned beyond the Bolchaia Gate on the Eastern front. Low-hanging clouds and dense forest merged, making an impenetrable darkness. Meanwhile, flickering lights dotted the Angara encampment, showing significant troop movements. For about a mile upstream and downstream from where the fortification met the riverbank, a low rumble suggested Tartar forces were mobilizing, awaiting their orders. Another hour crept by without incident, marked only by the occasional howl of winter winds through the trees.

The massive cathedral bell in Irkutsk was moments away from tolling 2 AM, yet the enemy forces showed no signs of launching their attack. Growing uncertainty crept through the ranks of the Grand Duke and his commanders, their breath visible in the frigid night air as they consulted in hushed tones. Had they misread the Tartars' intentions of a surprise assault on the city? Combat noise, the crack of rifles from forward positions and the screech of artillery shells overhead filled previous nights. But now, an eerie silence prevailed, broken only by the crunch of snow beneath patrolling soldiers' boots and the distant crack of river ice. The officers maintained their vigilance, prepared to issue commands as the situation developed, their hands never far from their weapons as they scanned the darkness beyond the fortifications.

Ogareff's quarters comprised a spacious ground-floor chamber within the palace, with tall windows that opened onto a side terrace. A short walk along this frost-covered terrace offered sweeping views of the flowing river below, its dark waters churning against ice-crusted banks.

The room lay shrouded in complete darkness as Ogareff stood vigil by the window, his breath disturbing the stillness as he waited for the precise moment to execute his plan. He alone held the power to give the crucial signal. His strategy was clear: once the signal drew most of Irkutsk's defenders to the assaulted areas, he would slip away from the palace like a shadow and make his way to the Bolchaia Gate. Should he find it unprotected, he would throw it open to the waiting forces; if not, he would guide the overwhelming force of attackers against its meager defense, ensuring swift victory.

He lurked in the darkness like a predator poised to attack, muscles tense with anticipation. before two o'clock, the Grand Duke requested Michael Strogoff, the only name by which they knew Ivan Ogareff. An aide-de-camp arrived at the closed door and called out, his voice echoing through the empty corridor.

Ogareff, standing motionless by the window and concealed in the shadows, remained silent, a cruel smile playing at the corners of his mouth. Palace staff were unconcerned by the Czar's missing courier, a fact duly reported to the Grand Duke.

At two o'clock, deep chimes resonated through the palace halls from the clock. It was time to start the planned diversion with the Tartars awaiting the signal to attack. Ivan Ogareff threw open the window with practiced stealth and positioned himself at the northern corner of the side terrace, his movements deliberate and controlled.

From high above, Ogareff watched the churning waters of the Angara River below, its dark surface reflecting the scattered moonlight like shards of broken glass. He retrieved a match from his coat pocket, struck it against the rough stone balustrade, (a **stone railing or protective barrier**) and used its flickering flame to ignite a small bundle of tow that had been bathed in priming powder. With calculated precision born of meticulous planning, he cast it into the rushing current, tracking its descent with cold satisfaction.

Ogareff, in his cruelty, had the river's surface slicked with oil, the rainbow sheen a testament to his merciless act. The region above Irkutsk was rich with naphtha springs, along the right bank between Poshkavsk suburb and the main town, a natural resource that would now serve as an instrument of destruction. Ogareff had seized control of the massive storage tanks containing the flammable liquid, positioning his men to guard them days before. A simple breach in the reservoir walls, executed under cover of darkness, was all it took to release torrents of oil into the river, his chosen weapon to set Irkutsk ablaze and bring chaos to its streets.

They executed the operation earlier that night, explaining why the raft bearing the genuine Imperial Messenger, Nadia, and the escapees now drifted upon a stream of petroleum. The precious fuel gushed from massive storage tanks through their ruptured walls, cascading downhill until it reached the river. There it formed a floating layer, buoyed by its natural buoyancy, spreading an iridescent sheen across the water's surface. Such were the ruthless tactics of Ivan Ogareff, a traitor who, in league with the Tartars, employed their savage methods against his own people with calculated precision!

Flaming oil spread across the Angara River's surface, igniting with the speed of lightning as if the water itself were pure alcohol. Blue fire raced between the riverbanks, sending spirals of vapor skyward, the heat so intense it scorched the air itself. The few remaining ice chunks, caught in the burning liquid, dissolved like wax over intense heat, releasing sharp hisses of steam that mixed with the acrid smoke billowing above.

artillery fire erupted from both the northern and southern edges of the town. Enemy guns blazed, their thunderous reports echoing across the water, while thousands of Tartar soldiers charged toward the fortifications with savage war cries. Wooden buildings along the riverbank burst into flames everywhere, their ancient timbers crackling and splintering in the inferno, and the night's darkness vanished in the brilliant conflagration that painted the sky an apocalyptic orange.

"Victory at last!" Ivan Ogareff exclaimed, his voice carrying the weight of weeks of careful manipulation and deceit.

His satisfaction was well-earned. The diversionary tactic he had orchestrated was devastating. Irkutsk's defenders now faced an impossible choice between repelling the Tartar assault and battling the raging inferno. Church bells pealed through the chaos as every able citizen rushed either to defend against the attackers or to fight the spreading flames that threatened to consume the entire city. The screams of panic and shouted orders merged into a cacophony of terror.

The Bolchaia Gate stood unprotected. Following Ogareff's cunning proposal, crafted to deflect suspicion by making it appear motivated, only a skeleton crew of guards remained, selected from among the exiles' small contingent. He had convinced the military command these men would fight with particular zeal to prove their loyalty, knowing full well they would be defeated within minutes.

Ogareff stepped back into his chamber, which was now bathed in an eerie glow from the burning Angara River. The dancing orange light cast grotesque shadows across the walls, reflecting his own twisted triumph. As he prepared to depart, the door burst open, revealing a woman with soaked garments and disheveled hair, her silhouette stark against the hallway's darkness.

"Sangarre!" he blurted out, assuming only the gypsy woman would dare enter his quarters . His hand moved toward the weapon at his belt, a habit born of years of treachery.

But he was mistaken, it was Nadia who stood before him, her face flushed with urgency and determination!

Earlier, when the flames had raced across the river's surface like a demonic serpent, Nadia had cried out in terror. In that moment, Michael had wrapped his powerful arms around her and plunged them both into the frigid depths of the river, seeking shelter from the encroaching fire. An ice floe carried them, drifting and spinning through the current to within thirty fathoms of Irkutsk's nearest quay, the flames reflecting off the black water around them.

After diving under the water one last time to avoid a burning patch of oil, Michael guided Nadia to safety on the quay, both of them gasping and shivering in their drenched clothes. At last, Michael Strogoff had completed his mission, he had made it to Irkutsk, though not in the manner he had ever expected!

"We must get to the governor's palace!" he told Nadia, helping her to her feet with trembling hands.

They rushed through the chaos-filled streets, dodging panicked citizens and falling debris, reaching the palace entrance within ten minutes. Though flames from the Angara River leapt against the palace walls like hungry crimson fingers, the sturdy stone structure remained unscathed. However, the wooden buildings along the riverbank were not so fortunate, they had erupted into an inferno, their structures crackling and groaning as they surrendered to the relentless fire.

The grand palace stood with its doors wide open, allowing Michael and Nadia to slip inside unnoticed. Their wet clothes attracted no attention amid the chaos within, droplets pooling beneath their feet on the polished marble floors. The vast ground floor hall teemed with activity, officers rushing to receive commands and soldiers hurrying to carry them out, their boots echoing against the high ceiling. In the swirling crowd of uniforms and stressed faces, Michael and Nadia found themselves pulled apart by the surging mass of bodies.

Frantic, Nadia raced through the corridors, calling out for Michael while trying to find her way to the Grand Duke. Her heart pounded against her ribs as she navigated the maze-like passages. Suddenly, a lit doorway appeared before her, golden light spilling onto the hallway floor. She rushed inside, only to freeze in horror, her blood turning to ice, there stood the very man she had encountered at Ichim and glimpsed again in Tomsk. The traitor whose treacherous actions would soon deliver the town to its enemies now stood mere feet away, face to face with her, his cold eyes widening in recognition.

"Ivan Ogareff!" Her voice pierced the air like a blade.

The man froze at the sound of his name, his shoulders tensing beneath his uniform. With his true identity exposed, everything he had plotted would crumble into dust. Only one option remained: silence the one who spoke it. He lunged at Nadia with the speed of a striking snake, but she pressed herself against the wall, brandishing a knife with unwavering determination, its blade catching the lamplight.

"Ivan Ogareff!" Nadia shouted again, her voice stronger this time, knowing the despised name would bring someone to her aid. The words echoed down the corridor like a death knell.

"Silence!" the traitor snarled through gritted teeth, spittle flying from his lips in his fury.

"Ivan Ogareff!" For the third time, she called out, her voice strengthened tenfold by pure hatred, each syllable ringing with years of accumulated loathing.

Blind with rage, Ogareff yanked a jeweled dagger from his belt and charged at her with murderous intent, forcing her to back into a corner. The cold stone walls pressed against her spine as death approached. Just as hope seemed lost, an unstoppable force seized the villain and slammed him to the floor with bone-jarring force.

"Michael!" Nadia cried out, relief flooding her voice.

Michael Strogoff burst into the room, having followed Nadia's desperate cry through the winding corridors. He had located Ivan Ogareff's quarters by tracking her voice, his keen hearing compensating for his blindness as he arrived through the doorway that stood ajar, his breath coming in controlled bursts.

"Stay calm, Nadia," he said, positioning himself as a shield between her and Ogareff, his stance betraying years of military training.

"Brother, watch out!" Nadia exclaimed in alarm, her heart pounding. "He has a weapon, and unlike you, he can see!"

Ogareff rose to his feet, brushing dust from his uniform as a smirk crossed his face. He sized up his blind opponent with predatory satisfaction. Confident in his advantage, he lunged at Michael with lethal precision. But in one swift motion, the blind man caught Ogareff's armed hand with uncanny accuracy, wrenched away his weapon with crushing force, and sent him crashing to the floor with a thunderous impact.

Ogareff's face flushed with fury and humiliation as he recalled the weapon at his side. Drawing his sword with a metallic hiss, he lunged forward again. His opponent was sightless, this would be an easy victory over a mere blind man! The thought of being bested by someone so handicapped made his blood boil with rage.

Nadia, watching in horror as her companion faced this deadly threat, rushed toward the door, crying out for help. Her fingers fumbled with the heavy latch as panic threatened to overwhelm her.

"Keep the door shut, Nadia!" Michael commanded, his voice cutting through the tension like steel. "Stay silent, I need no help! This scoundrel poses no danger to the Czar's courier today! If he has the courage, let him attack, I stand ready!" His words carried an authority that seemed to freeze the very air in the room.

Ogareff coiled himself like a tiger preparing to attack, moving in complete silence. He masked even his breathing, determined that the blind man would not detect his presence. His boots ghosted across the wooden floor as he circled his prey. His goal was to deliver a fatal strike before his opponent could sense him approaching, his sword gleaming in the dim light.

Nadia observed the dramatic scene with a mix of horror and awe, finding herself confident despite her fear. Michael's composure seemed to flow into her like a calming wave. Though armed with only his Siberian knife and unable to see his adversary's sword, Michael appeared to have divine protection on his side. Remarkably, how he stayed aligned with the sword's point while moving, his head cocked as if listening to some invisible guide.

Ogareff observed his peculiar opponent with unmistakable unease, his fingers tightening around the sword's hilt. The blind man's extraordinary composure unsettled him, defying all logic and expectation. Though his rational mind insisted that he held every advantage in this mismatched duel, his adversary's stillness left him chilled to the marrow. He had already chosen his target, decided where to strike, mapping out the killing blow in his mind. Yet something held him back from dispatching this sightless challenger, an inexplicable hesitation that gnawed at his confidence.

Finally, he lunged forward with practiced precision, thrusting his blade straight at Michael's heart in what should have been an unstoppable attack. With the slightest motion of his knife, more than a twitch, the blind man deflected the attack as if swatting away an annoying insect. Michael remained untouched, his stance unwavering, waiting for Ogareff's next strike like a statue carved from living stone.

Beads of cold sweat dotted Ogareff's forehead as he stumbled backward, his boots scraping against the floor, only to surge forward again with renewed desperation. But just like his first strike, this second assault proved futile against his opponent's supernatural defense. The knife had deflected the blow from his ineffective blade, the metallic ring of their weapons echoing through the space between them.

Consumed by a mixture of fury and dread before this immobile figure, he found himself transfixed by the blind man's wide-open eyes, unable to look away from their milky depths. Though these eyes couldn't see him, were incapable of sight, they seemed to bore into the depths of his soul with terrifying accuracy, holding him in their terrible, mesmerizing grip. It was as if those sightless orbs could perceive something far beyond mere physical presence, reading the very essence of his being.

Suddenly, Ogareff let out a piercing shriek that echoed off the stone walls. Understanding struck him like lightning, freezing his blood. "He can see!" he screamed, his voice cracking with hysteria, "He can see!" Like a cornered predator seeking escape, he retreated step by step toward the room's far end, gripped by overwhelming terror, his boots scraping against the floor.

The statue sprang to life as the blind man strode toward Ivan Ogareff, each footfall deliberate and menacing. Standing before him, mere inches from his face, he declared with cold precision, "I can see! I see the scar from the knout (a **harsh, heavy whip**) I struck you with, you treacherous coward! The mark of your shame is plain as day! And I see where I shall strike you now! Draw your weapon! I grant you the honor of a duel! Your sword against my knife!"

"He can see!" Nadia gasped, clutching her hands to her chest. "Could it be possible?" Her words hung in the tension-filled air.

Ogareff, realizing his doom was at hand, summoned every ounce of courage and lunged at his unflinching opponent with a desperate snarl. Their blades met in a shower of sparks, but with one precise movement of Michael's knife, guided by the skilled hand of the Siberian hunter, the sword shattered into glittering pieces. In the next instant, Ogareff crumpled to the ground with a dull thud, his heart pierced, his life extinguished, his face forever frozen in an expression of disbelief.

The door burst open with a resounding crash. The Grand Duke strode in with his officers behind him, their boots clicking on the wooden floor as they halted at the entrance. As he moved forward with measured steps, his eyes fell upon the lifeless form on the floor, the very man he had believed to be the Czar's messenger, now lying in a widening pool of crimson.

"Who handles this death?" he demanded, his voice sharp with anger, his hand gripping the hilt of his ceremonial sword.

"I am," Michael stated, standing tall and unwavering.

One officer pressed a pistol against Michael's temple, the cold steel contacting a metallic click.

"Tell me your name," the Grand Duke commanded, his face flushed with fury, moments away from ordering the man's execution.

"Your Highness," Michael replied, meeting the Duke's gaze without flinching, "perhaps you should instead ask about the identity of the man lying dead before you."

"I already know that man! He serves my brother! He carries messages for the Czar!" the Duke thundered, his voice filling the chamber.

"Your Highness, you are mistaken. This man is no royal courier. This is Ivan Ogareff!"

"Ivan Ogareff!" The Grand Duke's voice echoed with shock, his face draining of color as the implications dawned on him.

"Yes, Ivan the Traitor!"

"Then who in heaven's name are you?" the Duke whispered, taking an unconscious step backward.

"I am Michael Strogoff!" The declaration rang through the room with unmistakable authority.

Chapter Fifteen

CONCLUSION
Modern English

Michael Strogoff's eyes had never been burned. A remarkable occurrence, involving both mental and physical aspects, had prevented the searing blade wielded by Feofar's executioner from harming his vision. An extraordinary twist of fate had rendered the white-hot sword that should have destroyed his sight powerless.

During the execution, his mother Marfa Strogoff had been present, reaching out toward her son. Michael had looked at her with the intense love of a son believing he was seeing his mother for the last time. Her anguished face, etched with terror and despair, had stirred emotions so profound within him they manifested. Though his pride fought against it, tears welled up from his heart and gathered beneath his eyelids. As these tears evaporated across his corneas, they created a protective barrier. The vapor from his tears, forming between the glowing sword and his eyes, neutralized the blade's burning effect. This phenomenon mirrors what happens when metalworkers dip their hands in water vapor before handling molten iron, a principle known as the Leidenfrost effect that had saved his sight.

Realizing the peril he faced if his secret was revealed, Michael grasped that his safety depended on absolute silence. The Tartars would execute him immediately if they learned their punishment had failed. Yet he also recognized an opportunity, his apparent sightlessness could serve as the perfect cover for his mission. Since others believed him blind, they would grant him freedom of movement, considering him harmless and defeated. This meant he had to maintain the deception, fooling everyone including Nadia, and never letting his guard down for even a moment. Having weighed his options, he committed to risking everything to convince all who crossed his path that he could not see. The masterful way he carried out this deception proved his remarkable dedication, as he learned to rely on his other senses and move as though sightless, all while observing everything around him.

Only one person knew the reality of his situation, his mother, to whom he had confessed the truth during their reunion in Tomsk, as he embraced her in the darkness and covered her face with tender kisses. In that intimate moment, he had allowed himself this one breach of his careful deception, unable to maintain the pretense before the woman who had given him life.

Michael had read the Imperial letter when Ogareff displayed it before his eyes, the same eyes Ogareff wrongly believed he had destroyed. The letter revealed the traitor's vile schemes, explaining Michael's extraordinary determination throughout the latter half of his journey. It was the reason he felt such an overwhelming need to reach Irkutsk and deliver his message in person. He had learned the devastating truth: the town would be betrayed, and the Grand Duke's life was in grave danger. The fate of both the Czar's brother and all of Siberia now rested in his hands. Every step, every moment of pretended blindness had led to this crucial revelation.

Michael related the tale to the Grand Duke, his voice trembling with emotion as he described Nadia's crucial role in their journey. He spoke of her unwavering loyalty and courage, qualities that had proven invaluable throughout their perilous adventure.

"Tell me of this young woman," the Grand Duke inquired, intrigued by the remarkable companion who had aided the Czar's courier.

"She is Wassili Fedor's daughter, the exile," Michael explained, his voice filled with respect and admiration for his faithful traveling companion.

"Captain Fedor's daughter," the Grand Duke corrected him, "is no exile's child any longer. Irkutsk has no more exiles within its walls." His words carried the weight of authority and the promise of redemption for those who had served the city in its time of need.

Overwhelmed by joy after enduring so much sorrow, Nadia sank to her knees before the Grand Duke, her eyes brimming with grateful tears. He helped her rise with one hand while extending his other to Michael, a gesture that symbolized the integrity of their shared triumph over adversity.

Within the hour, Nadia was embracing her father at last, their tears mingling as they held each other close. Reuniting Michael Strogoff, Nadia, and Wassili Fedor marked the pinnacle of happiness for them all, their long journey complete after countless trials and tribulations that had tested their very souls.

The Tartars' two-pronged assault on the town had failed, their military strategy proving no match for the defenders' determination. At the Bolchaia Gate, Wassili Fedor and his small but resolute contingent repelled the initial wave of attackers, fighting with the fierce dedication of those protecting their homeland. Fedor had stayed and defend this position through sound military intuition, which proved to be the right decision as the battle unfolded.

Meanwhile, the townspeople got the fire under control through their coordinated efforts and unwavering resolve. The naphtha fuel burned across the water's surface, creating an eerily beautiful but dangerous spectacle, and the citizens' quick response contained the flames to the waterfront buildings, sparing the rest of the town from damage. Before dawn broke, Feofar-Khan's forces retreated to their encampment in disarray, leaving many casualties strewn across and beneath the town's defensive walls, a grim testament to the cost of their failed siege.

Sangarre, the gypsy who had tried to reach Ivan Ogareff, was among those who perished, her body discovered near the water's edge where she had fallen during the chaos of battle.

The attackers halted their assaults for two days, their morale shattered by Ogareff's death. He had been the driving force behind the invasion, the only one whose laid schemes could unite and motivate the khans and their warriors to attempt conquering Asiatic Russia. Without his strategic mind and manipulative influence, the various tribal factions began showing signs of discord and uncertainty.

Though Irkutsk's defenders remained vigilant and the siege persisted, dawn on October 7th brought the thunderous sound of cannon fire from the surrounding heights. This was General Kisselef's relief force announcing its arrival to the Grand Duke, their artillery echoing across the valley in a welcome symphony of salvation.

The Tartars chose not to await an assault. Unwilling to risk engaging in combat near Irkutsk's fortifications, they dismantled their encampment along the Angara, leaving behind supplies and equipment in their haste to avoid being caught between the city's defenders and the approaching relief force. At last, Irkutsk found itself free from siege, its citizens emerging to survey the abandoned battlefield.

Among the first Russian troops to enter the city were two of Michael's companions, the ever-united Blount and Jolivet. They had managed their escape by crossing the Angara's frozen surface before flames could engulf their makeshift raft, crawling and sliding across the treacherous ice while dodging burning debris. Alcide Jolivet later recorded this close call in his journal with characteristic wit: "ended up like a lemon in a bowl of punch!" His British colleague noted it as "a rather sporting adventure."

The group was overjoyed to discover that Nadia and Michael had survived unharmed, and especially relieved to learn that their courageous friend had not lost his sight. Harry Blount made a notable observation in his records: "Even red-hot iron sometimes cannot destroy the function of the optic nerve." Jolivet, not to be outdone, added his own flourish: "The eyes of a true Russian patriot cannot be dimmed."

After settling in Irkutsk, the two journalists focused on organizing their travel notes and experiences. They spent long evenings by candlelight, comparing observations and cross-referencing details. They sent detailed articles to London and Paris about the Tartar invasion, and, their accounts aligned, with no contradictions even in the smallest details. Their editors, long accustomed to their fierce competition, were shocked by this unprecedented collaboration.

The Emir and his allies suffered a string of defeats in the remaining days of the campaign. Like all who dared challenge the mighty Russian Empire, their invasion proved disastrous. The Czar's forces encircled them and reclaimed each captured town, pushing the invaders back across the steppes they had traversed months before. Nature itself turned against the invaders as a brutal winter descended, with temperatures plummeting far below zero. The bitter cold claimed countless lives, leaving only a handful of survivors to make the long journey back to their Tartar homeland, their dreams of conquest shattered like ice beneath the winter sun.

With the Ural Mountain passage to Irkutsk now cleared, the Grand Duke prepared to return to Moscow. However, he postponed his departure to attend a moving ceremony scheduled after Russian forces had retaken the city, one that would mark the beginning of a new chapter for two of the journey's most valiant survivors.

Michael Strogoff approached Nadia and, with her father present, asked her: "Sister Nadia, when you departed from Riga for Irkutsk, did you leave behind any regrets besides missing your mother?" His voice was gentle but carried an undercurrent of nervous anticipation.

"None whatsoever," Nadia replied, her clear eyes meeting his without hesitation.

"So your heart holds no attachments there?"

"None, brother," she answered, a slight tremor in her voice betraying her growing awareness of his meaning.

"Then, Nadia," Michael continued, his weathered face softening with emotion, "I believe God brought us together and guided us through these trials because He intended us to share our lives forever." His words hung in the crisp air between them, weighted with promise.

"Oh!" exclaimed Nadia, embracing Michael with the same fearless devotion she had shown throughout their perilous journey. She turned to Wassili Fedor, blushing, and said, "Father..." Her voice trailed off, filled with hope and seeking blessing.

"Nadia," Captain Fedor responded, clasping both their hands in his, "nothing would bring me greater happiness than to call you both my children!"

They held their wedding ceremony in the grand cathedral of Irkutsk, its golden domes gleaming in the winter sunlight. The same bells that had once warned of danger now rang out in celebration, their joyous peals echoing through the streets.

Jolivet and Blount attended the ceremony, intending to report on it for their respective readers, though for once their competitive spirits were subdued by the solemnity of the occasion.

"Doesn't this make you want to follow their example?" Alcide asked his companion, elbowing him as they watched the newlyweds emerge from the cathedral.

"Bah!" Blount responded, adjusting his collar with affected indifference. "Now, if I had a cousin like yours..."

"My cousin isn't available for marriage!" Alcide interrupted with a laugh, his eyes twinkling with mischief at their old joke.

"Ah, that's even better," said Blount, pulling out his notebook with sudden interest. "Word is there's tension brewing between London and Peking. Wouldn't you like to see the situation firsthand?"

"By heaven!" Alcide Jolivet burst out, already reaching for his own well-worn notebook, "I was about to suggest the same thing!"

And so these two inseparable companions, their competitive friendship as strong as ever, embarked on their journey to China, eager for their next grand adventure in the vast Asian continent.

Several days after the festivities, Michael and Nadia Strogoff, with Wassili Fedor by their side, began their journey back to Europe. The path that had brought such hardship on their outward journey now brought only joy on their return. They moved in a sleigh that glided like a speeding train across Siberia's ice-covered steppes, the frozen landscape sparkling beneath bright winter sunlight.

The group paused their journey at the Dinka's edge, just short of Birskoe. There, Michael located the burial site of their dear friend Nicholas. They placed a cross to mark his last resting place, and Nadia offered a solemn prayer for their loyal companion whose memory would forever live in their hearts. As they stood in reverent silence, snowflakes fell around them, as if nature itself were paying tribute to the brave man who had sacrificed everything to help them complete their mission. Before departing, Michael placed his hand on the wooden cross and whispered a quiet promise to honor Nicholas's courage by living the life of peace they had all fought so hard to secure.

In Omsk, they found Michael's mother Marfa waiting at the Strogoff family home, her weathered face beaming with joy through tears of relief. She embraced Nadia with overwhelming affection, having long considered her a daughter in her heart, and pulled both young people close as if afraid they might disappear again. On this momentous day, the resilient Siberian woman could acknowledge her son and declare her pride in all he had achieved, no longer forced to hide their connection from prying eyes.

Several days after their stay in Omsk, Michael and Nadia crossed into Europe, leaving behind the vast steppes that had witnessed their extraordinary journey. When Wassili Fedor made his home in St. Petersburg, his children remained close by, establishing themselves in a comfortable residence within walking distance, venturing out only to visit their elderly mother in her cozy Siberian cottage.

The Czar welcomed the brave courier into his service with grand ceremony, appointing him as a personal attendant and giving to him the Cross of St. George in recognition of his unwavering loyalty. As years passed, Michael Strogoff climbed to prominent positions within the Empire, his wisdom and courage serving Russia. Yet it is not his tale of achievement that merits telling, but the story of his hardships and ordeals, a testament to the strength of the human spirit in the face of insurmountable odds.

Epilogue

Michael Strogoff Books I & II

The Horizon of Duty

Irkutsk, Siberia, Twenty Years Later

The frost-laden winds of Siberia still whispered Michael Strogoff's name. To the villagers, he remained the "Courier of Iron," the man who had defied betrayal, blindness, and Tartar savagery to deliver the Czar's warning and save a nation. Yet in the quiet of his stone-hewn home overlooking the Angara River, Michael was simply a husband, a father, and a keeper of stories. Beside him, Nadia Fedor, now Nadia Strogoff, traced the lines of a map unfurled on their oak table, a gift from the Czar himself, its edges gilt with imperial insignia. Their children, dark-haired and sharp-eyed, played by the hearth, their laughter a testament to a peace hard-won.

The Czar's gratitude had been lavish: lands, titles, and a medal struck in Michael's honor. But the courier had asked only for a quiet post in Irkutsk, where he might serve as steward of the frontier he had bled to protect. Siberia, once a jagged tapestry of peril, now hummed with telegraph lines and nascent railways, threads of progress stitched by a regime eager to solidify its grasp. The Emir's rebellion had been crushed, his ambitions buried in the ashes of his own fortresses, but the memory of those flames lingered in Michael's dreams.

Historians would later write of this era as a fulcrum: the moment Russia's eastward march turned inexorable. Scholars marveled at how a single man's resolve had safeguarded Irkutsk, the linchpin of the empire's defenses. Yet in their monographs, they often overlooked the woman who had guided him through darkness. Nadia's diaries, discovered decades later, told a quieter truth, of fear dispelled not by valor alone, but by the unyielding grip of two hands clasped in trust.

On the outskirts of Moscow, a marble monument now stood, engraved with names of those who had perished in the Tartar revolt. Among them, Ivan Ogareff's was etched in smaller script, a cipher of infamy. The Czar, it was said, visited it once, his face unreadable as snow. His reign had grown heavier, tempered by the knowledge that loyalty was as fragile as it was vital.

As twilight draped Irkutsk in gold, Michael walked the riverbank, his steps sure, his gaze, restored by surgeons years prior, fixed on the horizon. Nadia joined him, her arm threaded through his. "Do you ever wonder," she asked, "what might have become of us if we'd faltered?" He smiled, the scar on his brow softening. "We did not falter. And so, the world turned."

In St. Petersburg, engineers drafted plans for a railroad that would one day span the continent, binding east to west. They called it the Trans-Siberian, a steel artery through the wilderness Michael had once crossed on horseback. Progress, he mused, was its own kind of courier.

**** From the journals of Pyotr Vassiliev, Imperial Historian, 1891**

Also by...

Juan José Piedra

The Dreamscape 2032 Steampunk Stillness Project

Coming Soon: An Eight Book Steampunk Science Fiction Novella Series

***Pre-Orders Coming Soon* Where You Can Witness the Birth of Legends!**

In the Age of Steam, the first dreamers dared to defy the earthbound chains of fate.

From coal and gear, spring and fire, they carved a path into the unknown, igniting an unstoppable journey that would stretch beyond the stars. Now, in a sweeping eight-book saga, **Juan José Piedra** unveils the epic chronicle of a civilization's ascent from humble beginnings to celestial destiny.

Across these novellas, heroes are forged in the fires of invention, secret protector races awaken from the ashes of forgotten wars, and the vast, hidden architecture of the cosmos reveals itself to those brave enough to seek it.

In this legendary series, you will find:

- **Worlds Reborn**: Steam-powered cities, lost technologies, and celestial frontiers.
- **Champions of Destiny**: Inventors, rebels, explorers, and guardians who defy the odds.
- **A Tapestry of Wonders**: From the tick of the first clockwork heart to the hum of quantum sails.
- **The Eternal Struggle**: Between freedom and control, vision and destruction, hope and despair.
- **A Journey Across Time and Stars**: Eight volumes, one living legend.

The spark of invention becomes the flame of destiny. The flame becomes a beacon across the void.

Be part of the Legendary Epic Saga! Pre-Orders Coming Soon!

Coming soon to all major bookstores & digital platforms including Book.io on the Cardano Blockchain!

Juan José Piedra

Forging Legends in the Age of Steam and Stars

ASIATIC RUSSIA
RUSSIA
ASIATIC
RUSSIA
Michael Strogoff
or, The Courier of the Czar
Jules Verne
Originally written in French
and published in 1876
Free Image Downloads &
NFTs for purchase
QuantumDigitalPublishing.io

About Jules Verne

Jules Verne

Jules Verne, one of the "fathers of science fiction," is renowned for his imaginative and scientifically plausible stories that have captivated readers for generations. Michael Strogoff, or the Courier of the Czar is a prime example of his mastery in blending historical accuracy with thrilling adventure.

Set in the late 19th century during the reign of Tsar Alexander II, the novel takes place in a Russia on the brink of turmoil. The political landscape is fraught with tension, particularly in the Siberian provinces, where a rebellion led by the traitor Ivan Ogareff threatens the stability of the empire.

The story follows Michael Strogoff, a dedicated courier summoned by the Czar to deliver a crucial message to his brother, the Grand Duke, in Irkutsk. Strogoff's journey is fraught with danger, as he must navigate through a war-torn landscape filled with physical and emotional challenges. The narrative explores themes of loyalty, sacrifice, and the resilience of the human spirit, making it a compelling read for fans of historical fiction and adventure.

Verne's writing style is characterized by vivid descriptions and a sense of urgency that keeps readers engaged. Michael Strogoff is a testament to his ability to create a rich and immersive world that resonates with contemporary readers. The book's enduring appeal lies in its timeless themes and the universal human experiences it portrays.

As you embark on this journey with Michael Strogoff, prepare to be transported to a world of intrigue, danger, and heroism. May this classic tale of courage and loyalty inspire and entertain you as it has countless readers before you.

Enjoy your adventure through the pages of Michael Strogoff, or the Courier of the Czar.

Michael Strogoff (Originally written in French in 1876) is an adventure novel set in the vast expanse of the Russian Empire during a fictionalized Tartar rebellion. Though often published as a single volume, some editions split the story into two parts. Below is a consolidated summary of the two-book structure brilliantly written by **Jules Verne**:

Book ONE: The Mission

The story begins in Moscow, where **Michael Strogoff**, a fearless Siberian-born courier for Tsar Alexander II, is entrusted with a critical mission: to warn the governor of Irkutsk, the Tsar's brother, of an impending invasion by Tartar forces led by the ruthless **Feofar Khan** and his traitorous ally, **Ivan Ogareff** (a disgraced Russian officer). The rebellion threatens to sever Siberia from Moscow and overthrow imperial rule.

Michael departs immediately, traveling across Siberia via the Ural Mountains and the vast steppes. Along the way, he meets **Nadia Fedor**, a young Lithuanian woman journeying to join her exiled father in Irkutsk. The two form a bond, and Nadia becomes his steadfast companion.

Their journey grows perilous as Tartar forces, aided by Ogareff's spies, close in. Michael faces natural disasters, betrayals, and ambushes. A pivotal moment occurs when he is captured and tortured by the Tartars. To protect his mission, Michael endures a searing-hot blade that blinds him (or so it seems). Despite this, he escapes with Nadia's help, continuing toward Irkutsk under the guise of a helpless beggar.

Book TWO: The Siege and Resolution

In the second half, the Tartar army besieges Irkutsk. Unbeknownst to the defenders, Ivan Ogareff infiltrates the city disguised as a fisherman, plotting to open the gates to Feofar Khan. Meanwhile, Michael and Nadia, now reliant on her guidance due to his supposed blindness, arrive at the city's outskirts.

Michael reveals his true identity to Russian soldiers and delivers the Tsar's warning, foiling Ogareff's plans. In a climactic confrontation, Michael's "blindness" is exposed as a ruse (his eyes were saved by tears evoked during the torture). He duels Ogareff, kills him, and ensures Irkutsk's defense holds.

The rebellion collapses, and Michael is hailed as a hero. Nadia reunites with her father, and Michael returns to Moscow, honored by the Tsar. The story closes with themes of loyalty, sacrifice, and the triumph of duty over personal suffering.

Key Themes

- **Loyalty and Duty**: Michael's unwavering commitment to the Tsar and Russia.
- **Resilience**: Endurance against physical and psychological trials.
- **Deception and Betrayal**: Ogareff's treachery contrasts with Michael's integrity.
- **Imperialism**: Reflects 19th-century Russian geopolitics and colonial tensions.

Legacy

While less fantastical than Verne's other works (*20,000 Leagues*, *Around the World*), *Michael Strogoff* is celebrated for its intense pacing, historical flavor, and vivid portrayal of Siberia. It remains a classic of adventure literature, blending political intrigue with a personal odyssey of courage.

Acknowledgements

I wish to acknowledge my wife and lifelong creative partner, Jessie Keener, N.D. A remarkable woman whose wisdom, heart, and intellect have shaped every step of this journey. A Naturopathic Doctor with over 40 years of experience, Jessie brings the world into every conversation. Raised by the sea and seasoned by her early years in Brazil, she is as well-traveled as she is well-read, with thousands of books under her belt and a passion for knowledge that's truly inspiring.

A gifted communicator, Jessie hosted her own public access television show for many years, always championing truth, health, and the human spirit. She's currently working on her own powerful book: Who Will Save Our Doctors? A timely exploration of how today's medical professionals are being compromised by outdated protocols and the overwhelming influence of Big Pharma.

Her brilliance, integrity, and creative fire continue to light the way for thousands.

Glossary Of Terms / Michael Strogoff I & II

- **Hasseurs:** Likely refers to a type of mounted irregular cavalry or horsemen, possibly of Central Asian or Tartar origin, known for their skill in scouting, raiding, and engaging in guerrilla-style warfare. These riders would have been lightly armed and highly mobile, adept at navigating the vast steppes and rugged terrain of Siberia. Their role in the novel aligns with the depiction of Tartar forces, who rely on fast-moving, opportunistic cavalry units to disrupt Russian defenses and terrorize local populations.

Verne's use of such terms reflects the historical reality of Central Asian warfare, where nomadic horsemen played a crucial role in military campaigns, relying on their superior horsemanship and knowledge of the land to conduct swift attacks and strategic retreats. In the novel, such forces would have contributed to the challenges faced by Michael Strogoff on his perilous journey across Siberia.

- **Chef d'oeuvre:** Is a French expression meaning "masterpiece" or "masterwork." It is used to describe something that represents the pinnacle of skill, craftsmanship, or artistry.

In the novel, Verne may use this term either literally, referring to an exceptional work of art or craftsmanship, or figuratively, to highlight a particularly remarkable event, strategy, or achievement, perhaps in the context of military tactics, deception, or a daring feat by Michael Strogoff or his adversaries. The phrase conveys a sense of excellence and perfection in whatever it is applied to.

- **Sang Froid:** Is a French term that translates to "cold blood" in English, but it is used figuratively to mean composure, self-control, or unshakable calmness in the face of danger or crisis.

In the novel, characters like Michael Strogoff exhibit sang-froid by maintaining a steady, fearless demeanor even in life-threatening situations, such as when he faces the Tartars, endures torture, or executes his mission under extreme pressure. His ability to think clearly and act decisively, without letting emotions overwhelm him, is a defining trait of his heroism.

- **Imperturbable:** describes a person who remains calm, composed, and unshaken, even in the most difficult or dangerous situations. It refers to an unyielding steadiness of mind and an inability to be disturbed or flustered by external pressures.

Michael Strogoff himself embodies imperturbability, as he endures extreme hardships, braving the vast Siberian landscape, outmaneuvering enemies, and even facing torture, without losing his resolve. His imperturbable nature allows him to complete his mission with unwavering focus, making him a true model of resilience and self-discipline.

- **Provençals:** Refers to people from Provence, a region in southeastern France known for its distinct culture, language, and traditions. The term typically evokes imagery of lively, warm-hearted individuals, often associated with Mediterranean influences, music, and storytelling.

In the novel, Provençals might be referenced to describe a particular character's background, temperament, or expressive nature. Given Jules Verne's attention to regional characteristics, a Provençal character would likely exhibit traits such as vivid storytelling, warmth, enthusiasm, or a strong sense of identity linked to their homeland.

- **Corps Diplomatique:** Refers to the collective body of diplomats representing various nations within a foreign country or at a government's court. This term encompasses ambassadors, envoys, ministers, and other diplomatic officials responsible for managing international relations and negotiations.

Jules Verne often uses such terms to highlight the presence of high-ranking foreign representatives or to emphasize the political and strategic elements within the novel's setting. In Michael Strogoff, the "Corps Diplomatique" would likely refer to the gathering of officials, correspondents, and representatives who observe and report on events unfolding in Russia, particularly regarding the Tartar invasion and the Czar's response. Their role in the narrative underscores the political weight and international implications of the conflict.

- **Physiognomists:** Refers to individuals who study and interpret facial features and expressions to determine a person's character, emotions, or intentions.

Physiognomy was a widely accepted pseudo-science in the 19th century, based on the belief that a person's physical appearance, particularly their facial structure and expressions, could reveal their inner nature or even predict their fate. In Michael Strogoff, Verne may use this term to describe characters who observe and assess others based on their facial traits, especially in tense or strategic moments when someone's true identity, trustworthiness, or intentions are in question. This aligns with the novel's themes of deception, disguise, and the ability to read people accurately in high-stakes situations.

- **Chasseurs:** Wore the simple uniform of an officer of chasseurs of the guard - "Chasseurs" refers to a type of light cavalry or infantry soldier in the Russian or French military, known for their speed, agility, and reconnaissance abilities.

The term "chasseur" (French for "hunter") was used in European armies to denote elite troops specialized in skirmishing, scouting, and rapid movements. In the Russian context, Chasseurs were often associated with Cossacks or other mobile forces that played crucial roles in frontier defense and rapid deployment during military campaigns.

- **Facade:** Refers to the front or outward appearance of a building, often designed to be impressive or decorative.

The term can also metaphorically signify a deceptive outward appearance, where something or someone presents a false or misleading exterior to conceal true intentions or feelings. However, in the novel, it is most commonly used in its architectural sense, describing the exterior of structures in Russian cities such as Irkutsk or Moscow, which are depicted with detailed attention to their grand and imposing designs.

- **Polonaise:** Refers to a traditional Polish dance of a stately and processional nature, characterized by a moderate triple meter and elegant, flowing movements.

It can also refer to a type of music composed in the style of this dance, often used to evoke a sense of grandeur and national pride. Given Verne's detailed descriptions of cultural elements throughout the novel, the term might appear in reference to a formal event, a piece of music played in a Russian or Polish setting, or even as an allusion to the refined customs of the aristocracy.

- **Imperial Fête:** Refers to a grand celebration or festivity organized by or in honor of the Russian Emperor (Czar) and the imperial court.

Such events were often elaborate and lavish, featuring ceremonial banquets, music, dancing, and military displays, reflecting the wealth, power, and grandeur of the Russian Empire. These fêtes could be held on various occasions, such as official visits, victories, coronations, or national holidays, showcasing the splendor and dominance of the ruling monarchy.

- **Steppes:** Refers to vast, treeless plains that stretch across Siberia and Central Asia. These landscapes are characterized by their flat or gently rolling terrain, covered mainly with grasses and sparse vegetation, and are subject to extreme weather conditions, including harsh winters and scorching summers.

In the novel, the steppes of Siberia serve as a significant setting for Michael Strogoff's journey. These vast, open expanses emphasize the great distances he must travel, the dangers he faces from both natural elements and enemy forces, and the isolation of the Russian frontier. The steppes are both a physical and symbolic obstacle, representing the endurance and resilience required to complete his mission.

- **Iemschik:** (or Yamshik), refers to a Russian postilion or coachman who drives a horse-drawn vehicle, such as a tarantass, along the czarist empire's postal roads.

The Iemschiks were an essential part of the imperial postal and transport system, responsible for ferrying travelers, couriers, and government officials across vast distances, particularly in remote regions like Siberia. They often worked at relay stations, known as "yam" stations, where fresh horses could be quickly harnessed to allow for continuous travel. These drivers were known for their hardiness, familiarity with the rugged terrain, and ability to handle their horses skillfully.

- **Versts:** Killometers or versts, Refers to a Russian unit of distance measurement, approximately equal to 1.066 kilometers (0.662 versts).

The verst was commonly used in the Russian Empire to measure long distances, particularly in the vast and rugged expanses of Siberia, where Michael Strogoff's journey takes place. Given the immense scale of Russia, travel distances were often measured in versts rather than versts or kilometers.

- **Tarantass:** Is a traditional Russian carriage or traveling vehicle, designed for long-distance journeys across the vast and rugged terrain of Siberia.

Description:
The tarantass is a large, four-wheeled carriage, typically constructed with a suspension system made of leather straps or wooden springs, allowing it to absorb shocks on rough roads.

- **Cravat:** A neckcloth; a piece of muslin, silk, or other material worn about the neck, generally outside a linen collar, by men, and less frequently by women.

"cravat" refers to a piece of cloth worn around the neck, typically tied in a knot or bow, serving as a decorative and functional accessory.

- **Kibick or Telga:** The term "kibick" is likely borrowed from Russian киби́тка (kibítka) and is an obsolete synonym for kibitka, a type of vehicle. "Telga" refers to a type of four-wheel horse-drawn vehicle used primarily for carrying loads in Russia and other countries. The telga is nothing but an open four-wheeled cart, made entirely of wood, the pieces fastened together by means of strong rope.

"kibick" (also spelled kibitka) and "telga" refer to types of Russian horse-drawn vehicles commonly used for travel across Siberia and the vast Russian Empire.

- **Overawe:** Means to intimidate, subdue, or control someone through fear, authority, or an imposing presence.

Explanation in Context:
The term "overawe" is often used to describe how powerful figures, military forces, or intense situations instill fear or submission in others.

- **Khanat:** Khanates were typically nomadic Turkic peoples, Tatar and Mongol societies located on the Eurasian Steppe.

"Khanat" refers to a territory or political entity ruled by a Khan, a sovereign leader of a Mongol, Tartar, or Central Asian tribal state.

- **Damascus Blade:** Refers to a sword or dagger made from Damascus steel, a highly prized metal known for its exceptional strength, sharpness, and distinctive wavy pattern.

Explanation in Context:
Damascus steel was historically renowned for its superior quality, capable of cutting through lesser weapons and maintaining a sharp edge.

- **Sesame par excellence:** Is a figurative phrase derived from the famous magical command "Open, Sesame!" from Ali Baba and the Forty Thieves in One Thousand and One Nights.

Definition in Context:
"Sesame" symbolizes a powerful key, something that grants access or opens doors effortlessly.

- **Podorojna Papers:** Refers to an official travel permit or passport issued by the Russian government, granting the bearer the right to travel freely and requisition transportation along their journey.

Definition in Context:
"Podorojna" (or Podorozhnaya Gramota in Russian) was an official document in Imperial Russia, primarily used for government couriers, military personnel, or officials traveling on state business.

- **Kwass:** A jug of kwass, the ordinary Russian beer.

"Kwass" (also spelled Kvass) refers to a traditional Russian fermented beverage made from black or rye bread, which is mildly alcoholic and widely consumed by people of all social classes in Russia.

- **Zingaris or Tsiganes:** Refers to Gypsies, or the Romani people, a nomadic ethnic group known for their distinct culture, traditions, and lifestyle.

Definition in Context:
The terms "Zingaris" (from Italian) and "Tsiganes" (from French and Russian) both refer to the Romani people, a traditionally itinerant group spread across Europe and Russia.

- **Copecks and Roubles:** Refers to the units of currency used in the Russian Empire during the 19th century.

Definition in Context:
Rouble (₽ or рубль): The primary unit of Russian currency.

- **Eccentric Curvette:** An eccentric curvette refers to an unusual or irregular version of a curvette, which is a light leap performed by a horse where both hind legs leave the ground just before the forelegs are set down. In the context provided, the horses in question galloped continuously but also executed many unconventional curvettes as they moved along.

"Eccentric Curvette" refers to a sudden, exaggerated movement made by a horse, particularly a spirited or well-trained one, while galloping or changing direction.

- **Na Pravo: To the right, Na Levo:** Are Russian directional commands used primarily to guide horses or riders.

Definition in Context:
"Na Pravo" (На Право) – Russian for "To the right" or "Turn right."

- **En Règle:** Is a French phrase that means "in order" or "according to the rules."

Definition in Context:
"En Règle" is used to indicate that something is legitimate, proper, or compliant with official regulations, laws, or procedures.

- **Moujik:** (also spelled "Muzhik") is a Russian term referring to a peasant or laborer in Imperial Russia.

Definition in Context:
A Moujik is a common Russian peasant, typically a serf or free farmer, belonging to the lower class of society.

- **Postilion:** Refers to a horse-mounted guide or driver who rides one of the lead horses to steer and direct a carriage, tarantass, or postal relay coach.

Definition in Context:
A Postilion is a rider who controls a team of horses pulling a carriage or relay post vehicle, often without reins, relying on voice commands, a whip, and their own riding skills.

- **Confrere:** Is a French term meaning "colleague" or "fellow member of the same profession."

Definition in Context:
In the novel, "confrère" is used primarily by the French journalist Alcide Jolivet to refer to his British counterpart, Harry Blount.

- **Na Vodkou:** Is a Russian phrase meaning "with vodka" or "to vodka."

Definition in Context:

It is typically associated with Russian drinking customs, where vodka is a central part of social gatherings, toasts, and celebrations.

- **Tsigane:** Refers to a member of the Romani people, also commonly known as Gypsies.

Definition in Context:
The term "Tsigane" (or "Tzigane") is derived from the Russian and French words for Roma people, who have historically been nomadic communities spread across Europe and Asia.

- **Pour-Boire:** Refers to a small gratuity or tip given as a token of appreciation for a service rendered.

Definition in Context:
"Pour-boire" is a French term that literally translates to "for drink", implying a sum of money given to someone, traditionally to buy a drink but more commonly as a tip.

- **Postmaster:** Refers to the official in charge of a postal station, responsible for managing horses, carriages, and relay services for travelers, particularly couriers and government officials.

Definition in Context:
In Imperial Russia, especially along the vast and rugged roads of Siberia, post stations were crucial for long-distance travel.

- **Discomfiture:** Refers to a state of frustration, defeat, embarrassment, or distress caused by an unexpected failure or setback.

Definition in Context:

The term is often used to describe the feeling of being thwarted in one's plans, whether in battle, strategy, or personal ambitions.

- **Incendiarism:** Refers to the deliberate act of setting fire to property, buildings, or other structures, often as a method of warfare or destruction.

Definition in Context:
In the novel, incendiarism is used as a strategic tool by the Tartars and their allies to cause chaos and destruction, particularly during their invasion of Siberia.

- **Saryn na kitchou!:** Is a Tartar battle cry that can be roughly translated to "Down on your knees!" or "On your faces!" in English.

Definition in Context:
This phrase is shouted by the Tartar invaders as a command to those they are attacking, demanding immediate submission.

- **Kreml:** The term "kreml," Often spelled as "Kremlin," refers to a major fortified central complex found in historic Russian cities.

"Kreml" refers to the Kremlin, which is a fortified central complex found in many Russian cities, most famously in Moscow.

- **Bivouacked:** A site where people on holiday can pitch a tent temporary living quarters specially built by the army for soldiers.

"bivouacked" refers to the act of setting up a temporary encampment in an open area, usually without tents or permanent shelter, often for the purpose of resting or preparing for further travel or battle.

- **Dipterals:** Refers to large swarms of insects, specifically two-winged flies or mosquitoes, which are commonly found in the Siberian wilderness.

Definition in Context:
The word "Dipterals" derives from the biological classification Diptera, which is the scientific order for insects with two wings, such as flies, gnats, and mosquitoes.

- **Deh-Baschi:** Is a Tartar military title referring to an officer or commander, likely in charge of a group of ten soldiers.

Definition in Context:
The term "Deh-Baschi" is derived from Turkic and Persian origins, where:

- **Pendja-Baschi:** Is a Tartar military title, referring to an officer in charge of a group of fifty soldiers.

Definition in Context:
The term "Pendja-Baschi" is derived from Turkic and Persian origins, where:

- **Beng:** Is a Tartar term meaning "prince" or "chieftain."

Definition in Context:
"Beng" is a title used to denote a high-ranking leader or noble among the Tartars.

- **Il est un petit homme, Tout habille de gris, Dans Paris!:** Is a French nursery rhyme that appears in the novel.

Definition in Context:

This lighthearted French song is sung by the French journalist Alcide Jolivet, one of the two European correspondents in the novel.

To Those Who Ride Into the Storm

A Poem for Michael Strogoff

Through winds that howl and rivers wide,
Where frozen specters stalk and hide,
Beyond the reach of hearth and home,
The lone courier dares to roam.

His steed is swift, his course unknown,
A shadow cast where few have flown.
The road is cruel, the night is deep,
Yet duty wakes where others sleep.

The sky is torn with icy breath,
The path ahead is laced with death,
Yet forward still, his fate is sworn,
For he who rides must face the storm.

No banners raised, no songs resound,
No gilded halls, no laurel crowned,
Yet kingdoms rise and wars are stayed
By those who ride and are not swayed.

So let the tempest rail and roar,
Let lightning lash the barren shore,
For empires stand, as they have sworn,
On those who ride into the storm.

Made in the USA
Coppell, TX
06 December 2025